CORK CITY LIBRARY

Tel: (021) **4277110**
Hollyhill Library: 4392998

This book is due for return on the last date stamped below.
Overdue fines: 10c per week plus postage.

Class no. .... *HAR* .... Accn no. ....

TT

CLOSED
MONDAY

Dublin Evening Herald

NOËLLE HARRISON

BEATRICE

PAN BOOKS

First published in Great Britain 2004 by Macmillan
and simultaneously in Ireland by Tivoli, an imprint of Gill & Macmillan, Dublin

This edition published 2005 by Pan Books
an imprint of Pan Macmillan Ltd
Pan Macmillan, 20 New Wharf Road, London N1 9RR
Basingstoke and Oxford
Associated companies throughout the world
www.panmacmillan.com

ISBN 0 330 43202 8

'The Lost Girl' by Ciaran Carson reproduced by kind permission of the author and
The Gallery Press, Loughcrew, Oldcastle, County Meath, Ireland.
From The New Estate and Other Poems (1988).
'An Old Woman of the Roads' by Padraic Colum.

Every effort has been made to contact copyright holders of material
reproduced in this book. If any have been inadvertently overlooked, the publishers
will be pleased to make restitution at the earliest opportunity.

1 3 5 7 9 8 6 4 2

A CIP catalogue record for this book is available from
the British Library.

Typeset by SetSystems Ltd, Saffron Walden, Essex
Printed and bound in Great Britain by
Mackays of Chatham plc, Chatham, Kent

All Pan Macmillan titles are available from
www.panmacmillan.com
or from Bookpost by telephoning +44 (0)1624 677237

For Claire, Corey and Barry

There is enough beauty, truth and nourishment
in one small flower to last a lifetime.

Amancio D'Silva

The Lost Girl

An open window, the door unhinged,
Its lintel gleaming like a silver bone—

A cold moon rises
Over miles and miles of empty space.

I search through all her chambers,
In dark recesses
Hope to find her face.

Ciaran Carson,
after Robert ab Gwilym Ddu

ACKNOWLEDGEMENTS

I am grateful for the creative guidance and editing of my writing angel Kate Bootle, and the passion of my agent Marianne Gunn O'Connor, as well as the genius editorial input of Alison Walsh at Tivoli and Imogen Taylor at Macmillan. My precious band of readers was Donna Ansley, Alice Barry, Anakana Schofield, Anne Duggan and Mary McGreal, who gave me valuable critique and friendship. I would also like to thank Dermot Bolger for his insightful critique.

I have been inspired by the wisdom of my late Uncle Amancio, the ethereal etchings of Cora Cummins as a source for Eithne's work, the vibrant art of Noreen Walshe, in particular the painting *In Anima Vitae — The Aran Kiss* which features in the book, and the evocative photograph 'Frozen Reeds in Mist' by Steve Neale, which was the visual catalyst for the passage on Lough Bán.

Thank you to old friends from England — Jo Southall, Dom Rotheroe, Ajith Hettiaratchy, Synnóve Bakke, Manoushka Gold and Niki Winterson — who pushed me towards the path of writing, and to those in Ireland — Eileen Blishen, Bernie McGrath, Therese Dalton, Jenny Brady, Emer Marron, Debbie Hutchinson, Carol O'Connor, Sarah Beardmore and Anne Hill — who helped me remain steadfast. I am also indebted to Maura Carty and her daughters Rosie and Mags, who helped me so much with stories of life in North County Meath, and by looking after my son while I wrote.

Most of all I thank my family for their unerring support: my mother Claire, my brother Fintan, my son Corey, my step-daughter, Helena, my old faithful Chloë and, finally, Barry, who brought me to North Meath and the beginning of it all.

PROLOGUE

All Souls' Day, dawn

She woke; mouth dry, heart thundering, limbs stiff, rose from the stone floor and wrapped a blanket about her shoulders. She was still in her dress. She felt the shadow of her sleep and wanted to climb back into it. The boarded windows made the cottage as dark as death. It restrained her fleetingly. She opened the door.

Birdsong enveloped her. A gentle mist had begun to rise from the fields, like steam, like breath, like life.

She walked down to the stream, following the cattle tracks, and stood on the muddy bank, dropped the blanket, pulled off her dress and slipped out of her clogs. She stood naked for a minute, feeling the early winter chill encircling her. Her skin goosepimpled but she did not shake. Steadily she walked into the stream and immersed herself in the cloudy water.

It was deep in the middle, and she could feel minnows brush past her body. The solitude of dawn made her feel safe. The world was not yet in motion.

When the tips of her fingers started to prune and she began to feel blue, she got out of the water. Carrying her dress and clogs, she walked back to the cottage with only the blanket around her. She left the door open to bring in the light, lit a fire, and brewed some tea. When she was dry, she put on her clothes and an old jersey that was lying on the single battered chair. She waited.

A breeze whispered through the trees behind the cottage; a solitary leaf spun down the chimney breast. She squeezed a small wild flower in her hand and smelt it.

An hour later a car pulled up outside. She picked up her blanket and her bag, went out and got into the car. She handed the driver her bag; he looked inside. There was a pearl necklace, a blue silk scarf, a pink beret, a red leather-bound sketchbook, a mother-of-pearl compact and an embroidered purse.

ONE: THE PEARLS

EITHNE

She is in the woods, burrowing into the earth, under a giant lime tree.

I found the pearls curled beneath a root; they gleamed at me. A delicate string, each pearl perfection, with an unopened gold clasp. Beatrice had bought them in Majorca that summer. Pearls. Belonging to somewhere exotic. I held them in my hands, still a child's hands, my skin soft and unblemished, my fingertips sensitive. I closed my eyes and fingered each iridescent orb. Such glamour hidden in my woods. What were they doing in this dark, wintry place? These treasures from the sea were so far away from their source. Were they a gift from my sister, like all the secrets she had shared with me in the dark, in our bedroom?

I stood in the woods, the pearls twisted around my wrist, silently stroking them. The land cleared around me then, and suddenly I had perfect vision. I saw a thousand trails which wound in and out of the trees. Zones of green ferns picked up patches of sunlight, and clusters of milky white mushrooms cleaved to the sides of gnarled roots, which looked like bony fingers gripping onto the dark earth for dear life.

I came here nearly every day. Walking about, observing, never being part of anything, looking in from the outside. The woods were just five minutes away from our house: take a left outside the front door, swing to the right, past the old dive of a pub, and then down the hill, climb the fence, edge round the field on a muddy track, and into the dark until the spindly broken-down trees surrounded you. My wood was not a place most would choose to walk in. It wasn't attractive – no broadleaved trees, or dainty beech, just churned up mud track and the bitter scent of spruce. Once you were inside, solitude enveloped you. I had always liked this, and I had never been afraid of being on my own . . . not until this day.

Now I had found the pearls, and with them I uncovered fear. In that instant, my innocent, thirteen-year-old mind conceived the inconceivable – I was not safe.

I stuffed the pearls into my pocket, and called the dog. We ran then, slipping and sliding – such a long way – to the field. Out in the open it had begun to rain – a bleak, lashing downpour. Only when I reached the hard tarmac did I slow down; then I could not hurry home. My feet dragged as I stomped back up the hill. Was I crying? It was hard to tell with the rain streaming down my face.

Mammy went white, then sank back in her chair.

'Beatrice,' she whispered.

She squeezed the pearls tight in her fingers, as if she could make them burst.

'Get her a brandy,' Uncle Jack said. I got the decanter.

The Garda shook his head.

'This does not look good,' he whispered to Jack.

Beatrice had been gone a week.

Beatrice's hair rippled over her shoulders and down her back like a waterfall of fire. My sister Beatrice was beautiful. She was tall, and she held herself like a dancer, although she had never been to a ballet lesson in her life. Even her imperfections were beautiful: the little scar by the side of her eye, where she had knocked herself on the side of the bath as a toddler; her nose was slightly crooked – my fault, playing handball. Her hands as well were incredibly elegant, with long slender fingers and perfect almond-shaped nails. And they were always busy: painting, drawing, holding a cigarette, tickling me . . .

I sit in my bay window, looking at night spreading across Dublin. I have walked a long way today, the length of the South Pier, hitting the Irish Sea and a sense of anonymity. I massage my sore feet as lights come on in the streets outside, and my reflection becomes clear in the glass. I scrutinize myself. I am thirty-two, although I don't look it. My eyes still hold their shocked innocence, the way they looked when I was thirteen. I have no child; I cannot begin to imagine how my mother felt when my sister Beatrice disappeared nineteen years ago. It was Hallowe'en and she was coming home for the weekend, but she never arrived. She left Dublin on time, catching a bus at half past eight and arriving in the village at about ten. She knew Mammy was working so, instead of waiting around, she decided to hitch the last few miles home. It's something we all did, although maybe not at night . . .

Who saw her standing there in the dark? Who stopped and put her into their car? Was it someone we all knew? Was there a monster among us? Who was it and where did they take her?

Beatrice was never found. Just some of her things: a string of pearls, a scarf, a hat, a sketchbook and a compact. She must be somewhere in the woods, but they dug and they dug, and they searched every nook and every cranny and never found her. It was a mystery; Beatrice had just disappeared. She was an open book, a life with no end that had hardly begun.

When the search for Beatrice began to slow, my mother sat down and it felt like she never got up again. Not for years. She kept vigil by the back door, staring out of the window across the bog as if she could will her daughter to return. At first, everyone came to see how she was – friends, neighbours, my father's family – but when they could get nothing out of her, so that they felt even more useless and redundant than before, they all gave up. After six months they began to say she was wallowing in her anguish, and she should pull herself together: for Joseph's sake; for me . . . but really, they just couldn't face the honesty. My mother's brutal misery was too much. It was not the way things were dealt with. A good Irishwoman shoulders her misfortune and carries on no matter what. But my mother was English. She was different.

There was one neighbour who didn't say or think these things. Her name was Assumpta Lynch. The very day after Beatrice disappeared, Assumpta came round. She came straight in the back door without even knocking, went up to the kitchen table, grabbed a chair and sat down next to my mother. She said nothing, just held her hand. She sat there for well over an hour, and not a word was said between the two women. Then just as suddenly she turned to me and said, 'Put the kettle on Eithne, there's a good girl.'

Assumpta came every day. She made tea for Mammy, lacing it with brandy. She cooked the dinner for us all; and then she just sat next to Mammy for hours.

On the third week Mammy began to cry. As Assumpta gripped her hand, Mammy shuddered and wrenched out deep, guttural sobs from her belly from some place close to her womb. It was desperate.

And where was Daddy? He was like a shadow, at that time, drifting in and out of the house. Mammy's grief lost him, and so he dealt with it the only way he knew how – in the pub.

One day when Beatrice was about twelve, Mammy sat her down and told her everything about her past. She did it because of Daddy's drinking. He had collapsed in the main street again, this time in the middle of the day. Mammy was so mad with him. He had shamed her, and she got back at him the only way she could think of; by telling his daughter she was not his. It was Mammy who broke up the family.

I was only eight then, and had no interest in their chat so I played out in the garden while Mammy and Beatrice sat huddled at the kitchen table, drinking tea and talking till way past dark.

That night, as we lay tucked up in our beds, Beatrice repeated the tale in broken whispers. I was completely absorbed by the drama and romance of my mother's past. This girl Beatrice talked about had passion and spirit, she was like a heroine from one of Beatrice's romantic novels. I could not identify her with the worn woman who was my mother.

'My real father is completely different from Daddy,' Beatrice whispered.

'Do you mean we don't have the same Daddy?'

'Yes, of course stupid. That's what I'm telling you . . . my father was called Jonathan. Not Joseph, but Jonathan. Mammy called him Jon.'

'But why didn't they get married? Why did Mammy marry Daddy?'

'That's a long, long story. You see, Eithne, things weren't that simple, especially then. Jonathan, my daddy, and Mammy came from very different backgrounds and well, in those days, it was very hard for the two classes to mix.'

'What do you mean classes?'

'Mammy's family were poor, they were what you would call working class. Her father had to work very hard to make not very much money, and then, she said, her mother used to spend it all.'

'Why don't we ever visit them over in England?'

'Wait and let me finish telling you about my father – you see his family were very rich, so rich in fact that his father didn't really have to work – he was a lord—'

'Wow! Did they have a castle?'

'No – they weren't those kind of lords – they were just very – posh – and Mammy worked for them so that's why they didn't want my daddy, Jonathan, to marry Mammy . . . he was very good-looking she told me. Very fair she said, blond hair with streaks of gold and thick like mine, and he was tall and elegant.'

I could sense her eyes closing and her mind dreaming. I wanted to know more – why didn't he fight for Mammy like a real prince? And where did my daddy come into it? Was he working class too?

SARAH

Sarah Quigley left for London on a bright sunny day in October 1962. She had packed one small case with a change of clothes, some stockings and underwear, her nightdress and a hairbrush. In her handbag was a new lipstick called 'Sweet Cherry', which she had bought the day before, some violet eau de toilette, which her mother didn't want, and the old mother-of-pearl compact which had belonged to her father's mother. Her father had also handed her five one-pound notes, the night before, which she had carefully folded into her new leatherette purse. She had the directions to her new home, meticulously written down on a large sheet of paper, which was also folded and in her handbag. She had everything she could need for her new life.

Her train was at ten o'clock, in exactly one hour. She looked around her sparse bedroom one last time, at the row of tiny china dolls from all over the world which her father had bought down at the docks – the Chinese one in its red silk top winked at her, and Sarah felt it knew she wasn't coming back. She went down the narrow staircase; her parents were sitting at the kitchen table with a pot of tea.

'Do you want a cuppa?' asked her mother.

'No, I think I'll be off,' she said. 'It's a bit of a walk; I don't want to miss the train.'

'Shall I come with you pet?' asked her father.

'No, Dad. It's best I go on my own, don't you think?'

He nodded, his Adam's apple rising and falling.

She walked towards the door; her mother's back was to her and all she could see were her father's watery eyes staring across the kitchen table. He looked very small, whereas her mother's back was a hulk, a giant boulder of flowered material. Sarah watched her pick up the pot and pour more tea.

'Well, mind you don't get into trouble now,' her mother warned her. 'You work hard, and be a good girl.'

Sarah bit her tongue. 'Yes, mother.'

'We'll see you at Christmas, then,' said her father. 'It won't be long. Be careful, love.'

'I will, Daddy,' Sarah said and left.

She stepped out into the narrow street, and walked its length for the last time, past row upon row of neat red-brick houses, and rounded the corner. She could see Southampton docks in the distance, cranes crowding the skyline, a heavy grey smog hanging over them. She breathed in, as relief began to warm her chilled hands: she was getting out of here. The fear had always been with her that she would never leave. But now, at only sixteen, she already had her first job, a good one in London. She and Sally Langley had been determined to move away, and the day they had finished school they had bought a copy of the *Lady* magazine between them. Inside its pages were all kinds of advertisements for nannies and housekeepers, cooks and gardeners, as well as more mundane domestic positions, which were what the two girls were after. Sally's long-term plan was to train to be a nanny. But Sarah's desire to go to London came from romantic dreams on rainy Saturday afternoons; it was the place to be, the hub of everything, where you'd be bound to meet someone and fall in love.

The two girls had spent a whole week labouring over their

letters of application but it had been worth it. Sally was thrilled to secure a position as an au pair in Tunbridge Wells, and Sarah had got the first job she applied for: doing general domestic duties for Sir Eric and Lady Voyle at their house in Kidderpore Avenue, Hampstead, London.

Sarah settled well into the Voyle household. Lady Voyle took an immediate shine to her.

'Aren't you a pretty little thing,' she had commented the day Sarah arrived. 'You'll certainly brighten the place up.'

The Voyles' house was at least three times the size of the houses back home, no, more like four, thought Sarah. It had four floors. There was a basement, which she was never asked to go into, but was told housed the wine. The ground floor was dominated by an incredibly grand dining room with a table which seemed to stretch for eternity. When Sir Eric and Lady Voyle dined at home, they sat at either end of the table, and Sarah had to walk between them to serve their food. Next to the dining room was a succession of different living rooms; Sarah couldn't work out which was which and what they were all for. Finally, there was the kitchen where Sarah spent most of her time, staring out of the window and looking at the trees out the back and the blustery London sky, while she topped and tailed vegetables, things she'd never seen or heard of like French beans.

On the first floor were the bedrooms – five of them. Sarah had to make the beds, but she didn't mind because it gave her a chance to make tiny forays into this magical world of privilege. She especially loved Lady Voyle's room, with all the perfume bottles and trinkets on her dressing table, and its rich odour of sensual fabrics and clean linen.

On the second floor – the attic – were the staff bedrooms, one for Sarah and one for Rachel, the housekeeper. Lady Voyle had been almost apologetic when she had shown Sarah to her bedroom, but to Sarah it seemed immense. She loved the view best of all: a tiny window looked out onto the roof, over which she could behold the sparkling, glittering night-time panorama of London. It made her catch her breath. At night, before she went to bed, she would repeat to herself again and again, 'I did it, I did it, I did it,' pinching her arm to make sure it wasn't a dream and that she really had escaped Southampton.

Sarah hated her home because her mother resented her. Betty Quigley always blamed Sarah for ruining her figure, and for making more domestic work. After Sarah was born Betty never let her husband touch her again. Sarah's father was a meek man at home and chose to stay away as much as possible, spending every daylight hour working down at the docks and, as a result, he was made foreman. Sarah was left on her own to face her mother's biting temper. She couldn't wait to get away from her.

At the Voyles' house everyone was nice to Sarah. Rachel was very kind and patient, and explained things carefully to her. She praised her often, and Sarah began to feel more and more comfortable.

Lady Voyle considered herself a bohemian, 'One of the people' she liked to say. She painted, often going on trips to Italy and France, and when she returned she would set up small private viewings of her watercolours in one of the living rooms. Lady Voyle was Sarah's first contact with art. When she noticed Sarah spending more time looking at her paintings than cleaning, she gave her a sketchbook and a set of pencils; it didn't even occur to her to tell her servant off.

Sir Eric was a politician. At home he was quiet, polite, and happy to leave Lady Voyle in charge of domestic affairs. Sarah hardly ever saw him during the day because he was always out, and every evening, religiously, he would head off to his club.

Rachel told her that the Voyles were a very old family with good breeding, which was why, she claimed, they treated their staff so well. Rachel had worked for a terrible nouveau riche family; never again, she said. But the Voyle household was a pleasant one, full of charm, good manners and peace, apart from the hourly chime of the grandfather clock, and the cherry trees scraping the kitchen window on windy afternoons.

The Voyles had two children – twins and both boys – who had spent the past seven years away from home at boarding school. Both sons had just entered the hallowed grounds of Oxford University in the footsteps of every Voyle male before them.

Sarah had met the twins briefly during her first weekend in Hampstead when the two boys had come down from Oxford to visit their parents. Anthony introduced himself stiffly and shook her hand rigorously before letting it go. He was taller than the other boy, and had short, dark hair, and a long, fine nose. The other one, Jonathan, was talking to his mother; he merely glanced over at her and continued laughing and chatting, his golden curls flopping all over his forehead, and his green eyes sparkling, while he thrust his hands into his jacket pockets.

'Did you meet the boys?' Rachel asked her later, as they were eating their own meal after the family had gone out.

'Yes . . . they're very different,' said Sarah.

'And not just in looks,' said Rachel. 'I've seen them both grow up, and they've turned into lovely young men, although it's Jonathan who's the real charmer. He's always coming in here and distracting me while I'm trying to work – making me giggle and such like.'

'What about Anthony?'

'Oh, he's a little more aloof – it's Jonathan I know better.'

At Christmas the twins were due back for the holidays. Sarah was cleaning the stairs with a hard brush. She turned as Jonathan burst through the front door, hallooing and full of Christmas cheer. She was hot and out of breath with rosy cheeks and rising chest, her eyes were bright and her hair was loose and falling in curls about her face. Tendrils stuck to her temples, and perspiration clung like dew to her forehead. Jonathan was taken aback.

'Who are you?'

'I'm Sarah Quigley. We met—'

'Oh yes . . . of course— Where is my mother?' His confusion made him suddenly rude.

'In her room.'

He brushed past her as he went up the stairs. A little too hard. What he really wanted to do was reach out and touch her with his hand. He bit his lip.

Sarah had not gone home for Christmas because Lady Voyle needed her, she said, for all of the extra dinner parties she had arranged. Rachel did all the cooking, but Sarah had to do all the legwork – vegetable preparation, cleaning, washing-up. She did not mind. Christmas at home was dull. She could not bear another year of her father's forced cheer, as her mother moaned about the size of the turkey and the price of everything. She pictured him as he valiantly put up the tiny plastic tree while his wife berated him about the inferior quality of the decorations. Here she was an outsider, she could watch others enjoy Christmas.

On New Year's Eve the Voyles went to a party and Rachel had gone home to spend the evening with her family, so Sarah was on her own in the house. She cleared the dinner plates, washed them, and prepared the potatoes for the following day, leaving them in a pot of cold water. Then she swept and mopped the floor, wiped the table and sat down to enjoy a glass of champagne. Lady Voyle had left an opened bottle for her – it was half full. Sarah looked at the clock – five minutes to twelve. She had never drunk champagne before. She closed her eyes and imagined a different life.

Disturbed by a tap on the window, she looked up and saw Jonathan standing there, with a tipsy grin on his face. She opened the door.

'I was thinking of you,' he said. 'On your own here on New Year's Eve. I couldn't leave you by yourself. Who would you kiss when the clock struck twelve?'

What was she supposed to do? She had never had a boyfriend; she had never even kissed a man, apart from her father – and now this attention from a young, clever, rich, but most of all, handsome man who was interested in her. All of a sudden she felt incredibly dizzy, the champagne made her sway. As she lunged towards a chair, Jonathan moved quickly, sweeping her off her feet.

He filled up her glass with one hand, while, with his other arm, he held her tight around her waist.

'Let's toast the new year in,' he said. 'Five, four, three, two, one. Happy New Year!'

He leant forward and kissed her: hard, needy, immediately pushing his tongue into her mouth. The girls in Oxford did not go all the way. He wanted all the way.

They were on the floor, her clean floor. Her skirt was still on. She had not said one word. She looked at his face; his eyes were closed. He was beautiful.

Afterwards he carried her up to her room. He wanted to see her naked and took off her blouse, her skirt and all her underwear. She lay still, breathless, watching. He stood in front of her and took all of his clothes off. Then he bent over her, scooped her up, and pushed inside her.

'You're so sweet,' he murmured into her ear. 'You smell so sweet . . .'

She said nothing, but gasped suddenly as she felt him in her, as she remembered what his naked body had looked like.

Every night after that Jonathan went to Sarah's room. It was their big secret. Every night Sarah went all the way.

The third day after new year was a Wednesday and Sarah's day off. Jonathan watched her from his bedroom window as she left the house, smothered in a dark green coat, gloves, hat and scarf, scuttling like a tiny beetle down the icy road. The sight of her touched him and without thinking he ran down the stairs, grabbed a coat and slipped along the icy pavement until he caught her up.

'Jonathan! What are doing here?'

'I've been watching you, Miss Sarah Quigley. Where are you off to on such a freezing cold day?'

'I'm going up to the Heath for a walk.'

'Oh, how boring! And how cold! Let's do something far more interesting, my sweet Eliza Doolittle.'

Sarah blushed. She didn't know why he was calling her that,

but he sounded so affectionate. She looked back nervously at the house, could anyone see them? Meanwhile, Jonathan had hailed a black cab. He held the door open for her; she got in feeling like a princess.

The taxi flew into town. They got out at Victoria Station and walked down to the Thames. It was freezing; a cold wind bit into them, and the river churned dark and swollen beside them. There were very few people about, since it was still the holiday season. Jonathan walked behind Sarah and thrust his frozen hands into her coat pockets. She could feel his body pressed against her back. He was so tall, he could rest his chin on the crown of her head.

'I am going to take you to see some art.' He spoke loudly against the wind.

He led her to the Tate Gallery. Once inside, the paintings became a blur; Sarah was dizzy with emotion.

There was one room where Jonathan called the work pre-Raphaelite. She did not ask him what the word might mean – she just nodded and looked. Jonathan talked and talked about the artists. It was the most he had ever said to her – she was his audience. They stopped in front of a painting of a beautiful young woman, bathed in a celestial light. Her eyes were closed. She looked to Sarah as though she were praying, no, more than just prayer – pleading. A dove delivered a flower into her hands. Sarah read the label by the painting: 'Dante Gabriel Rossetti – *Beata Beatrix*'.

'Who is she?' she asked.

'Dante's lover.'

Jonathan said it as though she should know who he meant. She felt stupid, but she did not care – here she was in the Tate Gallery, looking at paintings with a stunning young man. He wanted to talk about art with *her*.

They ate tea in the steamy restaurant in the Tate Gallery. Sarah had never been so happy.

Then the Christmas break was over. Jonathan went back to university and everything went back to normal. But there was something Sarah had not thought about, and now she was worried. The possibility of pregnancy had never been mentioned in their nightly trysts. Sarah had thought that if she washed well afterwards nothing could happen. But now she started to feel sick – it could not be true. She would wait a few weeks until Easter, then Jonathan would be home and he would know what to do.

The Easter break arrived and the twins came home. But with them came two girls – Harriet and Charlotte. Charlotte was Jonathan's girlfriend; she was petite, blonde and bubbly.

'What do you think of the gals?' Lady Voyle asked while Rachel and Sarah were laying the table. 'Nice gals, don't you think? Well raised, intelligent. They are both studying English literature at St Hilda's. I really admire gals who decide to educate themselves before they even think about marriage.'

Sarah was dumb with shock. She did her work like a robot.

'Are you all right, Sarah?' asked Lady Voyle, noticing her servant's stricken face. 'You look very tired.'

During the day Jonathan ignored Sarah. He went out with Charlotte, taking her into town to shop in Kensington, or to a lunchtime concert or an art gallery. Every day when they left the house, Jonathan helped Charlotte on with her coat, gave her a gentle peck on the cheek, and opened the door for her. They walked down the street arm in arm; she was so small she could rest her head on his shoulder. In the evenings, the family dined together. There was much giggling and touching of hands between Jonathan and Charlotte. To all outward appearances it seemed that Jonathan had completely lost interest in Sarah.

But he could not stop looking at her, furtively, incessantly. Sometimes after breakfast there would be a small square of paper under Jonathan's cereal bowl, which Sarah would find and shove in her pocket. As soon as she could she'd rush to the toilet and take it out with shaking hands. The messages were brief: 'Behind the greenhouse, twenty minutes' or 'In the basement, half an hour'. Concocting ever more ridiculous excuses each day, so that she began to sense Rachel was becoming suspicious, Sarah would sneak off to meet her lover. That's what he was to her – her lover. He was the most exciting thing that had ever happened to her, and she found it impossible to be sensible, or work out exactly what she was doing. Blind with faith in him, or in something intangible which she was sure existed between them, she would stumble down the basement steps and find Jonathan hiding between the rows of bottles.

'I've missed you, darling,' he would say, as he began to unbutton her top. 'I love you, I love you . . .' he'd chant softly. Here was her chance to speak, when he was tender and caring, caressing her and telling her he loved her, until his body arched and he came inside her.

Then he would become detached and it would be too late. The expression on his face changed perceptibly. It made her shiver.

After he had gone Sarah would cry, alone in the dark, shoving her fingers into the ancient dust which had gathered between the bottles.

Once, before he could leave, she caught his hand, and in shaking whispers asked him, 'Are you ashamed of me?'

Jonathan turned, his face a picture of concern, 'Sarah, dear sweet Sarah,' he said. 'Of course I'm not ashamed of you. I love you – but you see I made a commitment to Charlotte before I met you and I have to let her down gently. It would be cruel . . .'

Sarah nodded. He was so noble.

'It's you I want. You know that don't you? And one day we'll be together. You're an angel, that's what you are. I've never met anyone so good, so unselfish.'

Sarah remembered her mother saying that the only way a woman could keep a man's interest was by being demanding and self-centred, 'To keep 'em on their toes' she had said. But why should her mother be right? She let go of his hand; she let him go back.

Sarah never mentioned the baby. And Jonathan never talked about marriage. After two weeks he went back to Oxford with Charlotte wrapped around him. Sarah began to expand, and her limited wardrobe started to be a problem. Rachel teased her about helping herself to too much steak and kidney pie, but at times she looked at Sarah anxiously.

Sarah knew she was running out of time. She went to Oxford. By now it was May, but still cold. She sat all day opposite Christ Church College watching for Jonathan. She was shivering by the time she eventually saw him with a group of friends, laughing and carefree.

'Jon! Jonathan!' she called.

He looked over at her and his face clouded. He crossed the road, his hands in his pockets. His friends stared at her.

'What on earth are you doing here?' he demanded.

She recoiled as if he had slapped her. What had happened to him?

'I have to talk to you,' she stuttered.

'Sarah, I can't talk to you here, go home. We'll talk next weekend.'

'Please.' Her voice quavered.

'Oh, come on, then,' he said. 'Since you are here, we may as well get a cup of tea. I'll see you later!' he shouted over to his friends who drifted off.

Jonathan took Sarah to a cafe. He ordered tea and scones while Sarah took off her coat.

'Goodness, Sarah,' he said, 'you have put on weight.'

She started to cry.

EITHNE

Pearls should stay in their shells. Hide under a bush. Hide your light, your beauty, your irresistibility.

They dragged the lough, but Beatrice had not sunk to its bed. They searched the bogland, but she was not buried underneath the peat. They looked painstakingly in the woods, in every thicket, but the trees did not yield her up. Maybe there is a place we cannot see and that is where Beatrice has gone. Like Avalon, or fairy country. Beatrice believed in the fairies. Maybe she is away with the little people.

When I was thirteen I saw the film *Picnic at Hanging Rock*. It made a huge impression on me. It is set in Australia on Valentine's Day, at the turn of the century. A group of schoolgirls go for a picnic under Hanging Rock with two of their teachers. There is a strange energy in the mountain and some of the girls are drawn to the rocks. They dance in a circle, they take their clothes off and then they just disappear. No one can find them.

That film still haunts me. Is that what happened to Beatrice? Did the landscape just take her, digest her beauty and swallow her whole?

Leo comes into the room bearing a mug of steaming tea. I get down from my windowseat.

'I didn't hear you come in,' I say.

'You were deep in thought,' he says. 'I didn't want to disturb you.'

'I wasn't really, just looking at the lights.'

I go towards him, he puts down the tea, and we embrace. I kiss him.

'How did it go today?'

'Great,' he says. 'I got the commission for the Tullamore bypass.'

'Oh my God!' I screech. 'Leo, why didn't you call me?'

'I knew you were out walking. You didn't have your mobile, did you? I sent a text.'

'Sorry, sorry, my battery must have run out.' I am hugging him. 'This is brilliant. I can't believe they went for it.'

'The Arts Officer said it was the clear favourite. Apparently they loved the concept of the elemental forces – you know, all that stuff I wrote about Tullamore being the centre point of Ireland and drawing in the wind, the rain and everything. The sculpture itself is going to be quite simple really, just big, very big!'

'I'm so excited,' I say. 'I wish you'd come in and told me straightaway. I hate the way you can be so calm.'

'That's just the way I am,' he says, holding me again, 'but I'm very, very excited underneath.'

And his eyes are shining.

We cook. Leo has bought a bottle of wine to celebrate. We talk about our work. Leo is worried that his budget won't be big enough to cover the costs.

'But you're getting thirty-five thousand euros!' I say.

'You'd be surprised how expensive it is,' he says, nodding knowingly. This is his fifth public art commission; his second since we got married three years ago. Apart from this he has had three solo exhibitions of his sculpture, as well as a residency at the Irish Museum of Modern Art. No wonder he has problems squeezing in his day job at the college. For me it's been harder. Leo has a way with people, especially gallery owners, clients and students. They all love and admire him. I don't have that ease, and I'm constantly distracted. Sometimes I know that Leo is thinking that print-making is somehow less pure than sculpture; that I'm not quite as professional as he is, that maybe I'm just dabbling. I've never had a solo show.

'I've a meeting tomorrow with Eliza Wright,' I say.

'Wright Gallery?' he asks.

'Yes, I sent in a submission, ages ago. She rang me this morning.'

'That's great,' he says.

'Katie says Eliza likes print.'

'Katie?'

'Katie in the studio. You know, Katie Bryan.'

'Oh, yeah. But how would she know that?'

'Well, I don't know . . . she just said so.'

'I wouldn't believe a word that girl says, she's cracked.'

'Thanks for the encouragement,' I snap, taking the dishes to the sink.

The mood suddenly changes.

'I was only telling you that I wouldn't believe anything that mad Katie says, I'm not saying that Eliza Wright doesn't like etchings. I think you've got a really good chance . . . your stuff is excellent at the moment. Jesus, what's wrong with you?'

'Nothing . . . I'm just nervous.'

'Come here,' he says.

He holds out his arms and folds me into him. I am still annoyed but I let him pull me to him, and gradually my hostility ebbs away. I turn my face up to him. We kiss for a long time.

He leads me by the hand.

'The washing-up . . .' I begin.

'Fuck the washing-up, let's go to bed.'

I let him take me through the kitchen, into the sitting room and up our tiny little staircase into our loft. This is where we sleep. The lamp is on and it casts a golden glow around our den.

Safe is our bedroom. The walls are painted an ever so pale lilac; 'Spirit' on the can. We have a giant-sized futon, piled with a billowing duvet and opulent throws picked up on our honeymoon in India. There is only one painting in here – it is by Noreen, a friend, and is called *In Anima Vitae – The Aran Kiss*. A man, half human, half nymph, cradles his lover's head; her white arms reach up and touch his black, curly hair, as her own red glory tumbles and dissolves into their surroundings. Tiny white daisies frame the couple as little fish dart by.

Leo holds me, and I feel like this woman. I am completely in his grasp. My devotion is fragile, but now utmost. Maybe he senses this, as we slowly fall back onto the futon, as if in slow motion, and gently peel our clothing off. Naked, we rub our bodies against each other, until we are both brimming with expectation. I reach over to get the condoms out of the locker, but Leo puts his hand over mine and stops me.

'What do you think?' he whispers to me.

I freeze, shaking my head.

'No, not this time, Leo, I'm not ready.'

'Eithne, I love you – I want us to be a family.'

My body tugs at me to let him in, but my fear is stronger.

'But we are a family – you have Shauna.'

'Don't you want to have my child, ever? If we want to have children don't you think we should start soon?'

'Yes, I know. Soon – but not now – I . . .'

27

How can I tell him the truth? That I never want to have children – that he is all I want – he is enough.

I'm scared that a baby is something too precious. If I lost it, I might fall into a void, like Mammy did when Beatrice went. I know how much that hurt.

I look up through the skylight at the stars. I make a wish. It is the first time that I have wished for something other than for Beatrice to return. As soon as I think of her I feel guilty and turn my gaze back to the painting.

The reason I really like this picture is because it reminds me of her. Not that she looked like the woman in the painting, although the hair is similar, but because its abandon reminds me of her spirit. She never held back.

A pearl necklace bought in a small boutique on the Playa de Palma in Majorca by my sister Beatrice. She bought our mother one too, and a bracelet for me. In Majorca pearls are not expensive. These pearls I could almost eat, tiny drops of opaque pleasure from the sea. When Beatrice gave me my pearl bracelet I was only thirteen. I had never been outside Ireland. I had never swum in the Mediterranean Sea. Beatrice told me how warm the water was, how soft the sand, and how hot it was. She made me laugh with her descriptions of stacked-up tourists like sausages on a grill, and the fights for the sun loungers. She told me she had sunbathed topless and to prove her claim removed her top to show me the unbroken brown of her tanned chest and back. When I asked her what she and the girls did on their holiday she was vague, 'We just sunbathed and went out at night.'

*

Last year Leo and I went to Majorca for a sun holiday, a quick, cheap break. The second day there, when we had seen all we needed to of the rows of identical hotel blocks and the artificial beach, Leo suggested we take a bus into the interior of the island, to a place called Valledemosa. Perched on top of a mountain, this old monastic settlement was a breath of fresh air. Although there were still plenty of tourists, this was miles away from the bleak monotony of apartment blocks. Later that day we decided to go even further up the coast, and took another bus to a small village called Deia.

After a hair-raising drive, where the road wound tighter and tighter uphill, the bus ground to a halt in a tiny village, perched high up on the edge of a cliff. We had read that there was a way down to a tiny cove so we followed a long, hot and dusty trail downhill, past houses, parched gardens and terraced olive groves. We didn't see a soul – it was time for the siesta. Orange trees marked our route – it was a thrill to be able to pick an orange straight from the tree. We hopped across a ditch. Leo took my hand. His face was completely obscured by his sun hat and glasses, but I could tell he was concerned.

The night before I had drunk too much. One sangria had led to another, after all, we *were* on holiday. Before I knew it, I was up performing my own unique version of the flamenco with the amused dancers. But my high spirits were swiftly followed by gloom.

'I keep seeing Beatrice,' I said to Leo. 'I see her everywhere I look.'

It was true; there were lots of laughing, carefree single girls with big smiles in wild, heathen groups, just like Beatrice and her friends. Who would think a holiday to Majorca would bring her memory back so keenly to me?

Leo had said nothing; he just twisted his fingers through mine, and then got up.

'Come on,' he had said, 'let's go back to the hotel.'

So today I feel fragile. I had been sick all morning, but Leo made me go out. Now the heat was getting to me, I was so thirsty I could hardly speak.

'Jesus, where the hell is the beach?'

'It says a short ten-minute stroll in this guide book.'

'Well, either the guy must be the fastest hiker in the universe or he should be taken out and shot. Fuck!'

I had slipped and, to prevent myself falling, I had grabbed hold of a thistly bush. Leo examined me.

'All clear. No thorns in your side,' he said sardonically.

Finally, we came to a small, stony cove. It had been worth it. A few people were sunbathing, and some more were in the sea. I collapsed, and then abruptly sat up and looked about me. A tiny restaurant was to our left, on a slab of rock overlooking the sea. It was not a particularly remarkable place, but it looked familiar. Then I remembered.

'Leo,' I said excitedly, 'Beatrice was here. She drew this cove in her sketchbook. It looks exactly the same – the restaurant here to the left, and the flag.'

Leo put his arm through mine.

'Maybe it was a mistake coming to Majorca,' he said. 'Everything seems to remind you of your sister.'

'No, it's good for me. I have to remember.'

It was ironic. Here we were eighteen years later sitting in the same spot where she had sat drawing her picture. But still my sister did not feel real, not as real as the salt I could taste in my mouth or the sweep of the sea breeze through my hair. She was just a memory as elusive as a dream.

The rest of the holiday we spent walking. Leo paced beside me, witnessing the pain and the memories.

In my first and second years at art college, I did not fully catch on to my style. My tutors criticized me for being too distant from my work; they said I had to find my own individual voice. It was as if they were encouraging me to be tortured, hurt.

The vacation before my finals I decided to go home for the summer. At first I did not touch a pencil, I just spent a lot of time thinking. I started looking at the fields, at the trees, the river, the loughs, and the lie of the land, especially the bog. I took black and white photographs of the landscape and searched for a way through: a path. This was the cycle of life in its raw state. It was such beautiful countryside, yet with such darkness beneath. Like my sister. It began to make sense; she had become the landscape. Beatrice had disappeared into the peaty, midlands earth, and all my emotions, which the landscape raised, reflected my state of mind concerning her. That summer I began to mourn Beatrice for the first time.

I took pictures of myself in the bog using a tripod and timer. A commemoration. I sat in the bog plucking its cotton and letting myself grieve. I was obsessed with the tiny: a small stone, a piece of lichen, a leaf, a small flower. I examined my flowers: dead now, but so beautiful, at one time complete and nourished. This was enough for me; this was all I needed. For the first time I truly believed my sister was dead and would never return.

When the summer ended I was frightened to go back to the city. Why would anyone ever want to leave where they came from? My soul was there. But return I did, to complete my degree. That autumn I was transformed from mediocre student to promising young artist. I left my first print in the acid too long, but the lecturers thought it was great. It was of a bog near home, very dark with deep cuts. They said it had a real feeling of turf, it evoked the Irish countryside – it's density – the dark.

So here I am several years later, with only a few group shows behind me. My new work focuses more precisely upon my sister's disappearance. I am trying to remember everything, to keep a record of memory and emotion. I print my landscapes, but they are no longer merely just that. Objects enter the arena, all hidden in the woods behind our house, by the lough, under the aspen trees, on the bog, by the rag tree and under the yews: a string of pearls, a scarf, a hat, a sketchbook and a small compact.

TWO: THE SCARF

EITHNE

There is a series of paintings of Beatrice wearing the scarf. I only discovered this a few months ago.

The paintings are by a man known back home as the Artist. He was a sombre man, tall and dark with a shaggy, grey beard. The Artist was Beatrice's mentor.

Leo discovered the pictures. It turned out the Artist was called Jakob Rudin, who was an uncle of a childhood friend of Leo's called Mick. Mick's and Leo's mothers and Leo's father were Polish Jews, who had escaped the Nazis, and through this unique bond the two boys had become very close. Their childhood was spent in the south inner city of Dublin, where Leo's parents ran a Jewish bakery. Mick, on the other hand, had been brought up a Catholic, like his father, but the two boys shared the drama of their parents' past.

Jakob Rudin had escaped from being sent to the concentration camps in the Second World War along with his sister Gertie, Mick's mother. They went to London first, but soon afterwards moved to Dublin. As soon as Gertie was old enough to fend for herself, Jakob left her there and moved to the countryside. He preferred isolation. Now that his perimeters of humanity had been destroyed, he distrusted everybody.

I remembered that the Artist hadn't mixed with the locals. He didn't drink in the pub and he didn't go to Mass, so the only time you might see him was in the corner shop where he bought his groceries. He had a very old car, a Ford Anglia, which used to clatter up the hill, but it got him around, and sometimes he would disappear for days on end. Most of us would see him painting in different locations — by the river, at the top of a field, or even on the roadside, that's how he got his nickname, although as far as I know no one ever saw any of his work, apart from Beatrice that is.

Beatrice had always wanted to be an artist. I remember her saying so from the time I was tiny. Before she went to college, she decided she needed extra lessons, and so one day, no bother to her, she marched down the hill and knocked on the Artist's front door. Instead of turning her away, he looked at the drawings she had brought with her and agreed to give her tuition. I don't think he ever charged her — I think after years of solitude he enjoyed her company.

Jakob Rudin died last year, leaving a house full of dusty canvases and nothing else. We discovered the connection when Leo said he was coming home with me one weekend.

'I'm meeting Mick,' he said. 'His uncle used to live near you. He died last week.'

'What was his name?'

'Jakob Rudin. He was a Jewish refugee; like my parents. Mick told me that he was a painter. That's why he wants me to come down.'

'The Artist! I thought he died years ago.'

'You knew him?'

'No, not really. But Beatrice did, he taught her,' I said.

The Artist had lived in a large stone house about a mile down the road from us. He had a wild garden with a stream running through it, and a scrabble of mangy chickens. His house was a mess. Mick had roped Leo in to help him sort out his uncle's paintings; to see if he thought any of them were worth anything.

'Piles of unoriginal oils,' Leo said that night in the pub.

Mick sighed.

'Did you ever visit your uncle when you were a child?' I asked Mick.

'No. This is the first time I've ever set foot in the house. My uncle disapproved of my dad. He could never get over the fact that he was German. I never saw him, even though my mam sent him a monthly allowance. She did try to keep in contact. We drove down once, but he would not even open the front door. He just didn't want to know.'

'You can't really blame him after what he went through,' said Leo. 'I still can't get my dad to talk about his childhood – I know nothing about his family, who he lost and who survived. As for my mother – she does talk about the past – it's awful and she has a thing about Germans too. I don't think she can help it.'

'Yeah, but my father has never even been to Germany. His parents were German, and his name is German, but he's always lived in Ireland. He had nothing to do with the war. My mam was really hurt when Jakob rejected them.'

'He was older than her, wasn't he? Maybe he saw more than she did – people deal with trauma like that in different ways,' Leo said, taking a slug of his Guinness. 'If you met my dad you'd think he was grand,' he continued, 'always cracking a joke and full of beans. But that's on the surface. I used to think about the war a lot when I was a little boy. There were all those war movies on then, you know like *The Great Escape* and the *Bridge on the River Kwai* – I was obsessed with them. But my dad hated me watching them. I always had to do it in secret, when he'd gone out. Once I wasn't thinking and I asked him, just blurted it out, had he ever seen a dead body? I'll never forget the look he gave me – like I'd punched him in the stomach. Poor guy.'

'Yeah, I know what you mean,' said Mick. 'When my mother came to Ireland with my Uncle Jakob she was only twelve and he was sixteen. They had gone the whole way from Germany to Ireland on their own. I still don't know how they got here. She never told me, and I suppose I'm afraid to ask. I don't want to carry that burden too.'

Leo and Mick nursed their pints. My husband looked stern, he was almost scowling. Everything about him was light – his pale blond hair, cut short, like a shaved halo, and his skin, several tones lighter than mine, even his lips seemed bled of colour. His navy jumper made him look even fairer. He was not from this land. His family, his heritage of pain was as real as mine, but buried deeper, further away. And he had learnt to leave it behind. It hung around him, but he would not engage with it.

'Would you never ask your father, Leo, what happened in Poland? How he got away?' I asked him.

'I can't – I should have, I know – but it's too late now. He seems happy, I don't want to ruin that.'

The Artist had become a real person, with a history and a family. To me he had always been a mystery, someone tragic and strange. The Gardaí interviewed him when Beatrice vanished, and I don't think he ever got over the fright of three large uniformed men entering his home with their air of authority and their interrogation. He was a foreigner, always the prime suspect.

The following day, Leo and Mick went down to finish up at the Artist's house, while I stayed home with my mother. At around midday he phoned.

'You had better come down here,' he said.

'Why?'

'I'll tell you when you get here.'

Mystified, I pedalled down the hill on an old bike. Mick and Leo were in the attic.

'Come on up,' Leo shouted.

I climbed up the stepladder. Leo pulled me in. The attic was lit by a naked bulb. Leaning against one side of the roof were a series of vibrant nudes in differing shades of blue. In each picture the model was the same woman – gentle adolescent curves, soft auburn hair, and a blue silk scarf. Beatrice. I gasped. Leo put his arm around me.

'Now these are worth something,' said Mick.

Leo shot him a look.

'What's that?' I asked.

Behind one of the canvases, another showed. I could see a foot. Two. Four, in fact.

'I did not know whether you should see this,' said Leo.

He took out the picture. There was my sister, naked again. She was reclining, her head thrown back and her face was wearing an expression I did not recognize. But her legs were spread and there was a man between them. Although I could not see his face, he looked like the Artist by his build. He had the blue silk scarf tied around his waist, trailing onto the floor.

Mammy aged. Within a week her shoulders hunched, her mouth sank down and her eyes lost their shine. Her skin became very pale, almost transparent, and I imagined she was made of glass. If I came too close she just might shatter. In truth, I was a little afraid. Her grief was like a Siberian winter, and I didn't want to go there. So I watched her, willing her to look at me. But she never turned. Like an old woman saying the rosary, she would sit on her chair by the back door, twisting Beatrice's blue scarf around her wrists and her hands, on and on. She would mumble to herself, like a prayer, or a chant, but I could never make out what she was saying.

I remember every groove of that old chair, the worn seat with the ripped upholstery, and the soft smell of old pine. That smell would mingle with the crisp bite of winter mornings. I would find her always in her chair when I came down every morning. She must have gone up to bed at some stage, but she rose early, unable to sleep properly, and I always felt I left her where I found her. In the mornings, no matter how cold it might be, she would have the back door wide open. The fresh scent of the new day would waft into the kitchen; it's a smell that always arrests me. At that time it reminded me of adventures Beatrice and I had when I was really little.

On September mornings, before we went to school, Beatrice used to pull me out of my bed and we'd skip out of the house and across the fields, returning an hour later, our lips stained with blackberries and our bellies aching from the juice, unable to eat one bit of Mammy's porridge. She'd give out to us, but her eyes were shining, and really she was delighted by her daughters' abandon. We had kinship then . . .

Sitting at the kitchen table, trying to eat some breakfast, waiting to go to school, in those early days after Beatrice was gone, I looked at my mother on her chair as if I was watching something on the television. And the shot just went on and on, like a tortuous scene from a foreign film, all still, apart from the shimmering blue scarf, sliding between her fingers, slipping around her arms, on and on, the pattern and rhythm as constant as knitting. I wondered that the material did not wear away.

SARAH

'Why don't you go home?' Jonathan said as gently as he could. 'It is at a time like this that a girl needs her mother.'

'No,' said Sarah flatly. She imagined the horror on her mother's face, her father's disappointment. She would rather die than go home.

'You can't tell my parents,' Jonathan said, his voice rising. 'Sarah, there is no future for us. We are from different worlds, it would never work.'

'Please help me, Jon.' Sarah started crying again. 'I don't know what to do. I'm scared.'

'Jesus. What can I do! Go home! Why can't you go back to Southampton?'

'No. Never!' she was almost screaming.

People started to look at them.

'Okay. Calm down. Just let me think for a minute.'

They sat in silence. Jonathan lit a cigarette. Sarah sobbed quietly; tears dripped into her tea.

'It is a shame you did not come to me sooner,' he said, 'we could have done something about it then.' He looked down at her stomach. 'It's too late now.'

Sarah was puzzled. Then all of a sudden she realized what he meant, and her last precious piece of hope died. He had never loved her.

'It's okay,' she said quietly. 'I'll be all right.'

41

'You won't tell my parents, will you?'

'No. I have a friend. I'll stay with her,' she lied.

'I'll get you some money,' he said. 'If you need anything, just let me know. You're a good girl, Sarah – it'll be okay.' He thrust a one-pound note into her hand. 'I have to go. Take care.' He got up, ruffled her hair and fled.

Sarah sat in the corner of the cafe. She stared at the money in her hand. She was no better than a whore. How had she let this happen? Was she such a fool that she had really believed he would marry her one day? She had thought she was special but now she realized she was just another sad case. It started to rain outside. She shivered, and felt a sharp twinge in her womb. She should go to the doctor. She poured herself another cup of tea and stared out of the window. What on earth was she going to do?

As Sarah looked out, she saw a familiar figure walking briskly down the street, shoulders bent into the rain. Anthony. She looked away but it was too late, he had seen her. He stopped, a puzzled expression on his face and, smiling, came into the cafe.

'Hello, Sarah,' he said. 'What are you doing here?'

Sarah looked down at the chips and cracks in the formica table, the top spattered with drips of tea.

'I had a day off, I've never been to Oxford. I thought . . .'

A lump rose in her throat. Anthony was looking at her critically. They had never really had a conversation before. Sarah started to get up.

'I'd better go,' she said. 'The train leaves soon.'

'Were you meeting Jon?' His dark eyes pierced her.

'Not exactly,' she said.

The need to confide in someone was so strong that she sat back down again.

'You look very upset, Sarah,' said Anthony. 'I am sure my

mother would be worried to see you like this. She is very fond of you, you know. Tell me, what is wrong?'

Why had she never noticed this dark-haired brother, always quiet and now so kind?

'It is Jon, isn't it? What has he done to you? I love my brother but I know that he can be an absolute scoundrel. Has he made advances towards you?'

'No, it's not him. It wasn't him.' Sarah began crying again. 'I promised I wouldn't tell.'

She shifted in her seat. Whichever way she moved it pulled her dress tight behind her. Anthony saw a small but pronounced bump.

'Sarah,' Anthony asked her gently, 'are you pregnant?'

'Yes,' she whispered.

Anthony took a measured breath. 'Is Jon the father?'

She shook her head but her hands went up to her face. She tried to push the tears away.

'No – no – no . . .' she stuttered.

BEATRICE

She slipped out of the house that night. Her head still hurt. She got on her bicycle and cycled down the hill to her friend's house. He was the only one she could trust. There was a light on in his bedroom window.

'Jakob,' she called softly. 'Jakob.'

A head appeared. A few minutes later the front door opened.

'Beatrice,' the Artist said in his gentle voice, 'why are you crying?'

She walked into his front room and sat on the couch, took out a handkerchief and blew her nose. Jakob said nothing. He poured her some brandy and put the glass on the tiny table beside her. Beatrice sniffed; she took a sip.

'Jakob, can I stay with you? Mammy and Eithne aren't at home.'

'Of course,' he said gently. 'You go up to my bedroom and I will sleep on the sofa.'

'Jakob, will you sleep with me? I'm scared.'

'Well . . .'

'Please, Jakob.'

'Okay. Come on, it's late. But just sleep. We sleep.'

They went up to his bedroom, and got into his large mahogany bed. He had pyjamas on, and she was still dressed. But each hour shed a layer as the warmth of them embraced.

THE SCARF

By the early hours of the morning they were naked and
Beatrice kissed Jakob. He put his arms around her and then
healed the hurt the brute had made there. He took her heart
outside the pain.

EITHNE

Print-making is dangerous. You use acid and ammonia, so you have to wear a mask and gloves, otherwise all the fumes and toxins could poison you.

What I love about etching is that it is a little like working in the dark, using your intuitive instincts rather than your visual sense, even though this is art and you are producing something for the eye. And then there is the slight loss of control – you are dependent upon the technical process and anything could happen. Your print has a life of its own: it could be full of depth and mystery, or it could be flat.

At the moment I am making an etching in which I incorporate the scarf like a wreath of smoke around the mountain which is visible from the top of our village. When I made this print, I imagined myself and Beatrice standing in this spot, on the corner of the village, opposite the pump. We used to stand there nearly every night, after we walked the dog. Beatrice would pick out the hill with the 'nipple', as she called it.

'That's Sliabh na Caillaigh, Witch's Hill,' she said. 'There's ancient burial mounds up there. When I get a car, I'll take you. Jakob and I went to one called Carnbane East, the white cairn. It's called that cos it would have been covered in quartz. Imagine the sight on a sunny day. It would have been like a beacon of blinding white light.'

She paused to light a cigarette. I stared at the distant hill, imagining it all white.

'There were the most amazing carvings inside the mound. I thought they were flowers and centipedes but Jakob told me they were symbols of the sun.'

'Can't we walk there?' I asked.

'No, it's too far,' she said.

'Maybe Daddy could take us.'

'No. You don't want to go with him. I want it to be just us and then we can dance on the mountain top and shout and scream.'

I looked sideways at her.

'Are you mad?'

'Absolutely. People are so inhibited round here; I get sick of it.'

'Why is it called Witch's Hill?'

'Jakob told me that this old hag used to sit up there in her hag's chair. You can still sit in it now. It's a big stone seat. Anyway, the legend goes that if she was able to carry her apron full of stones and still jump over the three hills of Loughcrew she would rule over the whole of Ireland. So she started with Cairne Bawn, but when she jumped she dropped a handful of stones, which turned into hundreds of tons. She hopped to the next hill, Sliabh na Caillaigh, and dropped another handful of stones, and they turned into a huge cairn. She jumped to the third hill – I don't know what that one's called – and threw the rest of the stones there, and they turned into another great pile. She was jumping from the last hill to a hill at Patrickstown, but she fell and broke her neck.'

'Charming!' I said.

'It's a lucky place,' she said. 'If you sit in the hag's chair and make a wish they say it will be granted.'

I shook my head. 'It all sounds a bit weird to me.'

We went home and had tea and sandwiches before we went to bed.

Beatrice's scarf was found on Witch's Hill two days after she disappeared. It was inside the cairn, resting on a stone. A tourist found it and brought it back to the bed and breakfast in which they were staying. The owner immediately recognized the scarf, and rang the Gardaí. Beatrice was wearing it the day she left Dublin, people noticed her and her trailing silk scarf as she drifted around Busaras looking for her bus.

My mother has a blue scarf as well. She wears it in her hair when she paints now. This is when I like my mother: when she is quiet and meditative, painting in the garden on a summer's evening and my father is away. My mother likes painting with watercolours. She loves the paper, thick and textured, and the power which the water has over colour and form. She has painted a thousand sunsets, each one different and poignant with lost promise.

The Wright Gallery is a converted warehouse on the south side of the quays. Although it is all white walls and high-tech, you get a feeling of vast emptiness, of history, when you walk in. I suppose that's good for a gallery, there's nothing in the architecture to obscure the art.

The space is bare apart from a black and white video, which is projected on the back wall. I linger here watching, waiting for the appointed time of the meeting. The film has no story, hardly any content, just a roundabout loop of mouths and noses. It makes me nervous. She is hardly going to be interested in my stuff . . . it's too normal.

An assistant takes me up to Eliza Wright's second-floor office. The girl is wearing the most awkward-looking black dress, made of what looks like distressed PVC, with a baggy cut and a messy hemline. Yet she looks incredibly cool, her self-assurance turning the disastrous dress into something funky.

Eliza Wright approaches. She is more conventionally dressed in a black trouser suit. She shakes my hand, holding my gaze with warm brown eyes, which are shielded by a tiny pair of round glasses. We go into her office; she bends over her desk flicking through a large diary, while I seat myself opposite, preparing to sell myself. My throat is so dry I wonder whether I'll be able to speak at all.

'Would you like a coffee?' she says quickly.

'Thank you, yes,' I croak.

The assistant goes over to the corner of the room, and pours coffee from a steaming cafetière. Eliza Wright pulls open the top drawer of a large filing cabinet, and takes out a dark blue folder, which I recognize as my submission. I am embarrassed by the silence. Eliza Wright puts the folder down on her desk in front of her, opens it and flicks through.

'"Underearth", "Underwater",' she murmurs. 'Yes, I liked this – the personalization of landscape. Am I right?' She looks up, peering at me over her glasses.

'Yes,' I say. 'These places – ' I point at the slides I sent her – 'they're not real – they're more like landscapes of the mind – emotional places . . .'

The assistant is sitting down next to me, nursing a large coffee, and nodding knowingly.

'What do you think, Sasha?' Eliza asks her.

'I think they're very haunting,' she says. 'I love the way you've pared your prints right down just to the essentials, and then just put in a tiny bit of detail.'

'It's very effective,' says Eliza.

'Thank you.'

'But are these places really imaginary?' Sasha asks me. 'I mean what inspired you?'

'Well, I grew up in County Meath, in the north of the county. There are lots of bogs there, so they inspired me. All the tones I use in the prints are there in the landscape – the areas of bogland, and the woods and lakes.'

'Sounds beautiful,' Eliza says. 'I've never been that way.'

'It can be bleak as well,' I say.

'I understand the "Underearth" part – looking at what might lie beneath the bog – am I right?' Sasha says.

'Yes, that's it.'

'But what about "Underwater"? she asks. 'How does that connect to your other theme?'

I am beginning to wonder who is in charge, Sasha or Eliza.

'Yes,' Eliza joins in, 'you say here that the "Underwater" section will be a series of etchings inspired by the mythology of Atlantis – the lost city. How does that fit in with your other prints?'

The two women stare at me. How can I explain?

'The starting point of my project was looking at the question: where do all the missing people go?' I begin.

'What made you think about that?' prods Sasha.

'Well, I have personal experience of it.' I speak clearly, each word ringing out. 'My sister went missing when I was thirteen, we think she was killed.' I race on before they can say anything, 'Maybe she's buried out there somewhere in a bog, or in the woods – there are so many places she could be . . . but you see, when I dream about her, I dream about the sea – I don't know why, maybe because she loved it so much – and she always used to talk about Atlantis, it fascinated her like it did my father.'

'I'm so sorry, Eithne.' Eliza looks grave.

'You're very brave to put that in your work.' Then, turning to Eliza, Sasha says, 'I think this is going to be an amazing show.'

'I agree – I'm very excited about it,' Eliza says. 'We can offer you three weeks in October, how do you feel about that?'

I nearly spill my coffee.

'That's . . . wonderful . . .' I manage to splutter.

'Excellent.' She smiles. 'We'll send you out a contract as soon as Sasha has it typed up. I'm very much looking forward to working with you.'

She stands up and takes my hand.

'We need a few more artists like you,' she says, 'willing to bare a little more without being caught up in their own egos.'

Sasha is nodding again, a small cynical smile playing on her lips. I can't work out whether she likes me or not.

'Well done, Eithne,' she says. 'I'll be in touch.'

My legs feel shaky as I walk back down the stairs. I am astounded that I told them so much.

As soon as I leave the gallery, I ring Leo on my mobile.

'That's fantastic,' he says. 'Didn't I say that things were going to start happening for you if you just stuck at it?'

'I've so much work to do,' I say. 'I need to go out west for a while just to look at the Atlantic Ocean. God! I need to start painting . . .'

'We'll go for a couple of weeks later in the year. We can stay at Marta's.'

'And then I had better go home to study the bog, and think about what I'm going to do.'

'Don't panic,' he says. 'You've loads of time. It's not as if you're making a huge installation, or a public art commission.'

There it is. It slips out again. I had suspected but rejected the idea that Leo thinks what he does is more important than what I do.

'Eithne, are you still there?' he says, noting my silence. 'What's wrong?'

'Nothing.' There's no point starting an argument on the phone.

'Let's go out for a few drinks, to celebrate, I'll meet you in town.'

By the time I meet Leo, I am too excited about the exhibition to be annoyed. We make a night of it, clubbing until three in the morning. And then we come home and pass out on the bed.

It is the night before everything changes.

SARAH

Sarah was already beginning to show when she left the Voyle household. Over the previous couple of weeks Lady Voyle had begun to have suspicions, and had interrogated her house-keeper.

'Rachel,' she said, 'have you noticed a change in Sarah? I think she might be pregnant, she has got quite large, don't you think?'

Rachel was in no doubt that Sarah was in trouble, and she had easily guessed who the father was, but Sarah had told Rachel that she was leaving in a couple of weeks to stay with family, and the housekeeper saw no point in humiliating the girl. She never broached the subject of why she was going to Sarah, although in private she sighed and shook her head at the pity of it all.

'No, I don't think so,' she said to Lady Voyle. 'She's just put on a little weight. It's impossible that she could be pregnant, she doesn't go out at all, she's here every single night.'

Lady Voyle looked at her housekeeper. She thought for a second. A possibility flashed through her mind. She dispelled it.

'Where is she going again?'

'An elderly aunt in Clapham. There's no one to look after her and she's dying, so Sarah is doing her duty for her family.'

'Things will be difficult for her financially,' Lady Voyle said. 'I must give her a little present.'

And that was the last time Sarah was mentioned.

Since that dreadful day in Oxford she had not seen Jonathan, who had studiously avoided coming down to London, much to the puzzlement of his mother.

Anthony, on the other hand, had come home every weekend and, taking care not to be seen by anyone, had met her in local cafes to discuss her and the baby's future. He was an honourable man and had insisted that she be taken care of. He accepted that going back to Southampton was not an option when she explained how she could not face her mother's condemnation and her father's shame. She wasn't even sure that her mother would take her back, and so he had arranged a house for her and the baby. At first he had tentatively suggested that she might consider adoption, and that he could help her organize it all. But Sarah instinctively shook her head. For some reason the thought terrified her more than keeping the baby.

As the weeks passed, and the weather grew milder, Sarah found she thought less and less about Jonathan. When he had first rejected her she felt she would die. She remembered when she had returned to London from Oxford, curling up like a ball on her bed, sobbing and ignoring Rachel's knocks on the door. Now, strangely, she found she missed him less and less. Only at night, when she could feel the baby kicking, did she still get upset and panicked. Could she get him back? Was it really all over?

At the weekend, when Anthony was around, things never seemed so bad. Sometimes, after talking over tea, they would go for a little walk on the Heath, and sit quietly under a tree chatting. When he relaxed, Anthony wasn't as serious as he looked, in fact he could be really funny, doing impressions of some of his professors at college and some of the 'snobs', as he called them, on his course. It was good to laugh, and sometimes he had her in tears.

One afternoon they were sitting by the pond, feeding the ducks, when Sarah asked, 'What do you want to do, Anthony, when you finish college?'

'Travel,' he said immediately. 'I want to go all over the world, ideally as an archaeologist. I'd love to go to Egypt and Jordan. They're the two places I really want to visit.'

Sarah flung some bread towards a handsome drake.

'I've never been anywhere,' she said, 'apart from here of course, and where I grew up.'

They were sitting a few inches apart, their fingertips almost touching.

'It'll be all right.' Anthony turned to look at her. 'One day you'll see the world, I'm sure.'

How could he say that? thought Sarah. All she could see was what was happening in the present, that she was pregnant, going nowhere.

'I won't let you down, Sarah,' Anthony was saying. 'I'll always make sure that you and the baby are all right.'

But in the back of her mind Sarah knew that she was living on borrowed time. She could not depend on Anthony's charity for the rest of her life. She had her pride. She would have to sort something out.

Still, for the moment she was not going to worry. All she was going to think about was having the baby. The idea of giving birth terrified her, yet the fact that there was a little person inside her waiting to come out thrilled her. She would never be alone again.

*

Sarah moved out of her Hampstead home one wet Monday in early June. She was tired so she splashed out on a taxi. Besides, she seemed to have accumulated a lot of things over the past year. When she arrived in Clapham she did not expect anyone to be there; Anthony had given her a key and explained that he would be round at the weekend.

The taxi pulled up outside her new home. The driver got out and carried her bags up the path. She thanked him and paid him, and was just getting her key out when the door opened. It was Anthony.

'Surprise!' he said, picking up her bags and leading the way. 'In the end, I thought I should be here to give you the grand tour.'

The house was small, but it was all Sarah needed. Thent room had a sofa and a couple of pictures on the wall. A narrow corridor led to the bathroom and a tiny kitchen.

He already had the kettle on.

'Follow me,' he said.

Upstairs there were two bedrooms.

'I thought you might like this room,' he said. It was the back bedroom which had a view of a garden. He had made the bed.

'The front bedroom you can use for guests.'

Sarah laughed. 'What guests?'

'Maybe me sometimes, if that's all right. At the beginning, you might want some company.'

Sarah blushed, then she saw a narrow doorway on the landing.

'What's this?' she asked. She opened the third door. It led to a tiny bedroom, which was bare apart from a cradle in the centre of the room.

'It was already here,' said Anthony. 'I couldn't believe it.'

Sarah walked into the room and placed her hand on the cradle. It rocked.

'Oh my God,' she said.

'What is it? What's wrong?' asked Anthony.

'This is like a dream come true.'

Sarah felt safe in the house in Clapham during her pregnancy. Although Anthony stayed in the spare room on the odd occasion, she was mostly on her own. He bought her a dog for company; a cocker spaniel. 'The best dogs to have around children,' he said. Sarah called the dog Beth.

There was no telephone in the house and Sarah did not write letters, so Anthony was the only person she had any contact with. She walked Beth every day on Clapham Common. The exercise was good for her as she grew and grew. Every Friday she walked into Clapham village to do some shopping. On the way, on the right, there were some building sites and each week one of the men always whistled at her even though she was obviously pregnant.

He had black curly hair and shouted, 'Hello, beauty,' with an Irish accent.

Sarah had never before had so much time to herself. In the evening, she knitted for the baby or else she painted – hesitant still lives of a bunch of flowers bought in the market that day or a milk jug on the table. During the day she gardened out the back.

Sarah's pregnancy was a normal one. She went to the hospital once every four weeks for a check-up. As she got closer to her time, she started going every week. Anthony had given her a simple wedding band to make things easier for her. The doctor called her Mrs Quigley and treated her with a certain amount of respect, which other young, unmarried girls did not get.

'Will your husband be bringing you in?' the doctor asked Sarah one week.

'Oh, well, he will probably be away working,' she said. 'He is always away.'

'What does he do?' asked the doctor.

'He's a builder,' Sarah said quickly, thinking of the curly-haired Irishman. 'He is working on a site up north.'

'That's a shame, seeing as there is so much building work in London at the moment.'

'He is hoping to move down here once the baby is born,' she said.

It was Anthony who gave Sarah her blue scarf. It was not silk but chiffon. It was not as long as Beatrice's and it did not have a fringe on either end. It was also a different shade of blue, duck-egg blue. Anthony Voyle gave Sarah a pale blue chiffon scarf on her seventeeth birthday. The baby was due in a week.

Over the past three months Anthony and Sarah had become good friends. He had taken care of his brother's problem without the other's knowledge, at Sarah's request. As far as Jonathan was concerned, Sarah was staying with a friend in Clapham Common. He never came to see her, so it would be very unlikely that he would ever learn of his brother's visits to the house he had rented for Sarah. Anthony had dug into his own personal savings to pay for the house. He felt it was the least his family could do for her. He had been tempted to tell his parents; they were decent people and would want Jonathan to marry Sarah, no matter what her background was. However, it was not only Sarah's insistence that nobody should know, but also his growing feelings for her, which made him want to protect her from Jonathan. If she married his brother she would have a miserable life, he knew that for sure.

Anthony had not been surprised by his twin's bad behaviour. He had seen the way Jonathan had begun carrying on as soon as they had moved to Oxford. He was just sorry that someone like Sarah was paying for it.

He had been drawn to her immediately, from the first day he had been introduced to her. He couldn't stop looking at her eyes. They were incredibly dark, with long black lashes. He had felt something when he looked at her eyes. Something, which connected them. Just in that look . . . that one look. She was small, with creamy brown skin, and curly auburn hair. Her smile was wide, and she had tiny pearly teeth. He thought she was the prettiest girl he had ever laid eyes on. Of course, he had dismissed his attraction, concluding that their worlds were miles apart, but he couldn't help noticing the spell his brother had cast over her, and Jon's ensuing infatuation. He had worried about the consequences.

'Your birthday present is in keeping with today's events,' he said as she opened his gift.

'I can't have you riding in my car with dishevelled locks.'

'It's beautiful,' Sarah said when she saw the scarf.

'Here, let me help you put it on.'

She put it over her hair and he tied it at the chin.

'Happy birthday,' he said.

'How did you know?' she asked.

'Well, I was rather sneaky. My mother has all your details in her desk drawer. It wasn't hard to find out.'

'You are incredible,' she said.

'I aim to please.'

They got into the car, a red MG. Beth sat in the back. The roof was down. It was a perfect summer's day.

'I am going to take you to one of my favourite places,' said Anthony.

They headed west out of London. After about an hour they turned off the main road and went through a town called Maidenhead. They took another turn and drove by the river and across a common, until they came into a village called Cookham-on-Thames.

'We used to come here a lot as a child. My father is a member of the local country club.'

They turned off the main road and up a drive, parking in front of a grand ivy-covered house with baby turrets.

'Here we are,' he said. 'How about a spot of lunch?'

They went inside the house. The receptionist greeted them.

'I booked a table for two. Voyle,' Anthony said.

This had never happened to her before; Sarah had never been taken out for a meal.

She had the works. Roast beef, roast potatoes, Yorkshire pudding, carrots and horseradish sauce followed by sherry trifle and coffee. Then they walked down to the river.

They went punting on the Thames. Sarah lay back, closed her eyes and trailed her hand in the water, as Anthony pushed them down the river. The sun kissed her face. Although the baby was kicking continually and she had terrible heartburn, that just didn't matter.

'Thank you, Anthony,' she said. 'This is the best birthday I have ever had in my life.'

She looked up at him, but the sun was in her eyes and she could only see his silhouette against the sky. He said nothing, and she had no idea what he could be thinking.

Suddenly she felt like a beached whale lying on the cushions in the boat. How could she have thought even for a second that he would be interested in her? He was just doing his duty. He was doing what his brother should have been doing and that was all there was to it.

'Can we go home, please,' she said suddenly. 'I'm tired.'

EITHNE

Shauna, Leo's daughter, arrives at nine, bright as a button. Clara, her mother, looks at the two of us.

'What a couple of wrecks!' She shakes her head, smiling. 'Are you sure you can manage?'

'He's off the hook.' I grimace. 'He's sloping off to one of his art debates.'

'I'd rather be here, suffering with you, honey,' says Leo, as he attempts to eat his breakfast.

'Here,' says Clara, 'Solpadeine. I never go anywhere without them.'

'Cheers,' I say.

'You'll be grand,' she says. 'Just do the wicked step-mother act if she gets too much.'

'Daddy,' says Shauna, 'can we go to the cinema? Please, pretty please.'

'Maybe,' he says trying to get himself together. 'If you're good for Eithne, we might take you.'

'Yes, yes, yes!' Shauna goes flying off into the other room.

'Good luck,' says Clara, and she's gone.

Leo leaves a few minutes later. I put some music on, and Shauna tries to get me to dance with her, but I can hardly move.

'Come on, let's paint.'

It seems the quietest option. I get out brushes, paper and

paints and Shauna begins to splosh around. I really don't care how much mess we make.

The telephone rings.

'Hello?' No reply. 'Hello?' The phone goes dead.

'Who was that?' Shauna asks.

'No one,' I say.

'Maybe it was the bogeyman,' she says. Recently Shauna has become obsessed with ghost stories.

The phone rings again. Shauna looks up expectantly. Her eyes wide open.

'I don't think it's the bogeyman. Probably your dad in a ropey phonebox.'

'Hello . . . hello.'

'Is that Eithne Kelly?' says a woman's voice with an English accent.

'Who's that?' I ask.

'Hi – I didn't know whether I should just come round or whether I should ring you first. I'm Lisa Hayes.'

Lisa Hayes. Lisa Hayes. The name does not ring a bell. Was she someone I had met in London last year when I was over with Leo? Some of his family is in England. Maybe she's a relative. But I really could not place this voice.

'Lisa, hello,' I say. 'I'm really sorry, I can't remember where I met you. Are you a cousin of Leo's?'

'Leo?'

'Leo Zwalf, my husband. I am so sorry I'm terrible with names – did we meet in London?'

Another art student over in Dublin, bumming a bed.

'No,' she says. 'We've never met. Don't you know about me?'

'Sorry . . . I think you must have made a mistake.'

'You are Eithne Kelly, aren't you? You are from Crossakiel in County Meath and you have a sister called Beatrice Kelly?'

'My sister is dead,' I say flatly.

'Fuck. She's dead? Fuck, fuck.' Pause. I can hear her take a drag on a cigarette. I don't know why I do not put the phone down, but something stops me.

'When did she die?' the girl asks.

'Nearly nineteen years ago,' I say.

'But that's impossible,' says Lisa.

'What do you mean?'

'I'm her daughter – and I'm eighteen. She gave me up for adoption. I've come to find her . . .'

I slam the phone down, run into the bathroom and throw up in the sink.

'Eithne! Eithne!' calls Shauna, 'it was the bogeyman, wasn't it?'

SARAH

The way in which Beatrice was born surprised Sarah. Her doctor had told her that there was no point coming into hospital until the contractions were at the most ten minutes apart and had been so regularly for an hour or more, otherwise she was not considered, strictly speaking, to be in labour and would be sent home. Sarah wanted to get things right, so she remained where she was when the pain started. She had been cleaning the house when she felt the first contractions. They were infrequent so she did not worry. Anyhow, she was busy nesting. The pains went away, and came back two hours later. Then they went away again. This went on for two days. Sarah got tired of looking at her watch and trying to time the contractions. They came. They went. They certainly were not regular. On the third day, Sarah decided to go for a walk with Beth. The exercise would hopefully bring on labour, she was fed up waiting.

She circled the Common. It was a cold day, but she felt hot. Here came the pain again. Breathe. Focus on that twig. Breathe through the pain. She wished she wasn't alone. She wandered slowly to the other side of the Common, she was right by the building site. She looked up, and there was the Irishman above her. He waved; she waved back and crumpled. Water was trickling down her legs. Beth leapt up at her and started barking with fright.

'My waters have broken,' she whispered.

The Irishman was there by her side, panting.

'Are you all right?' he asked.

'My waters have broken,' she repeated.

'What? Are you having the baby?'

She nodded. A wave of pain broke over her. She whined.

'Jaysus!' the Irishman exclaimed. 'Mikey, get the van, will yer. She's having a baby!'

They arrived at the hospital, and the Irishman took her in while Mikey stayed in the van with Beth. The midwife examined her while the Irishman sat outside waiting.

'Three centimetres,' said the midwife. 'You'll be a while yet. Do you have your overnight bag?'

'No, I was in the park,' Sarah said.

'Don't worry, I'll get you a gown. Your husband can go home and get your bag.'

Sarah went out into the corridor; she was surprised to see the Irishman was still there.

'I'd better be getting back to work,' he said. 'Is your husband coming?'

'I don't have a husband,' she said.

'Oh. Your fiancé, then?'

Anthony flashed through her mind. No, she could not expect that. She did not want him to see her like this anyway.

'No, I don't have one.'

'Oh.'

Pause. Another contraction. She gripped his hand.

'Please . . . could you get my bag?'

Twelve hours later Beatrice was born. It had been a slow process. The hours had crept by and Sarah was exhausted, but the second stage had been uplifting. She had never felt such power as she delivered her baby. All the time the Irishman let the nurses think he was her husband. He had sat patiently outside, and when the baby was born they brought him in to hold her. Sarah did not even know his name, yet there they were: a family. He held the baby gingerly, peered down at her and said, 'How ya'.'

'What are you going to call her?' asked the nurse as she stitched Sarah up.

Sarah closed her eyes and for a second saw Jonathan's beautiful face. Sorrow overwhelmed her.

'Beata Beatrix,' she whispered to herself.

'Beatrice,' said the nurse. 'That's a lovely old-fashioned name.'

BEATRICE

Beatrice went to the secret garden to write her note. She took with her a torch and a small box. The box was made of tin and she had painted it with brightly coloured patterns, and stuck shells on it. Eithne could not miss it.

The secret garden was behind the shed. You had to squeeze through the shed past all the tools, the lawnmower and a huge machine which caught leaves, to the back door. This door was permanently locked. Their parents had told them that the key was lost, and that there was nothing behind the shed apart from a jungle of weeds, but the girls had been intrigued. A high wall covered in ivy ran from the wall of the shed in a semi-circle, encompassing a small hidden garden, and about two years ago Beatrice and Eithne had found the key in an old greasy jamjar under piles of old newspapers in the corner of the shed. It had taken them a long while to get the door open, but eventually the lock had turned. Getting through had been difficult, because weeds and ivy blocked the doorway; painstakingly they had cut their way through.

It was always night in the secret garden. A lattice of tree branches, weeds, evergreens and ivy were interlaced above the girls' heads. The smell of poisonous plants was almost overwhelming. Anything fragrant or delicate had long since been exterminated by heavy green foliage. Being here had not been comfortable, it was smelly and dark, but at least they had been totally safe. No one could find them here; no one could hear them.

Beatrice looked at the piece of paper for ages and sucked the end of the biro. How was she going to tell Eithne? But she should know the truth: that she had not meant to leave her; that she would come back. Afterwards.

EITHNE

I am in shock. I lean against the side of the bath gasping. Shauna is calling me from the kitchen.

'Was it a ghost?' she shouts with delight.

I feel as though I have seen a ghost. It is impossible to think that Beatrice is still alive after all these years. She would have come back. In fact, she would never have run away in the first place. She wasn't like that. She was proud; she would not have cared what people thought if she had been pregnant. And our mother, of all people, could not have judged her. Even our father could not have been so bad as to make her run away. All alone, and pregnant . . . It was inconceivable.

Shauna walks into the bathroom.

'Why are you sitting on the floor?' she asks.

'I don't feel too well.'

'I'll get you some water.' She troops back into the kitchen and gets me a lukewarm glass of water. There are bits of green leaves floating in it.

'I put some mint in it,' she says. 'Lovely glass of mint water.'

'Thanks, love.' I pretend to drink it and get up shakily. 'Let's get on with our painting.'

The phone rings. I freeze.

'Actually, why don't we go to the park?' I say.

'Answer the phone, answer the phone,' Shauna trills.

I go into the kitchen, lift the receiver and put it straight back down again.

'Who was it?' Shauna asks, as I hand her a coat.

'No one. Wrong number.'

'Bogeyman, bogeyman,' Shauna sings as we leave the house.

We stay out all day. From the park, I take Shauna to the cinema, and then we have a pizza. It's dark by the time we get back and Leo is already home.

'Did anyone phone?' I ask nervously.

'No. Why?' He looks at my face. 'What's the matter?'

'I got this really weird phone call.'

'You look awful, Eithne. Jesus, what's happened?'

'It's Beatrice . . .' I pause not knowing quite how to put it. 'This girl rang me, Leo. She was English – she said she was Beatrice's daughter; that she'd been adopted.'

Leo looks appalled.

'That means,' I continue, 'that Beatrice was pregnant when she disappeared – that means she's not dead.' I gasp. 'Oh, my God . . .'

I feel like I am falling away from my self, my body unable to stay erect.

'Sit down,' Leo says, taking my arm and forcing me onto the sofa. I put my head in my hands.

'It might not be true,' he says quietly. 'That girl might be making it up.'

'But why would anyone do that? Go to all that bother?'

'It could be a mistake,' he suggests.

'Yes,' I say, feeling a little better. 'You must be right. It doesn't make sense – Beatrice couldn't have done that, just gone away without telling anyone. She wouldn't have willingly done that to Mammy . . . She really loved her. It has to be some misunderstanding, don't you think?'

Leo doesn't look so sure now.

'Yes,' he says unconvincingly, 'absolutely — and anyway even if she was out there somewhere she obviously doesn't ever want to come back, so what's the point of torturing yourself any longer?'

I stare at him in disbelief.

'I don't believe you just said that!'

He looks uncomfortable.

'I'm sorry, it came out wrong. I'm sorry . . . I'd better get Shauna out of the bath . . .'

'You have no idea at all — how dare you be so patronizing!'

'Calm down, will you?' he says. 'Shauna will hear you.'

'You don't know what it's like to lose someone close to you — how could you possibly tell me to just stop thinking about it?'

'Eithne, the story of my whole family is based on loss — aunts, uncles, cousins, grandparents, all gone. I'm just saying that there is a point at which you have to let go — we can't live with your sister's ghost for ever. If you cling on to the past too much, you forget about the future.'

'I haven't forgotten the future — I think about it all the time.'

'Whatever,' he says taking the towel from his shoulder and going out of the room.

I am raging. How did he do that? Turn around my upset so that now I feel bad, self-indulgent.

I growl, turn on the telly and slump onto the couch. Leo comes back into the room and picks up the hairbrush. He pauses and is about to say something; he seems unusually hesitant, but I turn my back on him and he gets the message.

*

There is one last portrait of Beatrice, which is in the Artist's attic. This painting is not a nude but a copy of Rosetti's *Beata Beatrix* with Beatrice as Dante's lover. The picture is smaller than the others and painted in soft focus in oils. Beatrice must have told the Artist about Sarah and Jonathan, and about what her name meant and why our father hated it. The painting shows Beatrice's head and shoulders, she is at right angles to us and illuminated by a shaft of light.

In the painting, Beatrice is receiving a small flower from a dove. Is this her lot?

I picked the picture up.

'Can I take this?' I asked Mick.

'Of course. You can take them all,' he said.

'No, I just want this one.'

'Will we burn the others?'

'You can't,' I said, 'somebody made them. We can't destroy someone's work. Sell them, pack them away. I don't care. Just make sure my mam and da never see them.'

I took up the small picture and examined it.

This last painting is imbued with more doom-laden eroticism than all the nudes put together.

I am still cross with Leo the next morning.

'Get up, Daddy – Daddy get up.' Shauna comes tumbling into the bedroom and jumps onto the bed.

He moans and tries to hide under the covers.

'I want my breakfast.' She prods him. 'I'm hungry.'

'Go on, Leo, get up.' I push him.

'Okay, okay,' he says, his head emerging from the covers.

Slowly he pushes open the duvet and sits on the edge of the bed rubbing his eyes. Shauna is delighted.

'I'll get the breakfast ready.' She scampers off to the kitchen, while Leo pulls on his jeans. He is not a tall man. Slight, with blue eyes, which slant at the corners. The texture of his skin reminds me of the marble he chisels, and his features are sharply defined, particularly his cheekbones. He does not look Irish in the least. He leans over me and kisses my forehead.

'Are you okay?' he asks.

'Yeah, fine. It's just . . . I feel so confused.'

'It's probably all a big mistake,' he says again, unconvincingly.

I am surprised, it is unlike him not to know for sure just what to say.

'Do you mind if I don't come with you today?' I say. 'I just don't feel up to it.'

'Course. That's fine. Sure, there'll be plenty more dinners at my mam's.'

A crash comes from the kitchen and he dashes out of the room.

It is a sunny winter's day, the best kind, clear and bright, and I look at the crystal hanging from our skylight, sparkling and bouncing rainbows off the walls. I feel stranded. I try to dismiss the English girl from my mind but I keep hearing her voice saying, 'I'm her daughter,' over and over and over again. And with that voice, a tiny seed of hope, which had always existed, begins to flower.

After Leo and Shauna have left, I get out of bed, and wander round the house drinking a huge mug of coffee. Every few minutes I begin shaking. I am in shock. It couldn't be true, it has to be a hoax. But what if it is? And with that thought comes anger – why? Why? Why?

Now I wish I had gone with Leo and Shauna. At least I would have been distracted. I decide to go for a run; maybe the icy air will make me feel saner.

I walk to Phoenix Park and then I run through the woods. I see deer, unconcerned at my approach. When I can't run any more, I lie on the grass and look up into the sky. I frame my eyes so that all I can see is a blue void. I think about Beatrice.

And Beatrice's sister. Me.

Empty, annihilated. The lost girl.

Which girl is lost?

When I was eight my Uncle Jack gave me my first book of poetry. It was called *Songs of Innocence* by Willam Blake. Uncle Jack told me that William Blake was not only a great poet but a talented engraver as well. Following the instructions of his dead brother who he had seen in a dream, Blake had decided to combine both poem and illustration in one entity, engraved on a copperplate. Each page of the book was to be coloured with washes by hand. No two copies of the book were to be the same. Even the order of the pages was not fixed. This was my first encounter with print-making. I was fascinated. For hours I perused the book attracted by the delicacy yet depth of the engraving, by its deep shadows and translucent layers of colour. And the writing. I loved the old-fashioned lettering – the full curve of a 'c', a fat wholesome 'g'.

Beatrice read me the poems. I was particularly impressed with the story of Lyca, the little girl lost.

I loved her name and insisted on being called Lyca for two whole weeks until my father exploded – if I wanted to be called after the little girl lost, I could just go and get lost until I grew up and answered to my real name like any normal human being. Then Beatrice shouted back and said that it wasn't my fault that Eithne was such a boring common name and it was no wonder I wanted to change it to Lyca. Then my father became serious and said something under his breath about Beatrice and why her name was Beatrice – bastard – I think he said. And then Beatrice stormed out, and my mother said, 'For God's sake, Joe.' And she looked over at me and I felt it was my fault.

Later that night, when Beatrice was still downstairs watching telly with Mammy, Daddy came up and sat on the end of my bed.

'I'm sorry, poppet,' he said, and he picked up the poetry book and read to me, the words a little slurred, but each one said with love. 'You're my best girl,' he said.

'Daddy,' I asked, 'why don't you love Beatrice?'

'I do.' The words came strangled out of his throat, but I didn't believe him.

When my daddy read 'The Little Girl Lost', it made me think of my secret garden.

> *Seven summers old*
> *Lovely Lyca told,*
> *She had wander'd long*
> *Hearing the wild birds' song.*
>
> *Sweet sleep, come to me*
> *Underneath this tree;*
> *Do father, mother weep—*
> *'Where can Lyca sleep'.*

One day, soon after my eighth birthday, I tried to get lost. I got up early, put on a thick sweater and made a pile of ham sandwiches. Then I set out. I walked for hours. All day, it seemed.

I walked down the big hill and kept going until I did not recognize the road, then I cut across some fields and through a small copse. It was tough going, but I was determined to get lost. Finally, I came out onto another road, and headed up a hill. I saw a spire in the distance. I thought, I will sleep in the graveyard and walk again tomorrow. Then I will be utterly lost. Everyone will weep and come looking for me. But as I got closer and closer to the spire the road became familiar, and I realized that I was approaching my own village. I had spent the entire day walking in a circle. I was too tired to attempt to get lost again. Wearily I shuffled home. It wasn't even dinner time and to add insult to injury no one had noticed I had gone missing.

'There you are,' said my harassed mother. 'Will you lay the table, please?'

'Did you miss me?'

'What?' she said.

'Did you miss me?' I repeated.

'Why? Where did you go?' she said half listening as she put the kettle on.

'I got lost.'

'You should take the dog,' she said. 'Don't go out on those roads alone. You hear me? The dog will always bring you home.'

> *Frowning, frowning night,*
> *O'er this desart bright,*
> *Let thy moon arise*
> *While I close my eyes.*

Maybe Beatrice had decided to get lost and succeeded. Yet Beatrice would never have left me behind. We had shared a bedroom for twelve years. Every night I had listened to her breathing in my sleep, and our dreams had woven in and out of each other's mind. In the morning we moved to the same rhythm. Now a stranger arrives and tells me something different.

I get up and dust grass and leaves from my trousers. I walk home slowly. As I turn the corner I see a figure sitting on the wall outside our house. A tall girl with blonde hair slouches

77

against the magnolia tree behind the wall. She is wearing jeans, large white runners and a padded jacket. She is smoking a cigarette, and stares straight across the road. She does not look in my direction, but I know this girl is waiting for me.

I am not surprised.

BEATRICE

An Loch Bán. Lough Bane. Her childhood passes beneath you, like a tiny trout, dancing in your watery, speckled light. She remembers those swans flying with their long necks thrusting skyward and their splendid wings sweeping through the crystal air. She will always be here.

On top of the Noggin, in the company of the beech trees, she looks down at the white, land-locked lough. Two fat bullocks graze close by. Now they are docile, but come evening they will charge about the field and spar.

She has walked around your shores a thousand times, An Loch Bán. And she has looked for herself in your glassy depths. You pull her, and your bed is infinite. This morning the reeds are frosted and sparkling. This makes them shine like sticks of gold. They stick out of your surface, which looks like treacle. You are frozen. She places her bare foot upon you. You do not crack. She puts her other foot upon you. Both feet are stinging, stuck to the cold ice. Can she trust you?

She sees a little girl skating on the lake in her wellies. She waves at her, and the girl waves back, but you are cracking beneath her, so she shouts to the little girl to warn her. Then she looks back down at the ice; it has thawed so fast. She looks up again, prepared to rescue the child, but she's gone.

Was it a dream?

She jumps back onto the bank. You splash her ankles and your iciness burns. She is scalded. It is time to move on.

EITHNE

Do you know that painting by Whistler? The one of his mother? She's sitting on a chair, in profile, all alone. The picture is called *Arrangement in Grey and Black*. That was how my mother seemed for five whole years. A composition of funeral tones. From the time I was thirteen to the day I turned eighteen we hardly exchanged more than a few words. All I remember is her sitting on her chair, her back to the door, staring out of the window. She would scan the fields and the distant hills again and again, hoping for a speck, a tiny figure, to emerge out of her nightmare.

If you were to look at her, she looked half dead but she was completely alert. I know this because occasionally she would suddenly say something. She could hear me coming, as if she was straining her hearing above all of the sounds of the house, listening out for a foot to fall on our hearth, her footfall . . . but the only steps she heard were mine, and she'd yell out at me, 'Stop shuffling.' I knew she was comparing me to Beatrice, who walked on her toes, like a dancer. I was clumsy. This I could not help. But at the time, I felt it was a great failing. In fact, I felt I had let my mother down.

Why could I not make her notice me?

I had always thought that she loved Beatrice more than me, but now it became blatantly obvious. Every day she continued her vigil stung my heart. No one else would do but *her* Beatrice.

Stupidly, I envied my sister: even when she had gone missing, she stole the limeight.

My father disappeared too. He could not bear the atmosphere in the house, and was completely futile in his attempts to comfort Mammy. My daddy did not see me any more. And in a way that hurt more, as he retreated to the only sanctuary he knew, the pub; he anaesthetized his suffering. He forgot that I was suffering too, and that only he knew how to make me feel loved with the songs and the jokes and the tickling he had showered upon me when I was little.

The family came: Aunt Bríd, Uncle Jack, Aunt Aoife and Aunt Mary. But none of them were able to rouse Mammy. In desperation they brought Father Cleary, but he could not reach her either. They were afraid to bring the doctor; they thought that Mammy might be taken away. And then who would mind me?

Overnight I felt like an orphan, and there only seemed to be one person who really cared. Every day as I was coming home from school I held my breath in anticipation, jumping off the school bus and running to the door. I'd stop and listen. Sure enough, I'd hear Mrs Lynch inside, moving about with military precision. Then I could breathe a sigh of relief; there'd be something to eat, and there'd be someone to listen to me. There would be some semblance of normality. We would have probably all starved if it hadn't been for Mrs Lynch.

Every afternoon at three o'clock precisely she'd come over, give the house a shake and put on the dinner. Even though she had her own very large family to look after, somehow she managed to look after me as well. I think she left the eldest Lynch girls minding the little ones. These girls were the same age as me, but for some reason Mrs Lynch considered I needed minding too.

She's dead now. All those years she had cancer and she never told a soul.

Saint Assumpta Lynch.

Assumpta — isn't that such a crazy name? But it suited Mrs Lynch. She was very religious, and I don't just mean she went to church every day. She lived her religion. I would describe her as someone completely without artifice: pure and unblemished.

Isn't it strange that I remember Mrs Lynch so vividly, more than my own mother and father at that time? I remember her kind face, with the soft brown eyes, and her complexion: flushed cheeks and pale forehead. It looked as if she had scrubbed her face with a wire brush. She was so kind, always gently guiding Mammy: drink this, and a cup of tea would be put into her hand; eat that, and a plate of food would be placed on her lap; listen to this, and she'd put on the radio.

It was Mrs Lynch who bought me my first pack of sanitary towels, and my first bra. It was Mrs Lynch who helped me find a dress for my 'debs' (our graduation dance at school). It was Mrs Lynch who drove me to Navan, to the county library, so I could take out books on art. Then we'd have a laugh looking at them together. Mrs Lynch used to slag the abstract expressionists — in particular Jackson Pollock — she said her little Johnny could do better with his eyes closed and a few pots of poster paint. But she didn't mean anything by it. I think she liked talking to me about art.

I painted her a picture once of the view from the village as you stand looking at Witch's Hill. It wasn't very good; in fact, the perspective was wrong. But she absolutely loved it. She framed it and put it up in her hall. I only discovered this on the day of her funeral when we all filed through the Lynches' front hall. I remembered her when I had given her the picture. She had said nothing for a second, just stared at it. Mammy was in the room, stationed by the back door, but she didn't turn or appear to notice what was going on.

'Eithne, this is just great, darling. It's beautiful. But don't you want to give it to your mother?'

It was Mother's Day.

'No,' I said firmly. I did not care if Mammy heard. I was so angry with her then – she had never wanted my love. I knew this because she had always shown me very little, as if I was always in the way. If I wanted anything – a story or a song – she would always refer me to Daddy. It was like she willingly split the family: her and Beatrice on one side, and me and Daddy on the other.

I was eighteen when Mrs Lynch died. I hadn't even known she was sick. All I had heard was that she was going into hospital to have some tests. I was even planning to visit her the next day; I'd painted her a picture of some flowers specially. But she never came back – she was gone, just like that. The same thing all over again.

I remember Mr Lynch came to our door. His face was ashen and he spoke in whispers to Daddy. I knew something terrible had happened, and I started to cry even before he said anything.

Daddy came into the kitchen. 'Assumpta Lynch died this morning, God love her,' he said to Mammy's back. 'It was the cancer, awful quick.'

I stood shaking, the tears spilling out of my eyes.

'Eithne, are you all right?' he asked, confused.

'No! No! No!' I screamed and sank to the floor. Mammy spun round, she stared at me incredulously. She was looking at me as if she had never seen me before. 'Get her some brandy,' she ordered Daddy hoarsely.

Exactly three days after Mrs Lynch died, Mammy got up from her chair. It was raining and beating down so hard that she couldn't see a thing out the window anyway. One of my art books was on the couch. She picked it up and leafed through it. It was about the Renaissance, and there were lots of paintings of angels, with beautiful hair in golden curls, singing. It seemed so lovely to her – all the colours – after five years of grey. I was in the bathroom when I heard Mammy crying. I hadn't heard her cry since that day with Mrs Lynch, five years ago. Cautiously I entered the room.

'What's wrong, Mammy?' I asked.

She held up the book. 'Do you think that she's in heaven?' she asked me, wiping her eyes with her hankie and looking like a child. 'Do you think she's an angel?'

'Yes, Mammy,' I said gently. 'I think she watches over you.'

'She's never coming back, is she?'

'I don't know.'

'I'm sorry, Eithne . . . please forgive me.'

Tears began to well in my eyes; I ran over and hugged her.

'Mammy,' I whispered.

She pulled away, and kissed my cheek.

'Will you tell me about the pictures?' she asked me.

So I did. I told her about the beginning of the Renaissance, and Giotto's painted murals in Padua, I told her about the winding streets of Siena, and Duccio's magnificent altarpiece, and then I spoke about Florence and the glory and splendour of that ancient city. As I spoke her face began to respond to the art I was describing, light began to fill her eyes again and her tears almost gleamed gold, reflecting the fragile rays of sun, which were breaking through the rain outside the window.

'It sounds like such a beautiful place,' she said. 'I'd love to go there.'

'Me too,' I replied.

'Then we will one day.' She took my hand and squeezed it tight.

And that was how my mother began to love me again. It was through art.

THREE: THE BERET

EITHNE

It was a beret not a hat. I don't know why they called it a hat. Possibly 'beret'was too foreign a word for the local Gardaí.

'A pink hat decorated with beads,' read the description.

It was a cerise beret with stars on the top.

Beatrice had returned with the beret when she went to the rock concert with Phil.

'Where did you get that?' I asked her.

'I swapped it,' she said.

'What for?'

'My waistcoat.'

'That was *my* waistcoat!'

'You gave it to me.'

'I didn't!'

'Oh, well, we can share this.'

She dumped the beret on my head.

'Suits you,' she said. 'Look, it has stars on it.' She whipped it off my head and threw it up into the air. Little diamanté beads sparkled in the sunlight.

'It smells,' I said.

'This is the genuine hippy article,' she said.

We were standing in a sloping field a few miles from the village. Phil was there. We had gone on one of our 'walks' — empty summer-day rambles, which went in no particular direction and with no particular purpose. Beatrice and Phil had let me trail along behind them, although in fact they preferred to be alone.

'You look stupid,' I said.

I was thirteen and really into fashion. I was wearing stretch drainpipe jeans, loafers, and a huge white frilly shirt. My hair was short and layered, with a side parting and a monstrous flick. Beatrice on the other hand let her hair roam wild; it was soft and curly. She was wearing a long dress from one of those ethnic shops. It was pale blue with paisley patterns. She had purple clogs on, and loads of bells and bracelets. She reeked of patchouli.

'We don't need to follow fashion,' said Phil. 'That's for the masses. We are individuals, we create our own style.'

He looked just as bad in flared purple jeans and an embroidered hessian shirt. His blond hair was curly and unkempt. Beatrice's blue scarf was wound around his neck.

The village regarded the pair with a mixture of confusion and horror. As we tramped along the lanes and byways of our locality, as we stomped through fields, farmers and local housewives would slow their cars down to a crawl and just stare as if they had seen an apparition. Beatrice delighted in this, Phil did not care and I felt humiliated.

We had only known Phil a few weeks, although we had heard about him nearly all our lives. Phil is my Uncle Jack's son. The son he had had to leave behind in England when he separated from his wife in the late sixties and came back to live in Ireland. For Jack this had been the single most traumatic event of his life – leaving his little boy behind – but he had had to back away gracefully. In those days paternal custody was unthinkable. Still, Uncle Jack had never forgotten his son – religiously sending him Christmas and birthday presents, visiting him every year (followed by a tearful, boozy return in the pub with my father) and finally managing to convince his estranged wife to let Phil come to Ireland in the summer of 1981. At that time, Phil was in between school and university, Beatrice between school and art college. Both cousins were poised on the precipice of life; they immediately hit it off.

Phil and Beatrice had a lot in common: they were both outsiders; both lived with men who were not their real fathers. Phil had been sent to public school, reared to follow a serious profession and stifled by his step-father's right-wing beliefs. Similarly, Beatrice felt constrained by our rural lifestyle, the narrow-mindedness of my father and the village. Both were champing at the bit, desperate for the freedom and independence of an adult life. Phil claimed he was going to be a musician (and he could play the guitar well), and, of course, Beatrice was going to be an artist. Together they would take off for Goa, Kathmandu, Marrakech . . .

To me, they seemed totally out of date. While I was listening to Wham!, Funboy Three and Bananarama, Phil and Beatrice would play Led Zeppelin, Bob Dylan and old David Bowie songs.

'Ziggy!' Beatrice would screech in the middle of a sugar beet field, and the two of them would launch into a rendition of 'Ziggy Stardust', and all the songs from that album.

I don't know why I followed them around; I suppose it was boredom. The worst kind, when you're thirteen. I did not have many friends, and the few I had lived too far away for a bicycle ride. Beatrice and Phil were my summer's entertainment.

The two of them had a powerful charisma: they shone, they glowed, they had so much spirit and vitality. They had so many dreams, and really believed that one day they would be famous. Although I was only thirteen, I had already resigned myself to a choice of three careers – a nurse, a secretary or a school teacher.

These were the options presented to us through our school careers guidance. Beatrice was considered eccentric, but she was respected as a demanding and challenging student. She was special.

And there was something else as well.

Looking back I realize that Phil and Beatrice could have been in love. Nobody worked this one out – they were first cousins. Taboo. But Phil and Beatrice both knew they were not really cousins, not by blood. They played with each other – horsing around – and even with my inexpert eyes I sensed something more. There would be a still moment in the middle of the play fight, a look, a teasing movement.

At that point I would turn on my heel and walk home by myself, feeling miserable, alone and ugly.

The highlight of that summer was the concert at Slane Castle. Of course my father banned me from going and strictly speaking had not allowed Beatrice to go – he would not give her the money for a ticket – and he persuaded Jack not to give Phil the money either.

The duo was undeterred. They picked raspberries for three weeks so they could each save enough money to buy a ticket.

When the day of the concert arrived, Mammy was worried; she had heard there had been fights in Slane the night before.

'They'll all be gone now, Mammy. They probably didn't have tickets anyway.'

'Don't worry, Mrs Kelly,' said Phil. 'I'll take care of her for you.'

My mother shook her head, but she would not stop them – any action which undermined my father she would allow, without him knowing of course.

THE BERET

The two of them set out, hitching a lift in the back of Paddy O'Connor's truck. It goes without saying that they looked a spectacle. Beatrice wore a floor-length flowered skirt, a clashing pink blouse, my embroidered waistcoat and the purple clogs. Phil had on his purple flares and an Afghan coat.

'People'll think I'm taking ye to the funny farm.' Paddy O'Connor laughed. My father was down at the bog – just as well, he would have gone mad.

Beatrice and Phil did not return until the next day, grass sticking out of their hair, eyes dazed. The concert had been good, but even better had been their discovery – drugs.

A bog isn't just brown. I learnt this when studying the bogs at home. There is a kaleidoscope of colours – greens, greys, reds, deep purple, bluish black. One of my prints is called 'Glenamona' – the name of a bog at home. The paper is filled with all these colours – their dark, deep shades, which a bog feeds, nurtures and reveals. In this expanse there is a spot of pink. It sparkles – glitters in a hidden light. Everyone asks me, what is that? Is it a flower?

No, it's a hat. A cerise beret with stars on it.

SARAH

Sarah did not remember much about the first days of Beatrice's life. Learning to breastfeed occupied the first twenty-four hours – the baby would not take the breast at first, and Sarah was afraid she would have to bottle feed. But eventually Beatrice learned to latch on. As the child sucked on her breast, Sarah's womb contracted. It was painful, but oddly pleasurable. Night and day lost distinction: she slept when the baby slept. She had never felt so tired in her life.

Anthony came to see her in hospital the day after Beatrice was born. He brought the most exquisite bouquet of flowers – irises, gypsophila and lilies. He was quiet, but the flush in his cheeks, the shine in his eyes betrayed his pride. To Sarah he seemed distant. The baby had just fallen asleep and she was dying for a nap.

'She's beautiful,' said Anthony.

'Yes,' she murmured. The baby stirred. 'I'd let you hold her but she has just gone to sleep.'

'That's fine. She looks too delicate to be touched. Sarah, would you like me to tell Jonathan?'

'No.'

'Sure?'

'Positive.'

'Okay. Well . . . when are you getting out of here? Shall I pick you up?'

'Thanks, but it's all right, a friend is coming.'

'Oh.' Anthony was surprised. He did not know she had any other friends in London.

'I'll come again tomorrow,' he said. 'Do you need anything?'

'Please don't bother,' said Sarah. 'I'll see you back at the house, at the weekend.'

'Right.' He backed off and was gone, leaving a small pink envelope on her lap. Her heart sank. So this was it, he was here to finally pay off his family's debt. Sarah could feel the nurses watching her. As far as they were concerned that was *not* Mr Quigley. Her face reddened, she felt stiff and self-conscious. She quickly put the envelope into her bedside locker without opening it. What if Joe had turned up?

He said he'd come back this morning. She shuddered at the thought of the scene. Joe would probably have assumed Anthony was the father. He might even have hit him. And what would Anthony have made of Joe?

She closed her eyes and tried to push her confused emotions to the back of her mind.

Sarah drifted into a disturbed sleep. In her dream Beatrice was a grown woman and they were dancing in the open, on land she did not recognize. The ground beneath her feet was heavy, it gripped their ankles like something soft gone hard, like petrified moss. It made their movements laboured. With a great effort they held hands and slowly spun round. Beatrice was her sister, not her child. Her mother was in the dream. Her hair had gone completely grey and its effect softened her face. She smiled. Sarah had no memory of seeing her mother happy. She was pleased – no harsh words, just love. Her mother was so happy that tears streamed down her face, she was sobbing, gut-wrenching sobs, her body heaving, gasping to breathe, baby . . . cry—

Sarah woke with a start. The baby was wailing. She lifted her up and held her tight. She wished her mother was here, even though she would have been horrified. Her mother could hardly be described as maternal, but still Sarah felt a strong urge to go back to Southampton where everything was familiar and safe. Maybe she should go home.

'How's it going?'

Sarah looked up; Joe was standing there holding a bunch of red roses.

'I didn't hear you.'

'Ah well, they always said I'm light on my feet. That's why I work on the sites – climb like a monkey, so I do.'

She smiled, imagining him swinging on the scaffolding.

'You looked very serious. What were you thinking about?'

'My mother. Maybe I should contact her.'

'She doesn't know about the baby, then?'

'No.'

'Well, if she wasn't there for you when you were pregnant, why bother telling her now? That's what I say.'

'It's just that I feel so alone.'

'What about this friend of yours, the one who lent you the house in Clapham? Surely she'll help you out.'

Sarah looked at Joe. His blue eyes had a teasing glint. He was always smiling. His hair was black and curly. He looked like a right rogue. But something about him – his frankness, his kindness – made her feel she could trust him although they had only met a couple of days ago and certainly not under ideal circumstances. She watched him as he sat on the end of the bed and took the baby from her. He was so natural. There was not a trace of awkwardness as he rocked the small bundle.

'Joe, my friend is a man.'

He looked up.

'The father?'

'No. His brother.' She took a deep breath. Why not tell him?

So Sarah told Joe about the Voyle household, about Jonathan and finding out she was pregnant, and then how kind Anthony had been. By the time she had finished, Beatrice was asleep. Joe gently got up and put her in the crib. He stayed standing.

'I'd be careful of that Anthony fella,' he said. 'I'll come and get you tomorrow.'

'Are you sure you still want to?'

'I said I would yesterday. I never break me promises.'

He strode out of the ward with the nurses eyeing him. That was it then. She would always be alone. Who would want her now she had been ruined?

EITHNE

My father loves the bog. When I was small the bog appeared dull, flat and lifeless to me. It wasn't until Daddy let me go with him (I would have been about nine) that I discovered how much there was to it.

Once a month, on a Saturday we would go down with a trailer to collect turf. My daddy would have already gone down during the week and cut and stacked the peat into neat piles. As we drove along the waves of the bog road, we'd sing a song. He's a good singer, even sober.

At the bog we'd drive past a couple of dumps – old washing machines, bags of rubbish, the odd shoe – my father sighing and cursing under his breath at the bastards who'd blight such a beautiful place. Up close the bog was far from flat. It's surface fell into a series of pools, lawns and hummocks. Daddy would point out the bog moss, its variety of type and shade. He knew the names of all the plants on the bog – white-beaked sedge, bog asphodel, cross-leaved heath, bog cotton; on the hummocks he'd show me the ling heather and bog rosemary. Daddy would have made a great botanist. He loved the birds as well – there seemed to be so many different ones then – and in the winter he brought me down specially to look at the geese from Greenland who roosted on the bogs for a couple of months. I'd ask him about Greenland, but he couldn't tell me much. He just said it was very cold and Eskimos lived there. It was right on the edge of the world.

'What's over the edge?' I'd ask.

'Nothin',' he said. 'Nothin' but the sea.'

'What's at the bottom of the sea?' I asked.

'The seabed. There'd be all manner of things down there: seaweed and rocks and little creatures that crawl along the bottom of the ocean; fish that can swim deep and, of course, there'd also be a few shipwrecks.'

I was fascinated.

'They say that there's a lost city at the bottom of the ocean,' he continued. 'People live there – like us – and carry on their daily business. The only difference being that they live under the ocean and we live above. Because of that their place is magical.'

'Does it have a name?'

'They call it Atlantis.'

When I think back to that time I realize how sad and lonely he must have been. Things were bad at home. My mother hardly spoke to him. If they did talk it would quickly escalate into shouting. Beatrice hated Daddy. She made no bones about it. She would taunt him because he was not her real father and therefore not entitled to tell her what to do. She would threaten to tell the whole village. What did she care! Then she'd get smacked, but she would never give in. Beatrice was headstrong all her life. That was the only thing that came between us – Daddy. I could not help it – I loved my father no matter how bad he could be. With me he was different. He was gentle and funny and a person neither my mother nor my sister got to know.

Sometimes it felt like Daddy and I were on the outside looking in. I can picture the scene: Mammy and Beatrice sitting by the stove, chatting, laughing, drinking tea. Mammy would be brushing Beatrice's hair, as her child told her tales about school, and teachers and every single thing that happened to her. We were excluded. We both believed we were not good enough. I became Daddy's consolation and he mine.

I wish Daddy had come to my degree show, then he would have known how precious our time on the bog had been for me. I was so disappointed he never showed up. Mammy hinted that he'd had too much drink the night before, showing off that he was up to Dublin to see his daughter's valuable pictures. What was the good of all his bragging if he never came?

Mammy said that my etchings reminded her of 'soul music'. She surprised me, coming up with poetry like that. When we came to my series on bogs she said nothing for a long time. Just kept walking up and down, up and down.

'I never realized how much you liked the bog,' she said, at last. 'You make it seem so beautiful. Oh, look – ' she pointed suddenly – 'that's Bog Lane, isn't it? Oh, that reminds me of when you girls were very little and used to run down to the raspberry garden with your cousins. And there's the bog at Glenamona. Your daddy used to take you there . . . it's a shame, I really should have made him come.'

BEATRICE

Bog Lane was not a lane you could walk down straight from the house. Behind Granny's there's the field, and then there's the lane. But she always went by the field because the lane was too mucky. Strange, but better to get wet knees than muddy feet. At the end of the field, she climbed over the gate and got back on to the lane. This small piece of path, up to the bog, was a bit better.

When Granny was still alive there was a raspberry garden at the end of the field, just before the bog. All the children went there to pick raspberries. The garden didn't belong to anyone; it was just a no-man's-land. Beatrice never forgot the euphoria of stuffing herself with raspberries and then the belly-ache.

In the dark, dank old cottage she lies down to sleep and dreams about the raspberry garden. It is a field of red, a soft downy crimson, before an expanse of black, her father's bog. After the sweet, lies the bitter. She can almost taste the smell of the acrid spruce, which ring his marshy land, all lined up, smartly planted, so tight you wouldn't want to squeeze through.

When she was younger she used to test herself. In the summer evenings, when her shadow was long, she would chase it across Granny's field and down Bog Lane. She would wave at the overgrown raspberry patch, and then skid to a halt at the end of the lane. In front was the bog. It was so quiet there. The trees would be creaking, a few rooks cawing, that would be all. She'd lean on the fence, but she wouldn't climb over. She wasn't afraid. She just didn't like the place.

EITHNE

My father found the pink beret on his bog. It was like some-one had left it there as a statement. He had always hated that hat. The first time he saw Beatrice with it on he told her to take it off and throw it away. She just glared at him and did nothing.

'Take it off,' his voice rose. 'You look like a clown.'

'Good,' she replied.

He tried to take it off. She screamed and scratched him.

'Ye bitch!' he yelled and slapped her. Beatrice ran out of the house. I stood still.

'What are you looking at?' he growled.

I was older then and there were no more trips to collect peat. No more special time with Daddy. He had given up on us all.

Two weeks after Beatrice disappeared, my father went down to the bog to get some more peat. The beret was lying there, waiting for him by his turf cutter. He carried it back to the house, dragging his heels. When he walked in, my mother was sitting as always at the window. When she turned she saw something pink in his hands, then she registered the beret. Her mind's eye brought before her her daughter's pretty face, smiling.

'No!' she howled. She was a small woman, but the force of her as she threw herself at him knocked him back. 'No!' she screamed again into his face. He stood quite still, regaining his balance, his hands hung by his side, the beret dropped to the floor. I picked up Beatrice's beret. I smelt it. But there was no trace of my sister left.

Instead, it had a strong smell of earth, decay and death.

SARAH

The day Sarah was due to leave the hospital she woke early. Her bed was by the window and the sun was streaming in. Everything seemed golden outside and she couldn't wait to get home. She looked at her child and felt a tremendous tug inside her. As soon as she got back to Clapham she would write to her mother. Now they had something in common – they had both experienced this.

The doctor came round and checked her and the baby. Everything was fine. She could leave. She went and got washed. She only had night clothes and things for the baby with her so Joe had brought her a bag of clothes. They were not her own, but they weren't new either. She felt a bit odd putting them on. The dress was blue, and there was a green cardigan. She changed Beatrice and dressed her, then swaddled her in blankets, and sat on a chair next to the bed. It was nine o'clock.

She only had to wait half an hour. She heard Joe whistling in the corridor, greeting the nurses as he came into the ward.

'Well, there you are,' Joe said.

'You came, then?'

'Course I did.' He grinned at her. 'Ready, so?'

'Yes,' she said meekly.

She got up; still sore, a little stiff. They walked out of the ward like any other young couple with their newborn charge. Out on the street Sarah felt dizzy.

'Are you okay?' he asked.

'It's just so bright, so noisy after the hospital.'

'In ye get,' he said. He made a space for her and Beatrice in the old van. 'Let's get out of here.'

He took off. They didn't speak for some way. Sarah was busy with Beatrice, fixing her hat, making sure she was safe and tight in her arms. It wasn't until they were heading up Finchley Road that she realized something was wrong.

'Where are we going?' she asked.

'I want you to come with me,' said Joe.

'But what about Clapham?'

'Forget Clapham,' he said. 'Forget them people using you like you were their property.'

'But Anthony isn't like that. I said I'd be there.'

'Do you really think he cares? He's just using you, Sarah. He wants you to be his mistress, I know them sort. He'd never marry you.'

'Joe, please, I want to go home.' Sarah started to cry. It was all too much.

Joe took a sharp right. He drove up Hampstead Hill and parked opposite the Heath. He turned off the engine, and sighed.

'Sarah,' he said, 'look at me.'

She wiped the tears from her eyes and looked up at him. He stared back at her with such intensity; his eyes were the deepest blue ever.

'I'm going back to Ireland,' he said. 'I've had it here. I'm sick of being called a Paddy and working like a slave. Okay, so we make a bit of money, but it's not worth it. I'm needed at home. Sarah, you should see it. We live in a beautiful place, there's woods and lakes and bogs all nearby. You'd love it.'

'I don't understand,' she said shakily.

'I've enjoyed pretending. I've liked the nurses looking at us as if we're man and wife. Marry me, Sarah! I'll look after you and Beatrice. It doesn't matter to me that I'm not the baby's father. No one will know at home. You'll be me wife. We could be so happy. You'd never have to worry about anything again.'

'But, Joe, I don't know if I love you. It's too soon.'

'Ah, how could you resist me! Sure I'll grow on you like mould.'

They laughed.

'So what do you say?' he said.

'But what about Beth?'

'Beth, who's Beth? Don't tell me you've another child.'

'My dog.'

'Sure, bring the manky dog. She's at our place anyways. The more the merrier. Is it a yes? Yes? Yes?'

Sarah nodded; she did not know what else to do.

'Yee-ha,' he yelled. 'Let's go and get married.'

'Now!' said Sarah.

'Why not? There's no time like the present.' He took a ring out of his pocket. 'I even have the ring.'

They drove on to Finchley Register Office.

'We'll have a proper wedding in the church when we get home,' he said.

She felt very strange, very odd indeed. He had assumed she wouldn't say no. He had booked the registrar, got the ring, he had even arranged for Mikey and his wife Sinead (the owner of the blue dress and green cardigan) to be there and act as witnesses. It was all over in a couple of minutes. Sarah walked out a married woman, still holding Beatrice. The child had slept through the whole event.

'Let's go and sink a few pints!' said Mikey.

Joe put his arm around her. 'Howya doing, Mrs Kelly?' He grinned. He looked like the cat who'd got the cream.

She thought of Anthony and her little house in Clapham. What had she done?

'I can't go to the pub,' she said. 'The baby . . . I need to feed her.'

'You don't mind if I go, do ye? A man needs to celebrate his wedding day with a few drinks an' all. Sure, I never even had a stag night.'

'We'll make up for it now, boyo,' said Mikey.

'Come on,' said Sinead. 'I'll take you home. We'll have a nice cup of tea and let them two fellas do their worst.'

The men carried on into town. Sarah and Sinead walked back to the flat where the three of them lived.

'I'll put the kettle on,' Sinead said as they went in the door. 'You can clean up and feed the baby. Joe's room is the second on the left.'

Sarah walked down a narrow, dark corridor.

She heard whimpering. She opened the door and was greeted by a highly excited Beth.

'Good girl, good girl . . .'

The dog rolled onto her back. Sarah delicately placed Beatrice on the bed, and then crouched down and rubbed Beth's belly. She looked around the room. It was hardly neat, but clean all the same. It was very bare – the only trace of personality a postcard from Ireland signed 'love Mammy and the girls'. She sat on the bed with Beatrice. The child was screaming for milk by now and Sarah's nipples were leaking and sore.

'Okay, come on, come on.'

Beatrice latched on and sucked. Beth had calmed down, and was now lying curled up at Sarah's feet.

'Oh God,' Sarah whispered. She had opened her bag, looking

for a hankie, and saw the pink envelope lying inside. She had forgotten all about it. She picked the envelope out with her free hand. Inside, wrapped in tissue, was a beautiful locket. She opened it; it was empty. There was a card as well. It read:

> *This locket should hold two pictures —*
> *one of Beatrice and, hopefully, one of me.*
> *Sarah, will you marry me?*
> *I love you*
> *Anthony*

She gasped. The locket fell. She started to cry and felt she would never stop. Beth sat up and began to whine again.

Several hours later the men came home. Sarah and Sinead had been in bed for ages, although Sarah had been up with Beatrice most of the time. When Joe came in she had just fallen asleep. He woke her.

'Sarah, Sarah,' came the urgent whisper, 'how's me wife?' He laughed. He was totally slaughtered. The stink of drink off him was nauseating. He got into bed with her and started pulling her pyjama bottoms down and getting on top of her.

'Joe, stop!'

'It's our wedding night,' he said. 'Don't you want to?'

'I can't,' she said. 'Not for six weeks. The baby . . . you know.'

'Ah, Jaysus, I'm sorry,' he slurred. He hugged her. She felt she couldn't breathe. 'Just touch me, will you?' he said breathily into her face. She moved her head, the beer fumes turning her stomach.

He gripped her hand and placed it on his penis. It was rock hard. He worked her hand for her, pushing it up and down. His breathing got heavier.

'Yes, yes,' he whispered.

He pushed his nails into her hand and forced it up and down rigorously. Eventually he came, sighed and immediately fell into a loud nasal sleep. Sarah extricated herself and stumbled over Beth in the corridor as she crept into the bathroom. She washed her hands, and looked in the mirror. She was very pale. Next door she could hear Mikey and Sinead.

'Get off me, you drunken pig.'

'Who are you calling a pig? Look at you, the fat cow. Stuffing yourself all day while I go out to work. Least you could do is let me have me rights.'

'Get off me, I said.'

She heard a slap. Maybe she should wake Joe.

'Ah, you bastard,' Sinead said.

'I'm going to have you,' said Mikey. There was silence, then she heard the bed springs. She could hear Sinead. Her tone of voice had changed, 'Go on, go on, yes, yes.'

Sarah looked back into the mirror. This was not the kind of life she had wanted.

EITHNE

We go to the Foggy Dew; the last thing I want is to stay in the house and for Leo and Shauna to walk in and see her. It is still early, and the Sunday afternoon rush hasn't yet begun.

'What do you want?'

'Guinness will do. I've never tried it before.'

I get one too. I need fortifying.

The girl does not look like Beatrice. She is blonde, has blue eyes and a large mouth. We sit down, waiting for the pints. She takes out a packet of cigarettes and offers me one.

'No . . . yeah, okay.'

We sit in silence, puffing away. The pints arrive. What does this girl want with me? Beatrice is dead. She has to be . . .

'I like this,' she says, drinking the Guinness.

'Look,' I blurt out, 'you must be mistaken. My sister disappeared nearly twenty years ago. There were suspicious circumstances, very. The Gardaí all thought that she had been abducted. She would never have run away. I am convinced of that. I'm sorry, but you must have the wrong person.'

She pulls on her cigarette and looks me in the eye.

'Christ,' she says. 'I've walked into some heavy shit here.'

'She wasn't pregnant. I would have known.'

'How old were you when she left?'

'Thirteen.'

'There were loads of things going on in my house that I didn't know about when I was thirteen. Maybe she didn't want to tell you and that's why she left.'

'No. You don't know Beatrice. She was different. She didn't care what people thought of her.'

'Fuck it. Forget it,' she says. 'I mean, you know less than me. All I'm doing is upsetting you. Thanks for the drink.'

She gets up. Suddenly I change my mind. Something reawakens inside me, years of denial falling away. I want desperately to believe that she is right.

'Wait a minute. Just let me think.'

She sits down and looks at me.

'I'll get some more drinks,' she says and goes to the bar.

I drain my pint. Could it be true? Is Beatrice out there somewhere? I begin shaking again – I am hot and cold at the same time, I desperately want to throw up.

Lisa comes back.

'Are you okay?' she asks.

'Yeah,' I say, trying to pull myself together, and taking a big slug of Guinness. 'Tell me, then, why you think my sister is your mother?'

'I don't think: I know,' she replies. 'Last month I was eighteen and I went to the adoption agency. I knew which agency to go to cos I found the papers at home.' She opens her bag and takes out a sheaf of photocopies. 'It has it all here,' she says. 'Name of mother: Beatrice Kelly. Name of father: Not known. Address of mother: Crossakiel, Kells, County Meath, Ireland. Look.'

She points at a blur of type. I start to hyperventilate.

'Oh my God,' I begin to choke. 'Oh my God . . .' I stumble out of my seat, and dash to the toilet.

SARAH

The next morning when Sarah woke Joe had already gone. The men had to get up at five to get to work on the building site. Beatrice was still sleeping, so she went into the kitchen to make a cup of tea. Sinead was sitting at the table, feeding crusts to the dog.

'Morning,' she said chirpily. 'How's the bride?'

'Fine.'

'Joe says you're going on Saturday, and I've hardly got to know you.'

'Going where on Saturday?'

'Going back home, to Ireland.'

Sarah froze.

'Hasn't he told you yet? Anyway, we're bound to meet up at Christmas. You never know, Mikey and myself might come back soon as well.'

She poured Sarah a cup of tea.

'Oh, and you're not to worry about Beth. Joe said she'd get mauled by his farm dogs, so we've agreed to take her on. She's a darlin' aren't ya?'

Sinead tickled Beth under the chin, and the dog licked her fingers.

'She'll be our surrogate baby.' Sinead giggled.

Sarah had to see Anthony.

'Sinead, could you do me a favour?'

'What is it?'

'Can you mind Beatrice for an hour? There's someone I have to see.'

'Ah no, I don't know anything about babies. What if she cries?'

'Please. I'll feed her before I go. I'll be fast — just one hour. Please, Sinead.'

Maybe Sinead heard the desperation in Sarah's voice, because she said, 'Okay. But be quick.'

Beatrice was awake in the bedroom.

Sarah fed and changed her. Then she picked up the locket, putting it in her jacket pocket.

Sinead was on the sofa reading a book; the dog was curled up next to her. Sarah handed her Beatrice.

'She's just gorgeous,' Sinead said. 'I'd love one soon.' She looked up at Sarah. 'You're going to see the daddy, aren't you?'

'No . . . it's a friend,' and with that she fled.

'You know you could do a lot worse than our Joey,' Sinead called after her as Sarah disappeared out of the door.

Sarah headed up the hill. She felt very light now that she wasn't pregnant any more. She wasn't far from the Voyle house; she recognized the road — she must be only a few minutes away. Flat-land gave way to grand houses, gardens and drives. What if he wasn't there? Should she say something to Lady Voyle? Leave a note? What if she was too late? Anthony would have been waiting for her last night in Clapham. Why had she married Joe? What had she been thinking of? Her head spun.

'Watch it, lady!' a taxi driver yelled as she ran across the street.

'Please be there, please be there and tell me what to do,' she prayed.

She turned a corner and there it was – her home for a year, where she had first fallen in love, where she had lost her virginity. It seemed an age away now but it was only a few months ago. She went up the drive. Anthony's MG was there. As she approached the house another car passed her and parked next to the MG; a young woman got out and ran up to the door.

Sarah recognized her. It was Harriet.

Charlotte's friend . . . Anthony's girlfriend. Sarah hid behind a tree. Her heart lurched as she saw Anthony open the door. Harriet embraced him. She kissed his cheek and took his hand. They went into the house.

Sarah crept up the drive. She looked through the living-room window. Harriet sat on a footstool next to Anthony with her arm around him, and then she kissed him again. Sarah had seen enough.

She pushed the locket through the letterbox and ran down the drive. She kept on running, down roads and avenues, past grand houses, tiny mews and high-walled alleyways, on and on she ran with no thought to where she was going. She found herself high up on the Heath, looking down on London. She flopped onto the ground and, pulling at the grass around her, she tried to clutch on to life. She had had expectations; although she had tried to suppress them, in her dreams she had hoped.

'Stupid, stupid girl . . .' she berated herself.

Of course he had only taken pity on her. All those times they sat here, on the Heath, talking, he had only been kind . . . nothing more. How could she have let it happen again? This was worse than Jonathan.

She felt as if someone had jabbed a knife into her heart. This hurt more than anything, more than childbirth. She gasped. She would never see him again. She would always be lost now.

Sarah made a vow. She locked a part of herself away that day. All the love she had for Anthony she would devote to her baby. There would be none left for anyone else.

EITHNE

And then I get drunk.

The afternoon turns to evening which becomes more and more blurred. Lisa likes to talk; she seems oblivious to my shellshock.

'I love swimming,' she is saying. 'I swim every day – I'm training to be a lifeguard. It's a great job, really good money, and all you have to do is sit around all day. And hopefully I'd be working with Steve; he's my fiancé. We've only just got engaged; we haven't got the ring yet, but he's asked me. We met at the swimming pool – course my mum and dad don't know yet.'

'What do your parents think about this?' I ask.

'Oh, they don't know I'm here. They think I'm staying with a mate. They'd go fucking mad! They don't even know that I know I'm adopted – it's all so fucked up.'

'Oh . . .'

'They never told me I was adopted. I just always knew. Well, strictly speaking they never told me straight out, but I worked it out when I was really young. My dad let it slip. Bloody hell, and they never sat down then and talked to me about it – no wonder we don't get on.' She finishes her pint, and continues. 'I was about five and I remember it was raining, and we, myself and my brother, Gary, he's a couple of years younger than me – he's not adopted – well, we were playing inside. I was really

117

bored and I found some of my dad's old tins of paint, so I decided to redecorate . . .'

Lisa begins laughing; I am just staring at her. Everything about her seems totally alien.

'When my mum saw what we had done she completely freaked out. I mean it was Gary just as much as me, but she always blamed me. She was yelling at my dad, and giving out like mad, and then she screamed right in my face, "You're a bloody monster!" And then to my dad, "What are we going to do with her?" And do you know what he said? "It was your idea to adopt, not mine, you know I thought it was too soon." Out it plopped, just like that. Suddenly everyone was quiet. And my mum just hissed, "Shut up, will yer." And that's how I found out.'

'That's awful,' I say.

'Oh, I'm glad I know. I would have found out anyway. I couldn't wait till I was eighteen so I could get away from them. I never really fitted in – that's why I wanted to find my real mum, I was hoping we might get along.'

For the first time she looks a little shy. I don't know what to say. Everything has taken on an unreal edge – the fact that this girl, sitting next to me, is my own flesh and blood, my sister's child, my niece, seems ludicrous. As I glance around, the pub begins to look strange as well – garish – and I imagine everyone is looking at me. I begin to sweat.

'Do you want another drink?' Lisa is asking me.

'Yeah,' I say.

My mobile rings. I know it is Leo, but I don't answer. I am at a loss to know what to say to him, and I suspect he would tell me to come straight home, to ditch this girl, Lisa Hayes, but she is a link to the past, the only chance I have to exhume my sister.

'How did you find me?' I ask, when she returns with two large whiskies. 'Why didn't you just go straight to Crossakiel?'

'I wasn't sure how to get there, so I did a search on the Internet. I looked up Kelly and Crossakiel. You came up.'

'But how?'

'There was a website on you. You're an artist, right?'

'Of course, my website,' I exclaim. 'I had forgotten all about it . . . God knows the last time it was updated.'

'Well, the website said you were born in Crossakiel, Kells, and gave your address and number in Dublin. I reckoned Beatrice must be your sister. I was just taking a chance when I rang.'

'So what are you going to do now?' I ask, taking a slug of my drink.

'I don't know.' She shrugs. 'It's bloody typical. I think I've finally found my real mum – then I find out you don't know where she is either.'

'I thought she was dead.'

'Maybe she is . . . now.'

We sit in silence. The alcohol makes me brave.

'Why don't you stay with me,' I say. 'Tomorrow I'll take you down home. Someone must know the truth . . . we won't give up, we'll find her.'

'I'm not sure,' she says. 'Maybe this whole thing's stupid. If she'd wanted me to find her she'd have left her address with the adoption agency, and they would've told me when I came looking. It's clear she doesn't want to know me.'

'That's not like Beatrice. She would, I know she would. There must be some terrible reason why she's never come back. Of course – it must be something to do with whoever your father is. He could still be living down home . . . and we're going to find out who he is and why she left. Tomorrow,' I announce, standing up and wobbling. 'Come on, let's get a taxi.'

'You sure?'

'I need to find her just as much as you.'

We go out onto the street. It is raining. We walk some way, lights and cars swishing by us. Now I feel euphoric, at last it is all over – we are going to find Beatrice.

'I can't stay long,' Lisa is saying. 'It's Steve. He'll get pissed off.'

'Just a couple of days. Surely he'll understand?'

'Yeah,' she says, lighting another fag.

We stop at a chipper on the way. By the time we get back to the house, we are soaking and stink of wet vinegary chips.

We burst through the door, still clutching our brown bags. Leo is sitting on the couch, watching TV.

'Where the hell have you been?' he says icily.

'Foggy Dew . . .' I shake the rain out of my hair. 'This is Lisa,' I say. 'She's staying.'

Leo's jaw drops. 'Lisa?' he repeats slowly.

'Hi,' Lisa says, plonking herself down on the couch.

'Eithne, can I talk to you for a minute – in the kitchen?'

'Now?'

'Yes, now . . .' he says through clenched teeth.

I follow him out.

'What the fuck are you doing, Eithne?'

He is furious.

'She turned up on the doorstep today. We went out . . .' I clutch his hands. 'Leo, she really is Beatrice's daughter, she showed me her birth certificate.'

'That could be fake.'

'Come on now, who the hell would bother to do something

like that? I mean look at her, she's only eighteen – she just wants to find her mother. Wouldn't you?'

'It's nothing to do with us.'

'Of course it's everything to do with us. She's my niece!'

'She's a complete stranger, you don't know her.'

'You're so bloody anal! What would you do if some long-lost relative turned up from Poland? Would you turn them away?'

'No . . . but they wouldn't be staying here.'

'Well, don't worry, it's just for one night,' I say sarcastically. 'We're going down home tomorrow. We're going to find out what happened to Beatrice – we're going to find out who Lisa's real father is—'

Leo's anger dissipates. He looks horrified. 'No!' he says quickly. 'No, Eithne, don't do that.'

'But I was thinking – if I can find out who Lisa's father is, then he can tell us what happened to Beatrice.' I begin shaking again and clutch the kitchen counter for support. 'Leo,' I stare right into him, 'she's alive – she's alive!'

He is shaking his head.

'Eithne,' he strokes my face, 'come on; come to bed. Sleep on it. You might think differently in the morning.'

'Okay, yes you're right.' I steady myself. 'I'll just sort Lisa out with a duvet.'

When I go back into the sitting room, Lisa is asleep. Sprawled on the couch, she fills its length. Her long blonde hair is splayed on the cushions, and her mouth is slightly open. She looks young. The remote control has fallen from her hand, and a pop video is blasting out from the TV. I switch it off. She's only a kid really. I pull the duvet up over her.

I sit down in the armchair opposite and stare at her. I can hear Leo getting into bed, switching out the light; but I cannot get up. It is only when I see the dusk of dawn and hear the birds begin to chatter, that I pull myself up. Is Leo right? Am I insane to believe that Beatrice is still here, in our world? Beneath my joy lies anger in the pit of me. She left me, here on my own, and she never came back.

BEATRICE

Mullaghmeen Woods. She is a being of nature, flitting through the trees, gliding above the sticky path. She is pulled up the hill, like a presence rising towards a ghost-moon. But now it is the day. The sun is early and, while everyone is still asleep, it is at its brightest, full of promise and hope. Who could guess that later, when they eat their breakfasts, it will be grey and raining, and on the radio they will say she is gone.

She was never really here, but out there, living in the husk of an ancient oak, or babbling like a reel in the brook. These young beeches are her friends. Fine, pale and slender, they huddle on either side of the trail so that all vision becomes vertical. Their leaves have been falling, and now, at the departure of autumn, their colours are most dramatic. If only she had time to stop and look at them. She would carry them with her, wherever she was going. Like the last dance, the best, the most wrenching.

An ethereal mist weaves around the trees; if she were Eithne she would be afraid. But she's not. What more is there to fear? Her damage makes her careless. What is outside and wild is safe, what is in her home is most dangerous.

EITHNE

Beatrice and Phil had taken magic mushrooms at the concert in Slane. They had also bought a lump of dope and a small jar of dried mushrooms from the guy who had given them the free trial. After Slane, the summer took on an even more leisurely pace for the duo. Beatrice would sleep in late every single morning, while I'd be with Mammy, helping with the chores. It wasn't until we were eating lunch that Beatrice would appear in the kitchen, usually still in her pyjamas. If Daddy was in this would enrage him.

The bread would be stuck in my throat as I waited for him to snap. Some days he would shut up and eat quietly like a chastised child. But some days he would start roaring and stamping and storm out of the house. My mother would sigh, call the dog and give her Daddy's food.

It was one such day, and Beatrice sat on the kitchen counter, swinging her legs and eating cornflakes.

'Not only do you spend all day in bed, but you can't be bothered to get dressed when you do finally get up!' Daddy growled at her.

'Leave her, Joe, she'll be off to college soon. This is her last summer at home,' said Mammy.

'College to do what? Nothing useful, that's for sure. Tell me – how are you going to support yourself as an artist?'

'Philistine,' Beatrice muttered hopping off the counter and strolling upstairs with her tea.

'What did you say? I heard ya.'

'Can we not have our lunch in peace without you going on?' Mammy snapped.

Daddy slammed his knife and fork down and stomped out of the house.

About half an hour later Phil turned up.

'Good afternoon, Mrs Kelly,' he said, breezing into the house. 'Is the lady arisen yet?'

My mother loved the way he spoke. She smiled.

'She's up, if that's what you mean. Will you have a cup of tea, Philip?'

'Thank you, but no. Myself and Lady Beatrice are planning a big walk today, and she has promised to paint me sitting in a cornfield.'

'Eithne, go up and tell Beatrice that Phil is here for her.'

But Beatrice was already on her way down, carrying a basketful of paints, brushes and paper.

'Can I come with you?' I asked as they were on the way out.

'Don't you have friends of your own?' said Beatrice.

'Take her with you, God love her, she's so bored here with me,' said Mammy.

'Well, okay,' said Beatrice. 'But you'd better not moan – we're going for a long walk.'

'I like walking.' I smiled at Phil, and he winked back at me.

We set off through the woods at the back of the house, across the bog and through some sweet-smelling meadows. An hour later we stopped on the crest of a small hillock. Phil took out some tobacco, papers and the dope. He rolled a joint which he and Beatrice smoked.

'Can I have some?' I asked.

'No way. You're too young.'

They lay there then chatting. I would go off for a wander when it got too boring. They smoked a couple of joints. Beatrice did not even touch her paints. By the time I got back they would be giggling over something silly.

'I'm going home,' I announced.

'A bouquet for the young maiden, Eithne.' Phil laughed, handing me a dishevelled bunch of dandelions.

'Thanks a million,' I said gruffly. I was fed up, but at least they let me go with them, at least they trusted me.

I would tramp home feeling frustrated and useless, wishing I was old enough to leave home, and escape from this bog-hole. Beatrice and Phil never returned until after nightfall.

BEATRICE

The earth rolled around her in big green waves. The sky was a startling blue, she felt as though she was expanding like Alice in Wonderland after she drank from the little bottle. She looked at him. He was all different shades of blue, soft and smoky. He walked like a stallion. He was laughing.

'Earth goddess,' he said.

They lay down on the ground. All their senses were heightened. They watched the sky as it became twilight and the moon emerged. She could see the dome of the sky, the stars sparkling like rips in the dark felt of night, day peeping behind.

They held hands and then they embraced.

'Let's take our clothes off,' she said.

They took everything off. It felt wonderful, the wind against her chest, the wetness of dewy grass beneath her. She thought she was in the ocean at the bottom of the sea. They lay, side by side, holding hands and fell asleep. That is what they remember.

When they woke they were shivering. Phil and Beatrice got dressed quickly and raced down the hill. They stopped at the spring to drink, feeling clear-headed and free. The full dark of night was yet to descend. They looked at each other across the stream. The water gurgled beneath them, their eyes were bright, the silence between them was as precious as a rare gem.

SARAH

They took the boat. Sarah sat mutely with Beatrice in her arms. She watched England disappear, and all hope retreat. Joe didn't seem to notice her mood. He went up to the bar again and again. By the time they reached Dun Laoghaire he was twisted.

Sarah had left without contacting Anthony. Even thinking his name hurt. In all their months of friendship he had not mentioned Harriet. Yet there she was in his life, kissing him . . . Why had he brought her the locket? Why had he asked her to marry him if there was always Harriet? There may have been an explanation, but she had not stayed to find out and now it was too late.

They were met at Dun Laoghaire harbour by a fat ginger-bearded man with a dirty Ford Escort.

'Tommy!' yelled Joe. 'How's it going? This is my best friend Tommy O'Reilly – Tommy, meet me wife, Sarah.'

'You dark horse.' Tommy laughed. 'They're in uproar at home over your secret marriage. Imagine being married a year and having a baby and all, and not telling your own family? Joseph Kelly, your ma is fierce mad with you.'

Sarah looked at Joe – married a year?

Joe helped her into the back of the car and handed her Beatrice.

'It's easier this way,' he whispered. 'Please, just go along with it.'

Joe got into the front seat. He and Tommy chatted noisily the whole journey. Beatrice fell asleep. Sarah pressed her face against the steamed-up window. Houses gave way to fields; the roads were bad, bumpy and twisting. As they drove further into the countryside she began to notice how green the grass was. It wasn't this green at home. The landscape attracted her. It was less manicured than the fields in England. There seemed to be more space, and there were certainly fewer cars on the roads.

Just over an hour after they had left the port they passed through Kells. The shop fronts were dusty and ancient, the houses pressed in together, the road was narrow and twisted. They passed a huge cross in the centre of a crossroads; it had carvings on it and looked extremely old.

After Kells the land opened out. The countryside was alien to Sarah. She had grown up in the centre of Southampton, and from there she had gone straight to London. She remembered picnics on the beach as a small child, and day trips to Bournemouth, and once they had gone to Devon to visit an aunt. But this was so different. For a start there were fewer people about. Occasionally they'd pass an old chap on a tractor, who'd give them a wave, his collie dog perched beside him on the seat. Joe and Tommy's conversation seemed to be completely obsessed by who had left and gone to America, and what they were doing. It sounded to Sarah as if there was no one left in Ireland.

Eventually they turned off the main road and passed through a village on top of a hill. They turned again and passed through another village, with a beautiful old church. Tommy drove down a narrow road, shaded by large leafy trees. It was a warm day, and dry.

'This is Bog Road,' said Joe. It was the first thing he had said to her since they had left Dublin.

Tommy turned into a tiny lane and followed its meandering

course for a few miles. They took a sharp left and the car bumped up a pot-holed track to a stone cottage with tiny windows. Sarah's first thought was how dark it must be inside.

'Here we are,' said Joe. 'This is Glenamona.' He was excited and practically leapt out of the car. The door of the cottage opened and a woman with a crown of curly white hair came running out. Her face was a softer version of Joe's.

'Joey!' she cried and fell on him.

Tommy opened the door for Sarah, and she got out with Beatrice in her arms.

'Ma,' said Joe breaking free from her, 'this is Sarah, and my daughter Beatrice.'

'Oh, Lord.' The woman wept. She approached Sarah, looking at the baby first. 'Will you look at her?' she cooed. Then she looked up at Sarah and her eyes hardened.

'How do you do?' She extended her hand.

'Hello,' Sarah said.

'You could have told me.' Joe's mother turned on him. 'Married a year and not so much as blessed in the church. You heathen!' She clipped his ear, but she was laughing. 'Come in and have some tea, you must be exhausted.'

They went into the house; the family crowded around them. As far as Sarah could make out, Joe had three sisters, and a brother who lived in England – apparently a small family by local standards. Plans for their 'proper' wedding were already under way.

'I've spoken to Father Cleary,' said Joe's mother. 'And he said that Saturday three weeks would be grand.'

'Actually, ma, there's a problem,' said Joe.

'Oh, what's that?'

'Sarah isn't Catholic.'

'Oh.' His mother didn't know what to say.

'But she wants to convert – don't you, Sarah?'

'I . . .'

The whole family looked at her.

'Yes, please.' She felt as though she was asking for another cup of tea, not deciding she wanted to change her religion. Joe had never discussed this with her, and it had never even entered her head. Beatrice began to cry, she was hungry.

'Mrs Kelly, is there somewhere I can feed Beatrice?'

'Have you no bottle?'

'I'm breastfeeding her. Is there a room I can go into?'

'Oh, I see. Well, upstairs. The first room you come to, that's the girls' room.'

Sarah got up.

'And please call me Margaret,' Joe's mother said stiffly.

Sarah went upstairs. She could feel the family looking at her as she ascended them, and Mrs Kelly's disapproval burnt into her back – not only Protestant, but breastfeeding as well.

EITHNE

When I wake the next morning Leo has already gone. My head is spinning and my mouth is parched. I stumble out of bed and wander into the kitchen to get a glass of water.

'Oh God,' I groan, cradling my head in my hands. Feebly, I put on the kettle, and stand staring at my distended reflection.

I can hear music; I go into the sitting room. Lisa is awake, sitting cross-legged on the duvet, watching MTV and smoking a cigarette.

'Hi,' she says.

'Hi there.'

'Mind if I smoke?'

'No, it's okay,' I say, opening the window.

'You look rough,' she says brightly.

'I couldn't sleep. Do you want some tea?'

'Coffee?'

'Right.'

'Are we still going, then?' she asks, as I head towards the kitchen. 'Down to that village where you grew up?'

'Um, yes, of course.'

I don't feel so sure at all; maybe Leo is right.

'Can you do me a favour, Lisa?'

'Course.'

'Can I see that birth certificate again?'

She looks puzzled.

'Sure.'

She pulls it out of her bag, and hands it to me. I go into the kitchen and hold it up to the light. I scrutinize it and read it again and again:

*Births registered in the sub-district of St Pancras
in the London Borough of Camden.*

Date and Place of Birth: *1982, Twenty-second May, University College Hospital, St Pancras.*

Name: *Margaret* (Beatrice had called her Margaret, after Granny)

Sex: *Female*

First Name and Surname and Dwelling Place of Father: *Not known*

First Name and Surname and Maiden Name of Mother: *Beatrice Kelly*

Rank or Profession of Father: *Not known*

Signature, Qualification and Residence of Informant: *Beatrice Kelly, Crossakiel, Kells, County Meath, Ireland*

When Registered: *31 May 1982*

There is no denying it. This girl is family. I take a big breath and try to balance myself. Why was Beatrice in London? She didn't know anyone there — then it comes to me, of course, her father, Jonathan — what's he called? — Jonathan Voyle, that's it. Maybe Beatrice had gone to him, and maybe he had helped her. I still can't understand why she had turned away from Mammy, who would have walked through fire for her, probably reared the child as her own. It still doesn't make sense. But if I can find out where Jonathan Voyle is, he might be able to tell me where

Beatrice is now. I can't believe that none of us have thought of this before.

I go back in with the tea, and hand back the certificate.

'She called you after Granny,' I say, 'her name was Margaret.'

'I don't really like it,' says Lisa, 'I don't like Lisa either.'

'Lisa, can you tell me something?' I ask, changing the subject. 'Did the agency give you any other contact addresses for where Beatrice had lived in London at the time?'

'No, all they had was the address in Ireland.'

'Right. It's just I've thought of someone who might know where she is.'

She looks at me enquiringly.

'It's a really long story,' I say. I don't want to tell her about Jonathan Voyle, not just yet. 'I'll tell you if I get anywhere.'

'Okay,' she says. 'Can I give Steve a ring? I said I'd be back today.'

'Yeah, sure, go ahead. I'm just going to have a shower.'

When I come out of the bathroom she is still on the phone. I get dressed quickly. My skin feels sore, prickly, as if I have mild heat rash. I look at the insides of my elbows; hives are beginning to form on the skin. I scratch. The last time I got that rash was just before I got married – I was so stressed out then. This is worse. I can't think straight; instinct urges me on – a voice inside my head whispering, 'Go home, go home.' I know that Leo won't be happy, but it's not his business, that's what I tell myself, it's all up to me.

Lisa finally finishes her call and goes into the bathroom. I pick up the phone in the bedroom and dial home.

'Mammy, it's Eithne. Listen, I'm coming home today – I'm bringing a friend . . . She's over in Ireland and wants to see a bit of the country. Is that okay? Great . . . How's Daddy? . . .

It'll be all right with him, won't it? . . . Good. See you later
. . . Yeah, dinner. That will be great. Bye.'

Then I call Leo, it goes to call answering, he is probably
teaching a class. I leave a message on his voicemail to ring me at
home tonight.

Lisa is still in the bathroom. I eat some cereal and make
another pot of coffee. Finally she emerges in my dressing gown.

'You don't mind, do you?'

'No, that's okay. Coffee?'

'Yeah . . . you don't have any instant, do you? I don't really
like that stuff.'

'No, sorry, only ground.'

She takes a mug anyway, and we sit in silence.

'How's Steve?' I ask.

'He's fine. Not too pleased with me, though. He can't
understand why I'd want to find my real mum. He says she
isn't worth it.'

'I see.'

'Do you have any pictures of her?'

'Not really. Mammy has photos— Hang on a minute, I have
this.'

I go into the study. The small *Beata Beatrix*, which the Artist
painted, is on the desk. I pick it up and go back into the kitchen.

'This is her.' I hand the painting to Lisa.

'She's gorgeous,' she says looking at the delicate oil.

'Yeah, she was. Although there's a good bit of artistic licence
taken in that picture.'

I am scratching again.

'Right, are you nearly ready?'

'Just give me a minute and I'll get dressed.'

She goes back into the sitting room and comes out a few

minutes later in the same clothes she wore the day before. I notice that she is cleaning her flashy white runners with toilet roll. She catches me watching her. 'Nike,' she says as if I'd understand.

We drive into town, parking down a side road. I have an idea that I will take some things with me down home. I have my camera in the studio, some paper and inks and a couple of my sketchbooks. I have a vague plan to document everything – maybe use it in my show.

The studio is on the second floor. Noreen is at work on a steel plate.

'Eithne! How's it going? Are you in today?'

'No, hun, I'm going home for a few days. This is Lisa, a friend from England.'

'Wow!' Lisa says, pointing at our giant press. 'What is that? It looks like it should belong in a museum, like a giant thing they used for washing clothes hundreds of years ago.'

'It does look like a mangle. We use it to print – the paper goes here with the plate on top of it, then we put the blanket on and then we wind the press and it rolls across the top,' Noreen explains.

'Heavy work,' says Lisa as she tries to turn the handle.

'That's not the half of it,' says Noreen.

'And what are they?' asks Lisa, looking over at a stack of limestone blocks.

'They're lithographic stones. They're very, very heavy and a real pain to work with.'

Lisa fingers the weathered stones.

'Each one has to be ground completely smooth and washed down before you can use it,' says Noreen. 'Then it's touch and go whether the ink will take.'

'God, I never thought making a picture was so hard,' says Lisa, looking at the art around her.

Noreen exchanges looks with me – I know what she is thinking, what she'll say to me later.

'Do you have time for a coffee, Eithne?' she asks. 'We could pop over to Joy of Coffee.'

'Love to, but we're really in a hurry.'

There's no rush, but coffee with Noreen has implications. I just don't want her to know what's going on, not yet.

'Are you okay?' she asks. 'You look ever so pale.'

'I just couldn't sleep last night – I'll see you later.'

We go back downstairs with my stuff.

'Beatrice was studying art when she disappeared,' I tell Lisa. 'She was at the National College of Art and Design. She was good, very good.'

Lisa looks at me.

'Well, I didn't inherit that off her. I'm crap at art.'

'Maybe you never gave it a chance.'

'No, I'm really shit – matchstick people, that's all I can do.'

By the time we hit the Navan road it is lunchtime and people are running out of their offices, across the road into smoky cafes for soup and rolls. We pass a McDonald's.

'Hey,' says Lisa, 'can we get a burger or something? I'm starving.'

I go into the drive-by lane. Lisa orders a cheeseburger, Coke and fries. I just get a coffee. I can smell the place from inside the car and it makes my stomach churn. I pay, while Lisa digs in.

'You know, that food is complete crap,' I say.

She looks amused.

'You sound like my mum,' she says with her mouth full.

As I drive I begin to get nervous. I haven't been home in a few months. Leo and I had spent Christmas with his family, and then we had gone away for new year. Being home at that time of year is hard, there's booze everywhere, and Daddy usually gets out of control.

When I was little I used to love Christmas. Then, when Daddy drank he was funny. He'd buy box loads of crackers, and wear all the silly hats one on top of the other and turn all the stupid jokes into stupider songs. Mammy and Beatrice would join in, a bit. They'd start off playing Monopoly with us, but usually they'd get bored and wander off into the sitting room to watch the Christmas movie together. Then the battle would begin – Daddy and I could play for hours, bankrupting each other. He was always the top hat, Mr Posh he'd call himself, and I was always the little dog, Little Jordie he used to call me, because he said the dog reminded him of someone he used to work with.

After Beatrice disappeared, Christmas became pure torture. Daddy never even made it to the dinner table. After Mass he'd head straight for the pub. Mammy could hardly get it together to cook anything. I remember one year sitting in front of *The Wizard of Oz* eating cheese sandwiches. Another year the Lynches invited us. Mammy refused to go, but insisted that I should. It was awful. The Lynches were so nice to me. They had all bought me presents, and Assumpta gave me exactly what I wanted – a denim pencil skirt. Everyone was laughing and hustling and bustling – there was so much noise, so much love, that the contrast to my own home hit me like a force. I decided it would have been better not to know what I was missing each year. I never went again.

We drive past Navan, and it begins raining. A drizzle at first, but as the temperature drops the rain becomes icier and builds up momentum. I hope Daddy is busy, that he hasn't been in the pub yet. It is January, grey and cold. The land will be barren at this time of year, and there's not much to do. When it's that bleak, it's hard to take.

When I was a child, I wished we lived by the sea. The sea is so immense, so wide, so dazzling to a child's eyes. When you first see that chink of sea-blue on the horizon, it's a moment you remember for ever. But now I am glad we grew up in the heart of Ireland where, in the summer, the land is lush, the river wide, and we were surrounded by woods, bogs and loughs. Your childhood landscape never leaves you, wherever you end up.

A car pulls out in front of me.

'Jesus!' I slam on the brakes.

'He didn't even see you,' says Lisa.

'I suppose visibility is pretty bad.'

I am jumpy, like a cat. My heart is pounding as I begin to realize how much I am dreading going home. Since we were down with Mick, Leo has refused to go home with me. He says he's fed up trying with my parents. He says it's like they just don't want to get to know him, like they couldn't care less who I was married to. I try to tell him otherwise, but I lack conviction. Daddy does care . . . it's just he's not well; he needs someone to help him. As for Mammy, Leo is right. She is cold. Especially compared to Katy, his mother, who adores me, and plasters me with kisses and hugs every time she sees me, while enquiring when exactly am I going to produce a grandchild. Mammy never asks that. Thank God. But then she never asks anything specific about our lives, just how's work? And, not even listening to the answer, she'll move on to, how's the house? How's the little girl, Shauna? It drives Leo mad. I try to explain.

It's like she's standing behind plate glass, I say, and it's all steamed up, and she just can't see anything very clearly on the other side. She's lost inside her own pain. That's why she's distant. And he says, well, what's on her side? Beatrice, I say, the both of them, protected from reality. Well, Leo says, it's about time the glass was broken, it's about time you had your mother back. It hurts when he says that. It's too late now, I say, I'll never be Beatrice.

We pass through Kells. There's a line of traffic up the town.

'So did my mum have a boyfriend, then?' asks Lisa. 'Do you know who my father might be?'

Jakob Rudin springs to mind. And then Phil . . . I had worked out that Beatrice must have got pregnant round about the end of August so it was before she left for Dublin. It was definitely someone back home.

'It could be a couple of people,' I say. 'I'll have to ask Mammy. Beatrice might have told her if she had a boyfriend.'

'Are you going to tell your mum about me?' asks Lisa. 'How do you think she'll take it?'

'I think she always thought Beatrice would come back. I don't think she's ever believed she was dead.'

We turn left out of the town, already it seems to be getting dark.

'Because of the things,' I say. 'Lots of bits and pieces belonging to Beatrice were found all over the place – a necklace in the woods, a book down by the lake, a scarf on the hill. I always thought there was a killer out there and that was his trail but Mammy thought they were clues; she believed that Beatrice had left them there for us.'

'That's really weird,' says Lisa. 'What else was found?'

'Well, there was also a beret – that was found on the bog. It was pink and it had sequins on it.'

'God, people wore really disgusting things then, didn't they?'

I say nothing, and Lisa looks out of the window.

'I used to have a beret,' she says. 'I bloody hated it. My mum, who I'm going to call Lorraine from now on, used to make me wear it to school every day. I looked shit. So every day I'd take off the beret and hide it in a bush behind our bins. I also had another pair of shoes there as well. You can imagine the type of things Lorraine made me wear.'

I glance at her.

'You know, those really awful Clarkes things – really nerdish. Course, I was caught in the end. Lorraine was gardening one day and found the beret and shoes. But instead of getting angry with me, she just started to cry and ran up to her room to sulk. She was always doing things like that.'

It has stopped raining, and the sun vainly pushes through, although it is almost dusk. I turn off the main road, and drive up a steep lane. I need to walk. I park the car at the base of a hill – Witch's Hill – and switch off the ignition.

'Let's stretch our legs,' I say.

'Okay,' Lisa says unenthusiastically.

We leave the car park, and walk up some stone steps to a small gateway. A few sheep stare at us. We start to climb up the hill. There is a faint track in the grass. It is quite steep, but Lisa almost jogs along. It is hard to keep up. As we ascend, the clouds begin to clear, and we are able to look around us. The view is staggering. In every direction distant blue peaks frame the horizon. You can see Lough Sheelin, a wide pool of shining silver. Some of the land is rough, and knobbly, in other places fields have been levelled and cultivated. The hills nearby are the most fantastic shapes, one looks like a shark fin.

'Wow,' she says. 'What a view!'

'It's something else all right,' I reply.

We can hardly talk. It is so windy the words are being blown out of our mouths. Finally we reach the top. The main burial mound faces us; its surface is covered with sharp grey stones. To our left is a small burial chamber and to our right another ring of stones.

It is wild up here. The sun is setting and dusk creeps across the fields. We are being buffeted around by the wind.

'That's where Beatrice's scarf was found,' I yell above the wind, pointing to the entrance of the mound.

She nods and goes over to it. Peers inside.

'Spooky,' she shouts.

We walk round the windy side again, I am being pushed and pushed into the sky. It's hard to take.

Lisa climbs up onto the hag's chair, makes a loud whoop, and jumps down.

'Come on,' she says. 'It feels like you're flying!'

I shake my head.

'Come on.' She takes my hand and forces me up.

On the rocks the wind tries to beat us down, but we stand firm, and then jump out into it. Lisa whoops and I yell. The rage in my belly comes out as one big roar.

'Wow!' says Lisa. 'You're loud.'

We do it again and again until, completely exhausted, we collapse on the ground.

'That was great,' she says.

'We'd better go, it's getting dark.'

We pick our way down the hill. The rain has made it slippy as hell.

'Go down like a crab,' I say. 'Sideways . . . like this.'

She looks at me like I am bonkers, and at that moment she loses her footing and slips, landing flat on her bum.

'Are you all right?'

Her shoulders are rocking back and forth. At first I think that she is laughing, then I see the tears spilling off the end of her nose, trickling down her lips.

'Hey,' I say, and put my arm around her shoulders. 'Are you hurt?'

She shakes her head; then she lets out a wail.

'Why did she do it?' she screams. 'Why the fuck did she give me up!'

'I don't know, Lisa,' I say. 'I'm angry too.'

'I wish it had been you,' she says, and gives me a tremendous hug. Something about the way she does this, or the feel and smell of her as she hugs me, reminds me of my sister. Finally I can sense Beatrice in Lisa. She doesn't look like her, but she is beginning to look like someone familiar. I just can't remember who.

Back in the car we clean our shoes.

'Look at them, they're ruined,' Lisa sniffs, as she tries to pick the mud off her runners.

'Maybe we should wait till we get home. We can put them in the washing machine.'

I start the car.

'Lisa,' I ask, 'are you sure you don't want to go back to Dublin?'

'No, I'm okay now. I want to go on. I want to meet my real family.'

BEATRICE

'There is a wonderful world in the deep,' said Beatrice to Phil, as he stripped some bark off the tree. She stared at his hands. His fingers picked at the pieces of wood, which flickered all shades of brown.

'There are secret gardens and blooming sea-flowers unseen by human eyes,' she said. Phil paused, and looked up at her. His eyes were nearly as black as the bog-earth they sat upon. Her pupils were as dilated as his.

'There are forests of seaweed, groves of seashells, pools with pearls that shimmer and gleam,' she continued. 'The coral is as red as a poppy and shaped like a castle. And all manner of tiny sea creatures live within. It is a lovely country at the bottom of the sea.'

'When I was younger, when my step-father actually liked me, he used to take me fishing on the Thames,' said Phil. 'I liked it, we sat in silence, but it felt like family. Once he took me sea fishing. It was different. Kind of wild and noisy. I suppose there were other people there. I kept hearing this bell pealing like a church bell. I said to my step-father, "Why is the skipper ringing a bell?"

' "What bell?" he said. He didn't hear it.

'Afterwards I read in a book that some sailors say that they've heard church bells – peals from the ocean's depth, floating to the surface from towers below. These towers belong to submerged cities and sunken lands. There *is* somewhere else.'

SARAH

Every Friday Father Cleary arrived to instruct Sarah in the Catholic faith in preparation for her wedding while Margaret took Beatrice for a walk in the pram. Margaret really did seem fond of the baby and Sarah was, in a way, thankful for her support. She could not imagine how she would have coped on her own in Clapham – but maybe she wouldn't have been alone?

Sarah had never considered herself religious, thus she accepted what Father Cleary told her to believe in just as she accepted her lot. She still had not written to her parents and, though she knew she should contact them, as each day passed it became harder and harder to put pen to paper. Soon it would be Christmas and this year they were expecting her.

As the days shortened and Beatrice grew, Sarah was put to work around the house. It seemed to be her job to wash the floors, which were constantly dirtied by mud from the yard and outbuildings, every day.

Joe's father had died about five years earlier. It was shortly after his death that Joe and his brother Jack had set out for London. Both had started work on the building sites, sending money home to their mother every week. Jack had moved on about three years ago and was married, working in a bank and settled in Surrey.

The Kellys didn't own much land. A good part of it had been sold after the father died, but Margaret managed a few sheep, a couple of cows and some hens on the acres she had left. Joe's three sisters still lived at home. Aoife, who worked in the local chicken factory, was due to be married next spring. She was the fairest in the family and the friendliest towards Sarah. Mary was much like her mother. She always seemed to be going to church, as far as Sarah could tell. She was only at home for a while longer; in the new year she was going to Dublin to train to be a nurse. Bríd was the youngest. She spoke little and spent most of her time outside on the farm. She had been in charge of the livestock until Joe had returned and, although fond of her brother, her resentment towards him was perceptible. Towards Sarah she was unmistakably hostile.

At first Sarah found it hard to understand the Kellys' accents; they all seemed to speak so fast. Then she just stopped listening; they were never talking to her anyway. It was as though she was a shadow in the corner. Yet for the first time in her life she was vaguely aware that she was an important part of something – if only through her baby.

The women doted on Beatrice, showering her with little toys and hand-knitted cardigans. It certainly wasn't Beatrice's or Joe's fault, but somehow all Sarah's fault that they had never been told she and Joe were married.

The wedding day approached – the second week in November. Beatrice's baptism had been arranged for the same day. Joe and Sarah had been sleeping in separate rooms over the past six weeks. According to Margaret, 'They were not yet married in the eyes of the Lord.' Margaret had asked Sarah about her family. Were they not coming to the wedding? Sarah had explained that her father was too ill to travel. The subject was never raised again.

It was all happening too fast, yet each day felt impossibly long. Sarah went for walks, but there was nowhere to go. She would just stare at the sheep and their indifference and then turn back to the house. Her life was being lived for her. She felt utterly apathetic.

Joe more or less left her to it. Although she knew that she would never be able to love him, not in the way she felt about Anthony, nor even like the short-lived infatuation she had had for Jonathan, Sarah still wished he would spend more time with her. At least they could be friends. But he seemed always to be out and about on the land, or out someplace with Tommy O'Reilly, when they would usually end up in the pub and Joe would not get home until after she had gone to bed. Only on a Sunday was he around – for the big dinner.

The Sunday before they were married they went for a walk together after the meal.

'I'll take you to the bog,' said Joe. 'It's my favourite place.'

They walked across the field at the back of the house, climbed a fence and joined a lane, 'Bog Lane', he called it. They passed by a tightly knit wood behind which was an expanse of marshy land.

'Here we are,' he announced.

Sarah looked around her. It wasn't exactly what she would have described as stunning, but there was something about the sheer desolation of the bog which wrung her heart.

'Are you happy?' asked Joe. He looked at her with such earnestness. She turned away.

'Yes,' she said.

'You don't sound very happy, Sarah. What is it?'

'I just . . .'

'Give us time, Sarah. After we're married properly in the church, I'll work really hard. I've already seen the perfect site for our little house. We'll have more children, we'll be a family. You've fitted in so well – already Mammy likes you. And I can tell you she's a hard woman to please.'

'She's very kind, it's just . . .'

'I love you, Sarah.'

Joe came towards her and held her in his arms. Sarah did not pull back. She was so lonely that she needed his warmth, his love. He kissed her.

'Come on,' he said.

He took her hand and led her to a quiet copse of aspen trees to the left of the bog. He sat on the ground and pulled her down next to him. He unbuttoned her blouse, unhooked the heavy maternity bra and stroked her breasts. A little milk trickled from a nipple, he licked it.

'Are you ready?' he asked. 'Can we do it yet?'

'Yes,' she said. She needed him.

This was Joe's first time. She did not know much herself. They were clumsy. It only lasted a minute. Afterwards they lay side by side looking at the sky. Joe felt complete; Sarah felt even more alone than before.

EITHNE

I have started to work with shades of blue. Blue is a colour which immediately registers a mood. For me it conjures up solitude and a dreamy, floating feeling.

In 'Atlantis' I want the viewer to drift. Hopefully, the gradations of blue create a sense of depth. Using a technique called carborundum, I etch a seascape, very finely and with little detail. There is a breeze under the ocean and the seaweed is swaying. Tones of green and blue converge to create a pure Mediterranean blue at the heart of the print.

The girls had booked the holiday at the last minute. It had been Beatrice's idea to go to Majorca, the others had planned to go down to Tramore for the week, but Beatrice managed to find a cheap deal and persuaded the other three girls that they'd spend as much staying in Ireland. None of them had been abroad before. They were going the second week after the exams finished.

The week before they left the girls went on a big shopping trip to Dublin, they came back with summer dresses, hats, sunglasses, suntan lotion and bikinis. Beatrice modelled her stuff for me, her bikini was in a leopard-skin print and very skimpy.

'Jaysus!' I gawped.

'You should see Deirdre's — she's practically wearing nothing,' said Beatrice.

'Don't let Mammy see it,' I said, 'she'll never let you take it.'

The girls were booked into the Pillari Playa apartments on the Palma de Majorca. It was the cheapest place to stay on the whole island.

'I hope the apartment is all right.' Mammy was worried.

'It'll be grand,' said Beatrice. 'Sure we'll only be sleeping there. That is, if we get any sleep!'

Mammy gave her a chilly look.

'Stop, Mam! I'm a big girl now.'

'Just be careful. Those Spanish men are . . . different from the Irish.'

'I should hope so. I need a bit of fun, this place is so dead.'

I'll admit it, I was sick with jealousy. The furthest I had ever been was Galway. I had never even been to England, let alone the Continent.

'Don't look so glum,' said Beatrice. 'When you're older we'll go away together.'

'Promise?'

'I promise. We'll go somewhere really exotic like Tahiti or Jamaica. We'll work on the banana boats to pay our way.'

'Will you stop filling her head with such nonsense?' said Mammy, but she was laughing. Even Daddy smiled as he sat by the fire reading the local paper. It was before the summer turned bad, before Phil came. In fact, the holiday to Majorca had been a present from Daddy. Beatrice had studied hard for the Leaving Certificate.

The girls headed off on the Saturday afternoon. Immediately the house fell dead and silent. I trailed around the fields with the dog at my heels – there was nothing to look forward to, not until Beatrice came back next Saturday.

On the Wednesday, Daddy came home in high spirits.

'I've just been down with Jack,' he said. 'His son, Philip, is coming over for the summer. It'll be great to have the help, so.'

Mammy looked up from the table, she was painting a single red rose.

'That's great,' she said. 'I'm so pleased for Jack.'

'You'll be meeting your cousin,' Daddy said to me. He looked around then. 'Is there no tea ready?'

Mammy glanced up.

'Oh, is that the time?' she said casually. 'Eithne, would you run to the shop and get some bacon and eggs. My purse is there on the dresser.'

'A fry!' Daddy exclaimed. 'But that's breakfast!'

'Well, cook your own if you don't want it.'

'For Christ's sake, haven't you better things to do than paint that dead flower? Jesus!'

He stomped off into the sitting room and turned on the telly.

The phone rang. No one answered it, so eventually I picked it up.

'Eithne, it's Deirdre Maloney here. Can you put your mam on?' she said.

'Mam, it's Deirdre, ringing from Majorca!'

Mammy ran to the phone.

'Deidre, hello, yes, what's wrong?'

'Mrs Kelly, I'm sorry, I don't want to worry you, but Beatrice was out last night and she hasn't come back to the apartment. We don't know what to do.'

'Oh my God. Well . . . have you been to the police?'

'The tour operator said we had to wait twenty-four hours. I'm sorry, Mrs Kelly, it's just we thought we should ring you. She was only popping down to the hotel bar to watch the dancing, but she never came back.'

'Listen,' Mammy said. 'Give me your number. I'll ring you back in a while, I'll ask her dad what we should do.'

She put down the phone.

'Joe!' she called.

'What's wrong?' I said.

'Beatrice has gone missing in Majorca. Joe!'

Daddy came into the room.

'What is it?'

'That was Deirdre, she was ringing from Majorca. Beatrice went out last night and she hasn't come back. What should we do? Do you think we should call the embassy?'

Daddy held her shoulders.

'Calm down . . . come on now, I'm sure there's an explanation. Beatrice will be fine. You know what she can be like. Have they contacted the local police?'

'They have to wait until tomorrow before they can report her missing. Oh Jesus, anything could happen to her!'

'Well, let's just wait a couple of hours and ring again. I'm sure she's fine. Come on, sit down and have a brandy.'

Daddy reached for the decanter.

'I'll go and get the food,' I said and slipped out the door.

I walked around the village three times, my heart pounding. Beatrice was so much a part of me. There were just the two of us. We were comrades. I felt that if something had happened to her I should know about it, intuitively. I searched my mind, it was blank.

When I got back Mammy and Daddy were in the sitting room.

'There you are,' said Mammy. 'I thought we had another missing daughter on our hands. Everything's all right. Deirdre phoned just after you left. Beatrice turned up practically as soon as she had finished talking to us.'

'She couldn't find the hotel,' said Daddy. He was on the stout already.

'She went to a party last night, stayed over, and then spent the whole of the next day walking up and down the beach looking for her apartment,' said Mammy.

'That's the last time we let her go off on her own like that,' said Daddy. 'She can't be trusted.'

'She'll have something to answer for,' said Mammy. 'Not only for going off to a strange party but without the other girls.'

'You'd never do something like that, would you, Eithne?' asked Daddy, half jokingly.

'I'd never get the chance,' I muttered and went upstairs to stare at the ceiling and measure my boredom.

BEATRICE

She wondered if this was the right hotel. She had already been waiting an hour with no sign of her father. Of course, she wasn't quite sure what he looked like, but he would be looking for her as well. They'd know each other.

She played with her drink. It was already her second sangria. She knew she should go, the girls would be getting worried. Just a little longer. Surely he would come?

It had not been hard for Beatrice to find out that Jonathan spent the month of June in Majorca. Ever since she had found out that Joe was not her real father, she had made Sarah tell her everything including where the Voyles lived. Just before her Leaving Certificate she went up to Dublin for the day on the pretext of buying some study texts. But she also went into the central library and looked up Voyle in a London telephone book. There it was — the address in Hampstead and the telephone number.

Then it had just been a matter of phoning and pretending to be a relative of an old friend. She discovered that Jonathan had left for Spain that morning but his housekeeper had given her his number in Majorca. It was then Beatrice decided that she would go and see him, and nothing was going to stand in her way.

The day after the girls had arrived in Majorca, Beatrice had sneaked off to a phone booth and dialled Jonathan's number; a woman answered in Spanish.

'Hello, can I speak to Jonathan Voyle, please?'

'Who is it?' the Spanish lady said in heavily accented English.

'Tell him it's his daughter.'

She heard the woman calling him, 'Jonathan, it's your daughter.'

'Hello, Vicky darling.' He had a smooth voice, like cream.

'This is Beatrice,' she said.

'And who pray is Beatrice? I know no one by that name.'

He was about to put the phone down.

'Remember Sarah?' she said quickly. 'Sarah Quigley. She used to work for your family in Hampstead.'

'Yes, I remember Sarah,' he said cautiously.

'I'm her daughter.' Beatrice breathed deeply. 'Your daughter.'

There was silence, then he said, 'I thought she got married, and went to live in Ireland.'

'She did.'

'Well, what are you doing here? Is Sarah with you?'

'No. I'm on my own. I wanted to meet you.'

'I don't think so – I mean – why?'

'You're my father. I just want to see you.'

'I really don't think there would be much point. Sorry . . . what's your name again?'

'Beatrice.'

'Yes. Beatrice. I have nothing whatsoever to do with your life.'

'Don't you want to meet me?'

In the background she could hear the woman calling him.

'Look,' he said, 'I have to go.'

'Please, you owe it to me,' she pleaded. 'I just want to meet you once.'

There was a pause.

'Okay,' he said. 'Where are you staying?'

'The Pillari Playa.'

'I'll meet you in the Europa Hotel bar. Tuesday. 10 p.m.'

It was nearly midnight now and still no sign of him. Beatrice was rooted to her seat. A waiter came up to her.

'*Sangria, por favore*,' she said.

She wanted to drink herself into the ground. She was furious. How dare he stand her up? A gang of English lads came into the bar.

'Mind if we join you?' one of them said.

'Go ahead,' she replied, not caring.

They started drinking huge jugs of sangria. She joined in and got drunker and drunker. She had completely forgotten the girls would be getting worried. She didn't care at all. In fact, she couldn't give a damn.

The gang at her table grew and grew. Some girls from Germany joined them and they decided to go to another bar. Beatrice went with them. She started to drink vodka and Coke. There was a disco in the second bar and Beatrice began gyrating around the dance floor. All self-respect gone, she let anyone dance with her, and anyone shift her.

Later they all went back to the German girls' apartment and things began to get more out of control. One of the girls was extremely drunk; she took off her bra and let two of the lads fondle her breasts. The apartment was extremely crowded and Beatrice started to feel dizzy and hot. She stumbled into the bathroom. Another of the girls was on her back in the bath with one of the guys on top of her; they were in the middle of drunken sex. Horrified, Beatrice mumbled, 'Sorry,' and ran back out. She heard the girl laughing loudly behind her.

She stood swaying in the doorway of one of the bedrooms. Where the hell was she? She had to get back to her hotel. One of the lads approached her. He was completely drunk.

'Do you want to fuck?' he yelled at her, above the pounding music.

'No thanks,' she said.

'What?' he said, grabbing her as if he hadn't heard.

'No thanks,' she said, pulling away. Before he had a chance to say another thing, she fled.

Outside, in the dark, standing by the sea, her head began to clear. She cried. The tears tasted bitter on her lips. Why had Jonathan not come? Exhausted, she dropped where she stood and lay down on the sand. The sound of the sea was like a lullaby, it soothed her and made her want to be at home with her mammy.

When she woke the next morning her mouth was full of sand. She coughed and spat and sat up. It was early and luckily there was no one about. She hugged her knees and stared out at the sea.

What had happened? It hurt her head to try to remember.

It was already blazingly hot. She had no idea where she was. She went to a local shop and bought a bottle of water, then walked back to the beach, sat down and drank. She wasn't going to give up. It must have been the wrong hotel. He must have meant for them to meet somewhere else.

She had this dream about Jonathan and she still clung to it. He was so different from Joe: cultured, intellectual, someone you could be proud of. Maybe she would be invited to England. She could make friends with Vicky – her half-sister. She had a whole other family out there, all she had to do was find them.

It was very hot by now. Beatrice lay on the sand and closed her eyes. A wave swept over her. She was soaked, but cool.

She'd leave it for now and ring him another time, maybe one day she'd even go to London.

SARAH

Sarah was very alone at first in Glenamona. But then the magic of the place began to seduce her and her apathy lifted. It was certainly very different from what she had been used to. Sarah was an only child and, although her parents were far from well off, she had always had plenty of space – her own bedroom, and her own clothes and things. In London, when she worked for the Voyles, she had also had her own room and since all of her meals had been provided she had been free to do what she wanted with her wages. And then, of course, she had been spoilt by her time in Clapham.

In Glenamona, Sarah had no space and no money. Nothing belonged to her; everything was shared. At first she didn't like this; in particular the way in which Joe's sisters rifled through her stuff and felt they could wear her clothes without asking, dip their fingers into her precious face cream and dress her baby up in whatever they wanted her to wear. Sarah, Beatrice, Aoife, Mary and Bríd all had to cram into one tiny bedroom. To Sarah this seemed absolutely ridiculous. There was Joe with a room all to himself, while they were stuffed on top of each other. But Margaret was adamant – Sarah and Joe had to be 'properly' married in a Catholic church before she'd allow them to share a bed. It was crazy, but nobody challenged her authority.

There were just four rooms in the house, all of them tiny. Two bedrooms upstairs – one for the boys, and one for the girls

– and another bedroom downstairs which was Margaret's, and then the kitchen where everything else happened. There was no bathroom, and the family took it in turns to have baths in an old tin tub in front of the fire, with water which had been heated in big pots on the range. In the summer, if it was warm enough, they'd go down to the stream and bathe. The toilet was outside in a shed, it never occurred to the Kellys that it might be easier to move it inside.

As for domestic appliances – well, there were none. Sarah's mother had been a victim of post-war consumerism and had badgered her husband into spending most of his hard-earned cash on new and exciting appliances – an electric vacuum cleaner, electric cooker, electric kettle and, best of all, a twin tub. None of these things had been heard of in Glenamona, and everything was done the hard way. Sarah never forgot the hard labour involved in washing Beatrice's nappies: boiling pot after pot of water; scrubbing until her knuckles went red; then hanging them over the range to steam dry.

The only concession to the twentieth century in Glenamona was electricity; there wasn't even any running water in the house. The family used to get their water from the well by the brook at the edge of the yard. No one seemed to mind the chore, even in bad weather, because the water was beautiful. Sarah had never tasted water which was so sweet and so pure before. It was certainly worth the effort.

After a while, Sarah got used to her new life in Ireland. She began to feel as though she actually belonged somewhere. Gradually, she stopped minding when the girls took her clothes because they would give her something of theirs instead. Slowly she came out of her shell. In fact, sometimes she used to have fun with them when they brushed their hair at night, and talked about their fellas. Bríd continued to speak little, but her attitude had softened towards Sarah, and sometimes she would even ask her about England and what her life had been like there.

Sarah still often thought about her mother and father, usually at night, when everyone was asleep. Listening to the comforting rhythms of her sisters-in-laws' steady breathing, her own insides would run cold as she realized that she had grown up in a house with no mother love. The relationship which Margaret had with her daughters was so very different from Sarah's own experience. They were close, living in each other's pockets, and giving out and speaking their thoughts and emotions as if it was a right, like breathing the fresh air around them. She vowed that she and Beatrice would be like this one day.

The house at Glenamona was small and dark, but it ceased to be depressing. What it lacked inside was made up for by what was outside. Sometimes Sarah would stand in the yard at the front of the house and feel she was standing on the pin-head of a protected circle. Behind the house lay a field, and then the bog. In front of her was an orchard full of apple trees; their rosy scent filling her nostrils. In the distance you could see a new spruce forest which circled the land. They were in an enclave, removed from the outside world. It was somewhere you could stay hidden for ever. Maybe here, she thought, she could lick her wounds and forget about Anthony. Maybe here, she could devote herself to her child, be able to appreciate Joe, and be a good wife.

EITHNE

Lisa lights up. My mother says nothing. In fact she goes and gets an ancient ashtray.

'Cheers.' Lisa tips her ash.

She is still wearing her padded jacket, and is sitting slouched on my parents' sofa. She looks like a blonde giantess. I nurse my mug of tea. We are both cold. I had forgotten how the wind cuts you on Sliabh na Caillaigh. My mother stokes the fire.

'I can't believe you went up there today,' she says. 'It's gone so cold.'

An icy wind whistles around the house, backing her up. The light is failing. I begin to wish I had not come home.

'Where's Daddy?' I ask.

'On his way.'

She always says that. Sometimes he would appear, sometimes not. No one speaks. We can hear the trees beating the back windows, too close to the house. Daddy had chosen a bad site – boggy and damp in the winter, too dark in the summer.

'So where are you from, Lisa?' asks Mammy.

'Golders Green, in London.'

'I know it,' she says. 'I used to live in London. Quite nearby, in Hampstead.'

'It's lovely round there. There's a great swimming pool in Swiss Cottage.'

'Do you swim much?'

162

'Every day. I'm training to be a lifeguard.'

'Really?' Mammy is looking puzzled. 'So how do you know Eithne?'

There is a pause. Lisa looks stumped; she glances over at me.

'Lisa's at art college. They sent her on a study trip to Ireland, and she was placed in the print studio,' I say quickly. 'We just hit it off.'

'You must be very busy, Lisa,' says Mammy, 'studying full-time, and then doing your lifeguard thing.'

'Yeah,' Lisa says looking uncomfortable.

It is hardly surprising that Mammy is curious. Lisa is not like any of my other friends. For a start she's only a kid. I had been finding her hard to take. She's loud, talks too much and has bad manners. We have absolutely no mutual interests. Even her taste in music is completely different. I have almost decided that I won't tell Mammy who she is; that I'll tell her all about it when I find Beatrice. But after Lisa slipped on Witch's Hill, I feel differently about her. It's all an act. She appears brash, tactless, insensitive, but she does have feelings, she is vulnerable. And I can identify with that. I am beginning to feel protective towards her. It is a strange emotion; the only other person who has ever made me feel like this is Daddy.

'I hope you're hungry,' Mammy says, getting up and leaving the room. Lisa puts out her cigarette. She takes her coat off, and drops it beside her on the sofa.

'Did you grow up here?' she asks.

'More or less. We lived with my Granny till I was about four. When she died, Daddy built this house.'

'Is that Beatrice?' she asks.

A photograph hangs above the fireplace. It is my sister, in Majorca, just a few months before she disappeared. She looks stunning. Tanned, and with cascades of auburn hair. She smiles at us.

'She's beautiful,' Lisa, uncharacteristically whispers.

That holiday in Majorca was our downfall. If only she hadn't gone missing over there, the Gardaí would have taken her disappearance here more seriously. Not that they did not investigate it. But you could tell they thought she had run away, because of Majorca. People went missing every day.

And now this . . . Lisa sitting opposite me in our house. The Gardaí had been right, and my instincts had been wrong. I had thought she was dead. Lisa was a beacon, my angel of hope.

'I don't look like her, do I?' she asks me.

'No, not a bit,' I say.

'No wonder you thought I was lying,' she says.

'I would never have believed you unless I had seen it in black and white. I really thought my sister was dead.'

Lisa gets up, and stands in front of the fireplace. Hands on hips; head on one side. She stares at the picture. Then she traces Beatrice's smiling face with her finger. Imagine seeing your mother for the first time.

I hear the back door open, a gust of freezing wind blasts through the house. Daddy. He comes in.

'Eithne. Hello, darling,' he says.

He has been drinking.

'Hi, Daddy.' I get up and hug him. He stinks of cigarettes, although he doesn't smoke.

'Is Leo not with you?'

'No, he couldn't make it. I'm just down for a couple of days. This is a friend of mine, Lisa.'

'Hi, how are you?' she says staring up at him.

'Is that an English accent?' Daddy asks.

'Yeah.'

'So where are you from? Don't tell me . . . let me guess now
. . . North London would it be?'

'That's brilliant,' says Lisa, impressed. 'Howd'ya know?'

'Oh, I spent years in that part of England. I worked on the
building sites, see. Best part of ten year I was there. It certainly
never got this cold in London,' he says, stamping his feet.

'Would you have a jar, girls?' Daddy asks as he goes over to
the drinks press.

'What's a jar?' asks Lisa.

'It's a drink,' I say. 'Alcoholic.'

'No, thanks, I don't drink whiskey that much.'

'Eithne?'

'No, Daddy, I won't. Why don't you wait till after dinner?'

He pretends not to hear me and pours himself a drink.

Mammy comes back into the room. She barely acknowledges
Daddy. It is incredible how two people can live in such a small
space and so separately. It is painful to watch.

'Dinner,' she announces, and whips round out of the room.

We eat. Floury spuds, boiled, with the skins curling off them,
turnip, which has been boiled into oblivion and a pile of greasy,
nearly burnt, sausages. Mammy never took to cooking. Daddy
gets stuck in, I focus on the potatoes, I can see Lisa playing with
her food out of the corner of my eye.

'Do you not like sausages, Lisa?' asks Mammy.

'It's just they're very fattening, Mrs Kelly,' she says. 'I have
to watch my weight.'

Mammy stares at her, and then looks over at me. She can't
work out what this girl is doing here.

We eat in silence. I have always hated meal times at home.
My rash is burning through my top, and I can't stop rubbing it.
At least it's distracting me from possibly the most bizarre dinner
of my life. There sit my parents chomping away in front of their

granddaughter. Yet they don't know it. How am I going to tell them? Or should I at all? My head is pounding, and my stomach is heaving – it's hard to get the food down.

The phone rings.

'Will you get that, Eithne?'

I go out into the hall. It's Leo. He's furious.

'What the fuck are you doing, Eithne? You told me you were going to think about it.'

'Leo, I'm stressed out as it is . . . I don't need this.'

'You should have stayed here. Then we could have talked about it, worked something out.'

'What was there to talk about? It's my family business and I have to sort it out, Leo, not you, but me, on my own.'

There is a pause.

'I'm your husband, I *am* your family.' He is calmer now, no longer shouting. 'I want to help you.'

'I know, I'm sorry, but what can you do? Lisa is my niece . . . I checked all the papers again this morning. She really is Beatrice's daughter. All of a sudden my sister is no longer dead. Imagine how that feels?' He says nothing, and I continue, 'It's like one minute I'm happy, and the next I am so angry I could explode. I'm hot and throbbing all over, and then I feel as though ice has been trickled down my back. How could she do it, Leo? How could she leave me and never come back?'

'She must have had good reasons,' he says.

'But what? What could be so big that it stops you from contacting your family ever again? I just can't imagine what that could be.'

'Eithne,' he pleads, 'come home and talk this over with me. I don't like that girl, Lisa, I still don't trust her.'

'Will you bloody wake up?' I hiss. 'I don't care if you like her or not. She's my niece. For fuck's sake, why can't you support me, rather than do my head in?'

'You're losing it, Eithne,' Leo says, he is angry again, and his voice is tight and bitter.

'Well, if you can't understand what I have to do, that I have to introduce Lisa to her grandparents, then I don't see much hope for our marriage—'

'Don't do that,' he says quickly, ignoring my comment about our marriage. 'For God's sake, Eithne, don't tell your parents. Come back home tomorrow, please.'

'I can't deal with this,' I say wearily. 'It's hard enough without you trying to sabotage me. Go back to your precious commission — just leave me alone.'

And I put down the phone.

It rings again. I stand in the hall trembling, but I don't pick it up. Why is he doing this to me? It stops then rings again. I am shivering. An image of the sacred heart glares down at me from the wall. I hate tacky religious iconography, but suddenly this picture holds new significance. The heart is an entity in its own right, pulsing with blood, encircled with thorns, with pain, but it keeps on beating, it does not give in. I put my hand on my chest and breathe deeply. My sacred heart.

Later, I take Lisa to the pub. It is a relief to get out of the house, away from my mother's beady eyes. Daddy has gone down to the village pub, so I drive into Kells. I take Lisa to the trendiest place I can find. A jukebox blares out in a corner, but the pub is deserted. We sit up at the bar.

'Eithne Kelly!' says a voice.

Coming up from the cellar with a crate of Finches orange is Deirdre Maloney, Beatrice's old pal.

'Deirdre!' I say. 'Jesus, long time no see!'

'Well, I haven't seen you in ages,' she says, wiping her hands with a dishcloth. 'Last thing I heard you were getting married and up in Dublin. Are you settled there now, will you ever come back?'

'Oh, I don't know, Deirdre.'

'Well, do you have any kiddies yet?'

'No, not yet.'

'I've two myself now,' she says proudly. 'Darren, he's six, and Sinead, she's three. Darren's a little devil so he is. Sinead's great – a daddy's girl though, that's for sure. Maybe you'll come back when you have kids. A lot of folk do.'

'Maybe . . .'

'So what'll I get you girls?' she asks.

'This is Lisa, a friend.'

'Nice to meet you. So?'

'We'll have two pints of Guinness, please, Deirdre.'

She puts the pints on, and then comes back to the bar. Her voice drops an octave, and she is whispering although there is no one else in the pub.

'So,' she asks, 'did you ever find out what happened to Beatrice?'

'No – ' my throat tightens – 'no more clues.'

She turns to Lisa.

'Did she tell you about that?' she asks her. 'About her sister disappearing like that, all those years ago?'

Lisa nods.

'Awful tragic! Your poor mother – we were all upset – I was in bits. We'd just been on holiday together, and she was my best friend. Do you remember when she went missing that time in Majorca?'

'Yes, of course,' I say sparsely. I just want her to shut up.

'I was so mad with her . . .' says Deirdre, 'and then I found the sketchbook, do you remember, Eithne? You found the pearls, didn't you?'

She turns to Lisa, who is mesmerized.

'I was walking the dog about ten days after Beatrice disappeared, and I always go down by Lough Bane, because my parents' house is right on the lake. This day, I was right on the other side of the lake, on the opposite shore to the one we swim from, right by the woods. Well, I was walking along and I saw something red, at the water's edge, it was a miracle that it hadn't been swept away.'

Deirdre spoke with the ease of someone who has told the same story many times.

'I pulled it out, and my heart froze, it did. Because I recognized it immediately. Beatrice had brought it with her on holiday. It was her little red sketchbook. Well, I was terrified. I called the dog and ran back to the road. All of a sudden those woods seemed very dark, very evil. I was scared someone might have been hiding in them, watching me pick up the book.'

'What happened to it?' asks Lisa.

'I took it straight to the Gardaí,' says Deirdre, finishing off the pints and placing them down in front of us.

'It was no good to them anyway – they got no prints.'

FOUR: THE SKETCHBOOK

SARAH

In the end she had to wear Margaret's old wedding dress. It was too long for her, and too tight across the bust. Looking in the collection of hand mirrors which the three girls, Aoife, Bríd and Mary, held up, Sarah averted her gaze. She looked awful.

Not that Joe seemed to notice; he kept complimenting her. His flattery got more flamboyant as the day wore on: she looked pretty as a picture, she looked like a princess, she was his beautiful bride, stunning in virginal white. She shouldn't even have been wearing white.

It was the longest day of her life. The preparation, peppered with drinks; the wedding in the church and the exchanging of vows, that was the quickest bit. Then came the reception, which went on hour after hour: the meal, the band, the disco, the sandwiches, the residential bar. They had a room booked in the hotel, but Joe wouldn't let go of her all day. It was as if he was worried she might run away. Maybe he could read her thoughts.

Her stomach churned, she wasn't only sick with nerves, she really felt like vomiting. Every fibre within her body told her she was doing the wrong thing, but she was powerless to stop the Kellys and their tide of relatives and friends. It seemed as though the whole town was there but no one was on her side. She kept wishing a miracle would happen. In the church, she prayed for Anthony to suddenly appear, resplendent, demanding her return. But nothing happened.

Sitting in the hotel bar, dizzy from everything she had drunk, she looked around. Everyone was singing, swaying to and fro. She could go now, just run. What was stopping her? But then she looked over at Margaret, fiercely nursing Beatrice. When she and Joe had registered Beatrice's birth, Joe had made sure he was put on her birth certificate as Beatrice's father. Margaret would never give the child up and Sarah couldn't even consider going on her own.

It was daybreak before Joe took her up to their bedroom. She was exhausted, but there was no chance of sleep. For the past six weeks they had been sleeping in separate bedrooms; the only time they had been together was once under the aspen trees. He didn't even give her a chance to take off the dress.

'Mind,' she said, 'your mother's dress . . .'

But the skirt was pushed up around her head, and he was inside her before she could say another thing. She tried to join in, but she was hampered by the dress, and by the time she pulled it off her face, Joe had finished. He crashed out on the bed then, his pants around his ankles, snoring loudly. Now she couldn't sleep. She lay down in her dress and squeezed her eyes tight shut. She went through the whole day again, but turned it into a fantasy: Anthony and Sarah were walking out of an English country church, arm in arm, sprayed by confetti, and she was looking beautiful in a dress which fitted perfectly, and was ivory, not white.

After they were married in the church, Joe started planning for their new house. He kept on about it; his father had left him a small site, and now he wanted to get down to working out what the house was going to look like – how many bedrooms should they have, would they build one or two storeys? Sarah tried to be interested, but in her heart she could not find it in her to care. Her family had never owned their own house; it was an issue that was never a priority. She found the Kellys' interest in ownership quite alien. She knew the reason for it went centuries back: all the Kellys' ancestors had been evicted by their English landlords during the time of the famine. It was a very sore point. But still she found it hard to join in their obsession with land. Conversation around the dinner table constantly went back to what was happening with sites and land and property, and that field and this field – who had sold what and to whom and for how much. Besides which, everything in her life seemed so surreal she was afraid to see it transformed into bricks and mortar, and actually made permanent.

As winter progressed and made the landscape even bleaker, it became increasingly hard for Joe to find a permanent job. He was able to get bits and pieces of casual labouring but none of it was well paid. Eventually he decided to go back to London to work on the building sites.

'It'll only be for a few months,' he told Sarah. 'I'll not find work with such good money here. I can save up fast in London and then we can build our house.'

'Can't I come with you?' said Sarah.

'No. Sure, we'd spend everything just on living in London. You're better off here; it's the best place for Beatrice, and besides I need you to look after Mammy.'

'Don't leave me,' she pleaded.

'Sarah, you know I don't want to go, but we have to make these sacrifices so that we can build the house.'

'I don't care about the house.'

Her eyes beseeched him, but he looked straight through her.

'Don't be stupid, where would we raise our children?'

Joe left after Christmas. What was meant to be a few months

turned into six, then one year, then two, until the next five years had flown by. He visited, but never for too long, and so Sarah stayed waiting. He was always saving for the new house, yet whenever he was home he never had money to spare.

Meanwhile, not one foundation stone was laid of Joe's dream house. The truth was, that although he professed to love Glenamona, he could not bear to be there for long. He missed London and needed to be anonymous. At home, his mother's love swamped him, and although it was a tight-knit community, with good people around them, he never felt comfortable. Not after what had happened when he was at school. It took only twenty-four hours in Glenamona before he became restless and agitated. In London, he felt freer.

So why didn't Joe move back to London permanently and take Sarah and Beatrice with him? Because he was afraid. He believed that if Sarah went back to England, she would never stay with him. He was sure of that. Those people she had worked for would get their hands on her. Ever since his father died, Joe had been desperate to have his own family and now he had it, he was never letting go. Back in London, Sarah would have options, in Glenamona she had none. She was not a prisoner, but where could she go? She never talked about her family, and she never seemed to miss them.

For the best part of nine years Sarah continued to live with Margaret who, like most Irish mammies, doted on her sons, yet was sharp enough with the girls. But she was a decent woman, and although she never let Sarah forget that she was an outsider, at the same time it was against her nature not to draw her into the family circle.

As for the three sisters, Aoife married her childhood sweetheart Dermod on a wild, wet day the April after Sarah's own marriage. By October her first child was born, but no one was counting, not a mention of it. Sarah drew comfort from the baby's birth; at least she was not the only sinner in the flock, and now she could help Aoife and give her advice. How strange, she thought, that she, simple Sarah, should be the expert on babies. Sarah called on Aoife many times in the first year of baby Grace's life. She was able to give Aoife all Beatrice's baby clothes. It thrilled her to be consulted and admired. She and Aoife became quite close. But then things began to chill between them, just after Aoife became pregnant again. She kept hinting how great it would be if she and Sarah had their second babies at the same time. Surely it was time Sarah had another one? Beatrice was growing fast, and soon the gap between siblings would be too big. Sarah was horrified – the last thing she wanted was another child. She backed off, and started to visit Aoife less frequently.

Not long after Aoife had got married, Mary, the second sister, went to Dublin to work as a nurse. For someone involved in the caring profession, Sarah found her extremely cold. Mary kept her distance from Sarah. Whenever she was in her company the Englishwoman felt nervous; it was as though she *knew*.

So it happened that Bríd and Sarah were the only two remaining in the house with Margaret. Bríd's opinion of Sarah grew as she saw the other woman throwing herself into her daily chores. Sarah had always been a hard worker, but the unrelieved boredom of Glenamona made her embrace any distraction.

Bríd was a good teacher. Soon Sarah had mastered the mechanics of the family tractor and how to manoeuvre it over the bumpy land. As winter progressed, Bríd and Sarah would head down to the bog, the two of them crushed in the cab of the tractor with Molly, the family dog. They'd work non-stop for several hours, loading the trailer with peat. This was a different bog from the place Joe had taken her the first time they made love. That had been a place of colour and beauty. This land was dark and deadly. No birds sang, and the air was heavy with the odour of a nearby copse of spruce. It was from this place that they took their peat; never from Glenamona, never the home bog.

Sometimes Sarah and Bríd would see groups of men in the woods by the bog. They had shotguns and wore hunting caps.

'Shooting foxes,' Bríd told her.

It was a sinister place and Sarah did not care for it.

Bríd hardly spoke, but on the way back to the house she would sometimes take a small jar out of her jacket pocket, unscrew the lid and dip her finger in it.

'Want some?' she asked Sarah the first time she produced the jar.

'What is it?' asked Sarah.

'Primrose honey. I made it.'

Sarah dipped her finger in the jar then licked it. She could smell its sweet aroma before she registered its taste, then the delicacy of its flavour was incredibly powerful. She licked her finger again.

'Nice, uh?' laughed Bríd as she started up the tractor.

Most evenings the women sat in the kitchen by the range. Margaret knitting (usually for Beatrice), Sarah with the child on her lap and Bríd reading the paper. The ritual was always the same. Sometimes Margaret would turn on the radio, and they'd listen to music in silence. There was no television or record player.

On rare occasions, once Beatrice was asleep upstairs, Margaret would get out the best glasses and a dusty brandy bottle kept in a back cupboard. Giving each glass a wipe she would fill them with a good measure of brandy. At the same time she would fill a small jug with water and place it on the table. The three women would sit around the range sipping their brandy and water. Sometimes Margaret would tell stories about her childhood. Sarah enjoyed these. It seemed such a dramatic world, straight out of a film. When Margaret was a young girl there had been a war of independence in Ireland, followed by a civil war. The countryside had been streaked with violence. Many good men were lost, many heroes made. Margaret's own father had been killed fighting when she was only eight. It was a fact she constantly referred to. She had adored her father.

Then she would move on and talk about her husband, Padraig. They had lived just one field away from each other all their lives. He had been fifteen years her senior, but this had not daunted young Margaret in the least. At last she had found a man fit to replace the icon she had made of her father. Margaret worshipped Padraig. He had been her be all and end all. Sometimes, if she had too much brandy she would talk of the night Padraig died. At this point Bríd always left the room.

'I woke in the night and I heard him say, "Oh my God," and I thought he was just saying it in his sleep. But when I woke in the morning he would not move. Dead. Me darlin' Paddy had died right next to me in the bed and I did nothing. Just went back to sleep. Thirty years married and I still didn't know when he was lying stricken next to me.'

'There was nothing you could have done,' Sarah always said, but it fell on deaf ears.

'I'll never forgive myself,' Margaret lamented. 'When he needed me the most I let him down. Here I am now, all alone. My sons are both in England. Our family in bits.'

Inevitably she would turn her attention to Joe. 'Can you not get Joseph to come home?' she would plead.

'He wants to save for the house,' Sarah always said lamely. 'He'll be back soon.'

And he did visit frequently at first, but never staying too

long. Sarah could not say that she minded. His visits were an awful strain. Each time she saw him, he was less attractive to her. He was putting on weight and the heavy drinking had affected his general appearance. Even his eyes began to lose their intensity. Besides, she dreaded getting pregnant again. Usually she would pretend to have her period when he came home, but if he stayed longer than a week she had to concede. Joe would make love to her with the desperation of a man who knew he could never win. Each time Sarah lay down for him he could see an even greater distance in her eyes. A chill existed between them. Joe blamed himself. He promised Sarah that he would be back soon. The house would be built. They would make a family. Sarah hoped not. She liked it when it was just herself, Margaret and Bríd. For the first time in her life she enjoyed the company of women and being treated as an equal. Beatrice was growing into a lively little girl with soft auburn hair and a cheeky smile. She did not look like Sarah, nor did she look like Joe, of course. She had Voyle eyes.

This was something which confused Margaret, who constantly questioned Beatrice's looks. What colour eyes had Sarah's parents?

As Beatrice grew older Sarah gained a little more independence. Every Friday she cycled into town and visited the market. She always purchased some fish for dinner and afterwards she browsed in the shops. Sometimes she bought new wool to make a jersey for Beatrice, or ribbons for her hair. Every week Sarah went to a small cafe at the corner of the main crossroads in town. She would have a pot of tea and a scone with jam. She always brought a book with her, and for a full hour she savoured her solitude.

There were other folk in the cafe and sometimes a smartly dressed man arrived while she was there. He always sat at the table next to hers and ordered a pot of tea. Then he would take out that day's paper and hide behind it. When he was there Sarah smelt sandalwood. She found it a most delicious odour. And even though the man was not particularly handsome, Sarah found herself daydreaming about him.

About five years after Sarah came to live in Glenamona she set off as usual on her Friday trip to town. She was feeling low because Joe was due home the following evening. Margaret was in a flurry of excitement as she always was the day before Joe came, but Sarah dreaded seeing him. His last visit had been a disaster. As usual Sarah had pretended to have her period, but this time Joe had found out.

'You're unnatural,' he had spat at her. 'Don't you want to have a baby with me? Am I not good enough for you? Don't forget it's me who saved you and made you respectable.'

And then he had slammed out of the house and got slaughtered in the pub. That night he had slept on the sofa and had left early the next day. Sarah had not spoken to him since.

The weather matched her mood. It was wet and windy, and it was hard work cycling into town. She had a huge shopping list from Margaret:

> A couple of good chops for Joe
> Several bottles of stout for Joe
> The tobacco Joe likes
> A tin of the barley sugar sweets Joe likes
> A jar of Joe's favourite coffee
> A big sack of spuds

She would not have time for her tea and scone, and not a penny left to buy something for Beatrice. She ploughed on, soaked through, and completed all her chores in town. It was becoming quite stormy and Sarah decided to head for home before it turned really bad.

She faced head on into the gale, and spun down the hill. The wind knocked her breath, like someone was hitting her in the chest, and her headscarf was stuck to her scalp. Suddenly her bicycle jerked to one side. She stopped pedalling.

'Damn!'

She had a puncture, of all the bad luck. She began wheeling the bike along in the heavy rain; it would be hours before she got home. By then she would be exhausted and freezing.

A car passed. It pulled in.

The door opened . . . It was sandalwood man.

'Do you need some help?' he called over to her.

'Oh yes, thank you so much.' She approached his shiny green car. 'I've a puncture,' she shouted back against the wind.

'Oh dear,' he said, getting out of the car. He peered gingerly at the damaged wheel. 'I'm afraid I'm no good at that sort of thing, but perhaps I might be able to give you a lift home?'

'That would be wonderful, thank you.'

'Here, let me help you.'

He took the bike and jammed it into the boot of the car, using string to secure the open trunk. He opened the door for her and Sarah got in. By now they were both soaked, rain streamed down their faces. She took off her headscarf, which looked like a wet rag, and shook out her hair. It fell about her face in damp curls. The car began to steam up.

'Please, take this.' He handed her a handkerchief. It smelt of sandalwood. 'Where can I take you?' he asked.

'You're very kind. Glenamona. Thank you,' she replied, as she gently dabbed her face with his hankerchief.

'Right. You've plenty of shopping there,' he said, gesturing to her packages.

'Yes, my husband is due home from England tomorrow.'

She bit her tongue, she should never have said that. She was in a car, on her own with sandalwood man, now she had ruined it.

'Right,' he said again. 'Joe Kelly, would that be? My father knew his father well. Padraig Kelly used to work for us.'

'I always thought he had his own farm.'

'This was years ago, before he set up his own place. My father always had a lot of time for Padraig. Excuse me,' he said turning his head towards her, 'I haven't introduced myself properly – Noel Chaney.'

This was Mr Chaney, then. She had heard of him and his spectacular Georgian house. Noel Chaney came from old land-owning stock. They sat in silence for a while. Then he said, 'And where are you from, Mrs Kelly?'

'England. Southampton. I lived in London for a while.'

'London, such a wonderful city!' he said enthusiastically.

'A world away from here,' sighed Sarah.

They looked out into the beating rain.

'Yes, the weather can get you down, and the lack of culture, of course. But I find living here keens my senses. I do things I wouldn't do in town, like hunting and fishing, and I have time to contemplate. In London everything happens so fast you've no time to pause,' he said.

'I think I've done enough contemplating to last a lifetime,' said Sarah.

'Is that so? And what do you think about, Mrs Kelly?'

He glanced at her, and there was a twinkle in his eye. Was he flirting with her? She smiled at him.

'Nothing much.'

She gave him a sideways glance and he smiled at her. She noticed that his hands were smooth and golden with perfectly manicured nails; quite, quite different from Joe's rough claws.

They had turned down the lane. Noel Chaney drove her up to the house.

'Thank you,' she said. Neither of them moved.

'Any time,' he said. He suddenly leant across her, and opened her door from the inside.

'Your handkerchief,' she said, hardly able to speak.

'Keep it. I've plenty more,' he said.

He got out of the car, and took her bike out of the boot. The wind had abated slightly, and although the rain still fell hard and fast, it was easier to see his face. It shocked her, because he looked extremely handsome now she was able to look straight at him. They were standing very close to each other; he passed her the bike. They exchanged a glance just for a second, but it was enough for her to know that he liked what he saw too. Not saying another word he got back into the car. She could feel him watching her as she wheeled the bicycle round the side of the house. Then he turned the car and was gone.

Preoccupied with this tiny drama in her uneventful daily round, Sarah had not noticed Tommy O'Reilly's dirty old Ford Escort parked outside the cottage. When she walked in through the back door, she jumped, guiltily, she had not expected to see Tommy and Joe sitting at the kitchen table. The two men had just opened a bottle of whiskey.

Joe was facing the kitchen window. His expression was murderous.

'Who was that?' he snapped.

'Goodness, what a surprise,' said Sarah, ignoring his question. 'I wasn't expecting you till tomorrow.'

'Obviously,' muttered Joe.

'He thought he'd surprise you all,' said Tommy nervously.

'Where's Margaret and Beatrice?' asked Sarah, putting her purchases away.

'They went round to see my mother. She's dying to see the little girl,' said Tommy.

'Bríd?'

'She's not back. I haven't seen her yet,' said Joe. 'Who was that?' he repeated.

'Just a lift. A man called Noel Chaney. You see, I got a puncture—'

Joe got up from the table swiftly and gave her a smart slap across the face. Sarah staggered, shocked. He must have been drinking all day.

'Steady on,' said Tommy.

Joe ignored him.

'So that's what's been going on while I've been breaking my back for you, slaving on site after site in England. I should have known. Once a tart, always a tart.'

'Joe, it was raining, I had a puncture, the man gave me a lift—'

He shoved her.

'That's why you've gone off me. You've been having it away with that toffee-nosed bastard!'

'Joe! Come on now. Calm down,' Tommy said.

Sarah was scared. She ran out of the kitchen, out of the back door and into the lashing rain, across the muddy yard and down Bog Lane. She ran and ran until she came to the woods. Then she stopped under the shelter of the trees. The rain pattered above her, everything was slashed with grey. She took breath for a second. Then she heard a footfall behind her, but before she could turn she was pushed in the back. She fell onto the forest floor, a sharp stick stuck into her chin. She tried to scream but her mouth was muzzled by the earth. Joe was on top of her.

'Don't forget you're my wife,' he ranted. 'I've been faithful to you for five long years but all you do is reject me. I could have been having it away in London, but I never did, not once. Out of respect, see. And then you do this to me. Do you think I'm a fool? I know you've a soft spot for the gentlemen.'

He had her skirt up and was pulling her pants down.

'Don't think I don't know you've been with Noel Chaney all afternoon. I can smell him on you. Well, if you're going to behave like a whore, I'm going to treat you like one.'

He pushed inside her, she felt as though she was splitting apart. He cursed her and berated her, accusing her of all manner of things with Noel Chaney. It seemed to go on for ever. Eventually he came and lay quite still on top of her, silent, as heavy as a rock. She could not move.

'Sarah,' he whispered hoarsely. 'Sarah. Oh God, forgive me.'

He got off her. She pushed herself up off her knees, and pulled her pants up. He sat on the ground, his trousers around his ankles. He was sobbing. He could not look at her.

'Why can't you love me?' he wailed.

Her heart turned to stone.

'Don't you ever, ever touch me again,' she said. 'I'll take a pitchfork, and I'll shove it straight through your filthy heart while you're in one of your drunken stupors. I'll do it, Joe. Don't ever come near me again.'

She walked through the wood, and out onto the bog. It had stopped raining and the sun set weakly in front of her. Sarah held herself and wept. Then she took out Noel Chaney's handkerchief and dried her eyes.

That was the day her second child was conceived.

BEATRICE

Loughcrew. Her scarf flaps across her face and presses against her mouth. She sucks it in and blows it out. They climb the hill, pick their way up the uneven, mud-frosted path. They're wasting time, precious minutes, but she says they have to come here. The mist weaves around their ankles, rising off the field. Surely they are entering another world? The land is cowering from the winter, and gives off a pungent odour of earth like a frightened animal before the kill.

They go up, around a grassy curve, and up the final incline. The hag's chair faces them. But she doesn't go towards it – too late for wishing now. Instead, she takes his hand, and drags him behind a stack of fallen stones. She hops down into a narrow burial chamber, and pulls him after her. They are sheltered here.

She starts to kiss him feverishly. He tries to stop her, but she won't. She cries out, 'I need you, I need you now.' He looks frightened. She is like a wild thing. She will surely fly off this mountain if he does not ground her.

He complies, and lies on top of her. She breathes more easily now, relieved. 'Please,' she whispers. 'Please . . .' she begs, crying. Eventually he pushes inside her, reluctant, sad for her sorrow. He is too gentle and she urges him on. He is taken away then, and now there is no stopping them. She closes her eyes, and pushes the back of her head against the ancient earth. Then she opens her eyes again and looks in wonder at his dark silhouette against the early morning sky, which is picture-perfect blue, with tiny racing clouds. Faster they scurry, the shadows running across them. She closes her eyes again. She feels like a tree has taken root inside her, it grows, like Jack's beanstalk, bigger and bigger, taking her over, until it is exploding with blooms.

Then they are shaking and shivering they are so cold.

'Quick,' he says taking her hand. They climb out of the chamber, and the wind beats against them. They look about. Lough Sheelin is spread before them, immense and serene, its surface twinkling beneath distant blue hills. The land about falls into hillocky drumlins, and you can imagine entire settlements lying under them.

A whole civilization sleeps beneath their feet. An odd little tree catches her eye, she points it out. It is knobbly and buckled by the wind, standing on its own small mound. How much more can it take? All the life is beaten out of it and it is misshapen, a freak. This is how he feels, but he says nothing. They walk down the hill, he will not run. At some point her scarf is carried away by the wind. She doesn't stop. Let them take it, then.

EITHNE

This is no ordinary sketchbook, and no ordinary present. The Artist had made it for Beatrice. He made the paper himself, collecting iris leaves from the bog, mixing them into a pulp and straining them.

The cover is red leather. It is soft and weathered and came from a shoemaker in Berlin, or so he said. Beatrice carried it with her everywhere, with a small bundle of pencils. Her passion was drawing from life – people and the little details of our humanity. She had a real skill for likenesses and many local faces graced the pages. She drew from life at least once every day.

The red leather sketchbook is small, it can fit into a jacket pocket, but it is striking. Its cover is deep magenta, it looks like blood. Beatrice adored her sketchbook, and would not share it with anyone.

JOSEPH

He decided to go the long way home. Tommy had told him that he had seen some of the wire down, and a few of his sheep had strayed onto the road. He had better sort it out before he got home. If only he had a son, someone who could work with him, then he wouldn't be so tired, so lonely. He had been hoping that Philip, Jack's son, would have worked with him this summer. But the boy was totally indifferent to the land or any form of labouring. Joe felt awkward next to him. He was well spoken and full of clever words and sayings and Joe felt he was laughing at him, somehow. He didn't really like him and thought him spoilt. He never said so to Jack. His brother worshipped his son. But just to look at what Philip wore, skipping around the fields all day with Beatrice and Eithne like a girl, made Joe feel sick. Maybe the boy was homosexual. God, he hoped not. He didn't want that for his brother.

The sun was setting and Joe breathed deeply. This really could be the most beautiful place in the world. The sky was seared with the fiery colours, the landscape hushed and peaceful. He loved the smell of the land at this time of year; rich and ripe. The summer never felt long enough, the winter always felt too long. Joe fixed the fence and made sure all the sheep were in. It was getting dark. He set off for home and tea. He hoped Sarah had left something for him to eat. It was unlikely, as herself and Eithne had gone to see Aoife for the evening. He decided to cut across a small area of boggy land to save time. In the second field he crossed he saw movement in the half light. At first he thought it was an animal but then he heard human sounds, a woman sighing. He had never heard a woman sigh like that, but he knew instinctively what it meant. He crept closer. Just a quick look. Two naked bodies lay on the grass. They gleamed against the darkening land. They lay side by side, holding hands. The man had his other hand between the woman's legs. She sighed.

Joe looked at her face. It was Beatrice.

He froze. What did they think they were doing on open land, in full view of anyone! They did not notice him. They appeared drunk, in fact. Their movements were slow and their eyes were half closed. It was disgusting, scandalous – they were family, or so everyone else thought. He should storm up to them right now and give them both a good hiding. But for some reason he could not move, he was mesmerized.

Joe watched, horrified, as Philip slid his penis inside Beatrice. That was all he did, nothing else. Hardly any movement at all. Then they fell asleep, him tucked inside her.

It was too much. Joe turned and marched out of the field. He was shaking. Enough was enough. That girl was bad blood, not his blood, anyway. She had to be taught a lesson, she could not carry on just as she wished any more. He headed into the centre of the village.

First he needed a drink.

EITHNE

I wake late. There's still frost — it's one of those glittering winter mornings. I look out of the window. Mist is curling around the base of Witch's Hill, slowly vaporizing into the cold air. Everything about winter is more intense here. The sky is pure innocent blue, the trees, bereft of leaves, reach up like blackened limbs, and the ground is still green, but an old shade, not spring new, the earth beneath pushed up to its outer layer. This morning the grass blades are magical, twinkling like crystallized twigs.

Lisa's bed is empty, the quilt rumpled up into a ball in the centre of the mattress.

I go downstairs, pulling a large sweater of Daddy's on over my pyjamas. Mammy and Lisa are in the kitchen; Daddy has already left for the day. As I enter the room, I get the feeling that they have been sitting in silence for some time. Lisa looks relieved as I come in. Mammy glances at the clock — it's eleven.

'You must have been tired,' she says.

'Yeah, I'm exhausted,' I say. 'I've been working very hard.'

'That'll be for your solo show?' she asks.

'I've so much to do.'

'I'll make sure Daddy comes this time,' Mammy says. 'It's very exciting,' she turns to Lisa, 'isn't it?'

Lisa looks confused.

'I haven't told you that I have my first solo exhibition in Dublin in a few months,' I tell Lisa quickly.

'That's great,' she replies, but without conviction.

Mammy narrows her eyes and stares at Lisa, and then says, 'Well, I'm off out, girls – see you later.'

'Thank God, she's gone,' says Lisa as soon as Mammy leaves the room. 'She kept asking me all these questions about art. I just wanted to tell her who I really am.'

'We will . . . later,' I say.

I am rifling in Mammy's sacred kitchen drawer where she keeps everything precious. My fingers pass over the pearls, the beret, the scarf and the sketchbook. I push my hands right to the back and pull out a small pink envelope. I remembered finding this when I was very little and, as I had hoped, it was still in the same place.

'What's that?' Lisa asks.

'It's Mammy's. I'll be back in a minute – help yourself to more coffee.'

I go out into the hall, and read the back of the envelope. An address is embossed on its surface – *A. Voyle Esq., Kidderpore Avenue, Hampstead, London NW.*

I pick up the phone and dial directory enquiries.

We dress up in big heavy jackets, scarves, hats and wellies. The dog comes with us.

'Where are we going?' asks Lisa.

'Glenamona,' I say, 'where my Granny lived. Where Beatrice lived until she was nine.'

I drive down the hill out of the village, the road twists and turns and we take a sharp left. Here, heavy chestnut trees and evergreens lean over the road creating a tunnel. I turn down Bog Road, and then into the top of Bog Lane, until we come to the drive. I stop the car and park.

Jack and Bríd only moved out five years ago. It got too hard to keep the place warm, so they built a smart new bungalow, a mile down the road. Daddy wouldn't let them sell the land, so the family still farms it. He keeps saying that he is going to do up the house and live in it again one day. But it looks wretched now.

We walk across the little bridge over the stream, which is all but dried up. The orchard at the front of the house is completely gone, and the land lies fallow. The house is dingy grey, several slates have slid off the roof, and the glass has fallen out of the tiny windows, so that they're boarded up. I push the front door open, and Lisa follows me in. A few bits of furniture litter the house: a paint-stained table in the front room, and a rickety old chair in the downstairs bedroom. There is a letter on the windowsill addressed to Mrs Padraig Kelly, and a dusty, battered copy of Patrick Kavanagh's poems. I pick that up and pocket it.

'Yuck,' says Lisa. 'It really stinks in here.'

I can see that at some stage someone has let cattle in, there's bits of hay everywhere and dried-up pats.

'Let's go to the bog,' I say.

We go round the back. Brambles have taken over so that we are forced to walk some way down Bog Lane. As soon as I can, I climb into the field.

'It's better this way,' I say. 'Not so mucky.'

'I'm glad I didn't wear my trainers,' says Lisa.

As we plunge through the wet grass, Lisa turns to me. 'Have you *any* idea who my father is?'

'Well . . . Beatrice had this friend, Jakob Rudin, but you don't look a bit like him, and anyway she wouldn't have run away if it was him. Then there's Phil . . . but they were cousins, I'm sure nothing actually happened.'

'It's just a big bloody wind up, isn't it?' She continues, 'I've been thinking – I'm going to go home tomorrow, this is all doing my head in.'

'Already?'

'When I was speaking to Steve yesterday he said I should come back. He said this was all pointless, you know?'

'But it's not, Lisa – we got to meet. You have me now.'

'It's not the same – I just wanted to know where I came from, so that I could tell my kids. I wanted all this shit sorted out in my life before I got married.'

'But nothing is that simple,' I say.

'I know that now, that's why I don't want to find her any more. Lots of people are adopted and never get to find their real parents, and they're fine. We're just stirring up shit.'

We have begun to walk through the spruce copse – it goes incredibly dark. Her eyes and teeth gleam in the half light, and her head has fallen forward slightly. She stops and lights a cigarette. I feel sorry for her. She doesn't seem so tall now.

'Hey,' I say. 'You can always come back when you're ready. I'm going to keep looking . . .'

'But what about your husband? Do you think it's a good idea? I mean I decided it wasn't fair on Steve. I have to think about my future with him, isn't it the same for you? Don't you want to have kids?'

'Not really,' I mumble.

'I can't wait to have my own family. We've even decided how many – two girls and two boys so it's all even.'

I laugh. 'You can't order them!'

We come out of the wood, and we're on the bog. It is severe here now. The sky has turned white, and the land is darker than mud. Lisa shivers.

'I don't like it here,' she says. 'It's horrible.'

'Don't you want to walk across the bog? It's my favourite place.'

She looks at me as if I am mad.

'No thanks, I'm freezing – let's go back.'

Mammy is home when we get in. I can smell baking in the kitchen – she is attempting bread. Lisa says she's tired and is going upstairs for a lie down. I go on into the kitchen. My mother stands with her back to me, stirring a big pot.

'What's that?' I ask.

'Irish stew,' she says. 'Something traditional for our English guest.'

I hang up the coats and dog's lead, and fill her bowl with water.

'Did you have a good walk?' she asks.

'Yeah, it's cold though.'

'I think it might snow,' she says. 'Look at the way the sky's gone.'

We stand side by side, looking out of the back window. It reminds me of the days when Beatrice was first gone, and how we memorized the landscape.

'Who's that girl?' Mammy asks all of a sudden.

'A friend . . . a student, I told you,' I say awkwardly.

'But she can't be an art student,' says Mammy. 'I mean, I don't know much myself but that girl is completely ignorant of the basics. I asked her did she prefer to use watercolours or oil or acrylic and she was completely stuck. She had no idea what any of them are. Art student, she is not. Maybe she's your friend, though she doesn't seem your type— Now, why would you lie to me, Eithne?'

I want to tell her . . . but I don't know how to begin.

'Mammy, let's sit by the fire.'

She sits down by the range, and I sit opposite her.

'Who is that girl?' she repeats, irritated. 'I don't like her, she's very rude.'

'Mammy, do you remember you always thought that Beatrice would come back?'

'Why are you talking about that now?' Her voice squeaks, and she looks frightened.

'I thought she was dead,' I say. 'I really did. But you always believed she was out there somewhere, didn't you?'

She cannot speak. Just nods her head. Her face has turned grey; she looks worn out, her eyes are large opals of sadness.

'I think you were right,' I say softly. 'I was wrong, and you were right.'

'But . . . why?' The words come strangled out of her. I pause, unsure of how to phrase the next sentence.

'Because of me,' says a voice from across the room. Lisa has come in behind us. She sits down on a stool by the kitchen table and lights a cigarette. Mammy looks from me to Lisa. She is shaking. I take her hand, but before I can speak, Lisa comes out with it.

'I'm adopted. A few months ago I had my eighteenth birthday. That meant I was old enough to get my birth certificate. I found out who my real mum is.'

Mammy looks at me. She still has not twigged.

'No, not me,' I say quietly.

'The adoption agency couldn't really tell me that much. My mother had left no forwarding address, and she hadn't contacted them since the day she signed me over. All I have is what's on the birth certificate.'

She takes the certificate out of her pocket and gives it to Mammy, who stares at it in disbelief.

'There it is.'

Mammy reads in slow motion.

'She named her after Granny,' I say. 'When Lisa was adopted they changed her name.'

Mammy grips the paper, staring at it, she is unable to look up.

'That's why she disappeared, Mammy,' I say. 'Beatrice was pregnant.'

Mammy gasps, she is beginning to hyperventilate.

'Are you okay, Mammy?' I take her hands. Gradually her breathing slows down. She looks up then, at me, and then stares at Lisa.

'I think Beatrice could be alive,' I whisper.

'Why?' she chokes. 'Why?'

Suddenly we became aware of the draught. Daddy is standing in the doorway. He is still in his boots. I don't know how long he has been standing there but he must have heard what Lisa said. His face is as red as Mammy's is white.

'Get out of my house!' he shouts, and lunges forward grabbing Lisa by the hair.

'Get out of my house!' he repeats. 'You're lying! You're evil!'

Lisa screams.

'Get the fuck off me!' She still has a cigarette in her hand and, as my father begins to drag her out of the room by her hair, as Mammy and I stand up, frozen by shock and fear, Lisa takes the cigarette and stabs my father's free hand. He yelps and lets go. There is sudden calm. Everyone stares at each other, unsure of what will happen next.

And then we see a surprisingly sorry look on Daddy's face. He looks at Mammy and then at me, and then he turns on his heel and walks out of the house, leaving the door swinging open.

BEATRICE

Innocence does not last for ever.

Everything was fine until they passed the Artist's house. By then the effects of their high had completely worn off. They felt sluggish, low and, worst of all, plain dull, and they had their first argument.

'Let's call into Jakob,' said Beatrice, taking Phil's hand and guiding him towards the house.

'No.' Phil pulled his hand away.

'Why not?'

'I just don't want to go in.'

'But why, Phil? You've never met him. He's totally cool. He's got some brandy, we could have a drink.'

'It's not that.'

'Well, what is it, then?'

'I just don't think it's right.'

'What do you mean?'

'He's old enough to be your father.'

'So? He's my friend, Phil. There's no age limit on friends. Why are you so uptight? Jesus, look at you.'

Beatrice started to laugh. A red rag to a bull.

'What's so funny?'

'You! Dressed like the essence of free love, and behaving like an uptight prig. What a contradiction!'

'I do have principles, Beatrice.'

'So do I.'

'I don't sleep around.'

Beatrice stopped laughing.

'Nor do I,' she hissed.

'Everybody knows, about you and the Artist. What you do is your business, but I don't want to meet him. I don't want to shake his hand.'

'Jakob is my friend. He teaches me about art. I've never slept with anyone. I told you that. How could you believe such utter crap.'

'Everybody says—'

'Everybody says, everybody says. Don't you know better than to listen to them? You think that you're so high and mighty. You're just an English twit.'

Before Phil had a chance to reply, Beatrice had turned on her heel and headed back the way they had come. Phil stood in the middle of the road, watching her, powerless as she disappeared, emphatically, into the night.

His head throbbed. He could not remember why they had argued, all he knew was that it was irredeemable. A light came on in the Artist's house. Phil thought about it. Then he thrust his hands into his pockets, and stomped up the hill home. He was empty, sad and very hungry.

SARAH

Sarah's second labour was worse than the first. What she remembered most about it was not so much the pain as the loneliness. At least when she had had Beatrice she had been in a busy London hospital with plenty of student midwives to hold her hand. Eithne was born in Cavan hospital where there was no pain relief and no comfort. Joe would have been there if he had been allowed. He even came back from England when she was due. But he was the last person Sarah wanted to see. So he spent the long labour in the pub with Tommy O'Reilly. Margaret was ill again, and the three sisters were busy looking after their mother. They were tough women — to them child-birth was no big deal, so Sarah suffered alone, mute with pain, angry at her grief.

Eithne's conception was something Sarah had wanted to forget. But as life took hold inside her she could not deny her own. Even so, her swollen belly was like a dagger hanging above Joe's head. He could not bear to see Sarah pregnant and so he spent nearly all of the next nine months working in London. Margaret could not understand this — especially as she was not in the best of health herself, and wanted her family round her. Mary came back from Dublin for good and got a nursing job in Navan hospital. Aoife was beside herself with excitement. At last her sister-in-law was catching up. She already had three, with another on the way. There was news of Jack, marital difficulties and a planned move home, but no word from Joe. When Margaret rang he was never in, when she wrote he never replied. She began to turn on her daughter-in-law.

'Why can't you go over to London and persuade him to come home? Doesn't he want to be here when the baby comes? Doesn't he realize his old mam doesn't have long to go?'

Sarah would admonish her, 'You mustn't talk like that. You've another grandchild on the way to spoil, don't you be saying rubbish like that. Besides, I can't go over to London. Joe is working hard and we'll have another mouth to feed soon.'

All lies. There had been no money from England for weeks, and Sarah was making ends meet doing a cleaning job. She told Margaret it was just for pocket money, but really it was keeping them going.

Sarah had only spoken to Joe once since the 'incident'.

He had rung his mother on her birthday, and before Sarah could get out of the room Margaret had pushed the telephone into her hand.

'Tell him,' she hissed.

By then Sarah was four months gone. The women had known for a while, but she had still not told Joe.

'Hello, Joe,' she said flatly.

'Sarah.' He was drunk.

'I'm pregnant,' she said quickly.

She could hear him knocking against the wall.

'What? But how? I mean when?'

'You know when.'

'Oh, Sarah . . . I – I can't stop thinking about that. If only . . . Will I come home?' he gushed.

'No. Please don't, not on my account anyway,' she said

coldly. She handed the telephone back to Margaret, who was staring at her strangely. Sarah went upstairs. Beatrice was painting. She was sitting at the landing window with her paints and paper spread out on the wide sill. She was making butterfly shapes. Sarah put her arms around her tiny daughter.

'What are you painting there?' she said huskily.

'Butterflies. Look.' The child splashed paint on to the paper, folded it in half and then opened it out again.

'That's brilliant,' said Sarah.

One of her mother's tears slid down the little girl's cheek.

'Mammy, why are you crying?'

'I'm not, love, I just have something in my eye.'

The next day Sarah started a new cleaning job. It was for Noel Chaney, of all people. His housekeeper had gone on holiday for two weeks, and Mr Chaney needed someone to do some light cleaning work every day. Sarah had seen the card in a shop window in town. Her heart had missed a beat when she read his name and number at the bottom. At first she thought she had better not ring, and then she said to herself, 'What's the harm? I can give him back his handkerchief.'

But deep down she knew something else was motivating her. When she phoned, Noel Chaney did indeed remember her. He was delighted that someone he knew, and therefore could trust, would be working for him.

Sarah arrived early that first morning, with the memory of her bitter announcement on the telephone still fresh. The house was everything she had expected it to be; not as opulent as the Voyles', but larger and older. Two hounds greeted her as she made her way to the back door. It swung open and Noel Chaney stood before her, smiling, with a cup of coffee in his hand.

'You're early,' he said.

He had grown a moustache since she had last seen him. He looked older, and he was fair, like Jonathan. She wondered where Jonathan was now. Did he remember her?

'Are you all right?' asked Noel Chaney.

Sarah had paled. She lost her balance and stumbled over the threshold. Noel Chaney caught her by the arm.

'I'm so sorry,' she said, mortified.

'Sit down, please. Would you like a cup of tea or coffee?'

She nodded.

'Which?'

'Oh, tea, please.'

He put the kettle on. The colour gradually came back to her cheeks. Her hair shone, and her skin glowed in the way it does when you are pregnant.

'You look very well. What I mean is, you don't look ill,' Noel Chaney said.

'Thank you,' said Sarah. 'You see, I'm expecting.'

It just slipped out. She felt so comfortable with Noel Chaney. He was like Anthony.

'Congratulations,' he said smiling.

After she had had her tea, Noel Chaney showed her what he wanted done in the house. Then he went into the library. She heard him rustling the paper, and smelt his pipe. The sandalwood odour was everywhere. She breathed in deeply.

Sarah started upstairs. She made his bed, and dusted his dressing table. There was really not that much to do, he was very tidy. There was a picture of a young woman on his locker. She was fair with blue eyes. Beside the photograph was a beautiful old hairbrush; it was old, the silver slightly tarnished, smooth with age and the bristles were so soft it was practically useless. She picked it up, and gently pulled it through her hair, looking in the mirror on the dressing table and wishing she was the girl in the picture. The clock on the landing struck ten. She jumped.

'Snap out of it,' she whispered to herself.

For the following hour she became a whirlwind of activity. She brushed the stairs, swept the hall and dusted the sitting room. By then it was time to prepare Noel Chaney's lunch. She got going in the kitchen. He had asked for shepherd's pie. She managed it fairly well, although she knew she wasn't the best of cooks. At least it was on time. Loading the food onto a large tray she took it into the dining room and laid it out on the table. Then she walked hesitantly towards the library. The house had been so completely silent, apart from the clock striking, that it was hard to imagine anyone else was there. She stood outside the library door nervously. She could hear a newspaper rustling, a short cough. She knocked.

'Come in.'

She went in. Noel Chaney looked up from his desk.

'Your lunch is ready. Would you like me to serve you?'

'No, that's fine, Sarah. Thank you, I'll help myself.'

Her hand on the door knob she paused.

'Is everything all right?' he asked.

She walked up to him, and took his handkerchief out of her pocket.

'I just wanted to give you this back,' she said.

'Oh, but you can keep it, Sarah.'

There was an awkward pause.

'Would you like to stay for lunch?' he asked.

'I can't . . .' She pushed the handkerchief into his hands.

'Sarah . . .' he began. Sandalwood pervaded her. Before she could stop herself, she leant forward and kissed him.

'I'm sorry,' she said, and made to leave.

He caught her arm, pulled her towards him and kissed her. Sarah took off her cardigan and her blouse. He unclipped her bra. Her breasts were heavy. He undid her skirt and put his hands around her thickening waist. She stood naked, a woman in early pregnancy craving love.

'You are absolutely beautiful,' he said. Then he kissed her again. He led her to the couch, where he undressed. Their naked bodies unravelled, and opened up to each other. Sensation shot through her. She had not felt like this in so long.

When they had finished, Sarah was shaking.

'You must think I am terrible,' she said.

'Oh no, Mrs Kelly. You are a magnificent woman.'

He handed her back the handkerchief.

'I hope you'll come back tomorrow,' he said and, getting dressed quickly, he left the room.

Sarah sat for a second, stunned. She looked across the couch at a large gilded mirror. She did not look wicked. Then she got dressed, and raced out of the house. She ran down the lane, forgetting her bicycle. She ran and ran until she came to the bog. There she stood in the centre of its bleakness and laughed and laughed. Loud, mad, unabashed laughter, releasing five years of captivity.

JOSEPH

He stood among the rushes, swaying. He was here, in his beloved bog. He was trying to reconcile himself. It had taken him all evening and many pints to bring himself to this point. The wind had dropped and it was freezing. The bog-earth beneath him was hard, an icing of frost sparkled above its black innards. It was a full moon, and Joe could see clearly about him. The landscape was silent, as if touched by a spell that held time still. Not even the animals were out in the fields. Too cold. Everyone was inside.

Joe did not feel the cold. All he could feel was anger. It was an anger which had coursed through him for as long as he could remember. It wasn't about Sarah, or Beatrice, or the girl that Eithne had brought down with her. They were all casualties, the outcome of his rage. He could not go back, he knew that. Now the truth was out, now they would surely find Beatrice, he could not bear to face them all. Not again.

No.

It had all started with Miss Lundy. It was all her fault. They always said, of course, that he should have known better. He was thirteen, for goodness' sake; practically a man in rural terms. But Miss Lundy, his teacher, had frightened him.

She made him a teacher's pet and had forced him to stay after school every day, to help her with her marking. He would never forget his school mates' sniggers as they left the room, and his frozen terror as Miss Lundy, a hefty, middle-aged spinster, came towards him.

It would always start the same way.

She didn't whip him, or strip, or do anything dramatic.

'Sit down next to me, Joseph, and pass me the copy books as I mark,' she would say.

He sat next to her and, not saying a word, she would put her hand on his trousers, her fingers splayed over his penis. She would rub and rub as she marked with the other hand. He was terrified, yet he did not know what to do. Was he imagining this? Miss Lundy never said a word, her face was expressionless, she did not even raise an eyebrow. All of a sudden she would stop. He was left torn. She would order him to go. Joe would stumble out of the schoolroom. He would run home, sobbing and emasculated.

This was Joe's dark secret. He never told anyone about Miss Lundy, but of course there were rumours. The other children would jeer at him in the school yard, everyone knew – although they never saw it as abuse. Nor did Joe. He just wondered what was wrong with him, why did she pick on him?

When Joe returned from England with Sarah by his side, he thought that everyone would think he was normal, at last he might gain a little respect. Miss Lundy was long gone. Forgotten.

But she came back. On that awful day when Sarah returned from town with Noel Chaney, Joe had seen Miss Lundy in his wife's face. Had recognized her cold indifference. It blinded him to all reason, to all sense of himself.

And Beatrice. Miss Lundy was there that night too. Turning his mind.

Joe sighed. He gripped a whiskey bottle in his hand. It was almost frozen to his fingers. He raised it to his mouth. He looked again across the bog, and wondered about its infinite appeal to him. He drank the whiskey as though it was nectar, and then, having drunk himself unconscious, he fell forwards into the rushes.

He landed face down, rigid, like many of the trees he had once felled on the marsh.

EITHNE

I adore hand-made paper. I know how to make it myself. I did a paper-making workshop a few years ago, but somehow it never works quite as well as it should. Like baking bread, paper-making is an intuitive craft, a skill you need to be born with. When we were in Majorca we found a shop selling hand-made paper in the old part of Palma. It was tucked away behind the Gothic cathedral, in a narrow alley sitting in a pretty row between an antique shop and a book store. The shop sold paper of every colour, texture and size imaginable. It sold it in single sheets, in reams, in writing blocks, as well as envelopes, notebooks and sketchbooks. It was expensive, but I couldn't resist and bought a pile of sketchbooks.

When I first owned these precious books I could hardly bear to mark the pages. I'd spend hours fingering them, letting the tips of my fingers rub their rough edges. And I'd smell them too. They smelt profoundly ancient and earthbound; I imagined them drying outside, sun-baked and golden. After a while, I shyly started writing a few notes in pencil accompanied by the tiniest sketches. However, after I was given my solo exhibition, my confidence surged and I started using pen and ink. My sketchbook is my constant companion. I never go anywhere without it. I stick photographs in it – Polaroid shots of different landscapes, as well as more carefully composed photographs. I write in pencil, ink, even biro or marker. I press leaves and flowers, add splashes of paint, cuttings from papers and magazines, even smears of bog-earth. It is my definitive scrapbook: a collection of all my random thoughts and observations. This is the foundation to anything I print. It is its primary layer – its conception.

Beatrice's sketchbook is very different to mine. She was not, maybe I should say not yet, a conceptual artist. She loved life drawing. Beatrice's feelings were expressed through the gesture of each figure she drew or painted, how the head was held, and how people moved their bodies.

Beatrice's life drawings were nearly always faceless, ending at the chin. But she did not shy away from portraits. She just preferred to separate the head from the body. She had a skill for likenesses, something I'm no good at.

Her sketchbook is full of portraits of me. I was her most convenient model. I remember not wanting to be drawn and being irritated by her insistence but then I always gave in. I had to sit still for ages. It used to drive me crazy.

When I was thirteen I was good at art at school, but I lacked confidence. I let Beatrice's talent overshadow mine. Beatrice loved the Romantics. The Artist had given her a book on Delacroix. I remember each page as we leafed through that book: *Dante and Virgil in Hell*, *The Death of Sardanapalus*, *Jacob Wrestling with the Angel* and all those Algerian women.

I always thought the pictures were over the top, but Beatrice loved them. She was always talking about Delacroix as if she knew him. She loved quoting a sentence from the book – that he was 'A volcano artistically concealed beneath a bouquet of flowers'. She said that she wanted to marry a man like him. She even wrote a poem about him. It's lost now.

After Beatrice disappeared, Mammy burnt that book. I don't know why she didn't give it back to the Artist.

When Beatrice was gone, I started to read all her art books. I was avid; hungry for knowledge. It was as if what she had read might somehow deliver up clues. Then I started to draw properly and with intention. They were angular rough drawings of places, not people. I never wanted to draw people. Grief gave me an edge that most of my contemporaries at school could barely identify with. I took solace in painting.

But my way is different from Beatrice's. I don't want to engage with humanity. Instead I walk – in the city or at home down to the bog, the woods, the lough, carrying my box of charcoals, and then I create violent and bleak compositions. I remember when I was a teenager I would sit for hours marking the paper with thick, black lines, an abstracted view of a wood on the horizon. There was little comfort in this landscape, but then that was my view of the world at the time.

BEATRICE

Beatrice's anger made her walk fast. Why was she so mad? Nobody got to her the way Phil did. She had really thought they were kindred spirits – soul mates. But he had turned out to be like all the others, thinking she was something she wasn't, just because she was different.

Beatrice had always stood on the outside. She could not help it. She had never been shy – always speaking out and saying what she thought. She always seemed to view things from an altered angle. Beatrice had thought Phil was the same as her. Now it seemed he was not. Tonight she had seen an expression on his face which she did not like. He thought he was better than her – that was it. She had told him her story, about how she had always known that Joe wasn't her real father in her heart of hearts. She had told him about the day her mother had told her everything . . . she had told him about trying to meet Jonathan. She had turned inside out for him. Now she felt as though he had punched her in the stomach; she was winded, knocked back and hurt. She would never forgive him.

It's true she had never talked about Jakob, but what was there to tell? He was her art teacher and her friend.

Beatrice stopped walking. Where was she going? What had made her go back? She was so tired now, she felt she could drop where she stood.

The moon lit the road ahead of her. The shadows of the

distant mountains spread around her, inky blue and insolent. Their presence reminded her of her elders – Mammy and Daddy. She wished it were judgement day, so the hills would crack open like volcanoes and everything suppressed would be released; like hot molten lava. Mammy's true feelings for Daddy would be out in the open, and that would be so much better. Then they could all stop pretending.

A cloud drifted across the moon. It was suddenly very dark. Beatrice climbed over a gate and ran back home across the fields as noiselessly as any other animal of the night. By the time she got to the front door it had begun to rain. Heavy, humid drops splattered her face. She tossed her hair.

The house was in darkness. Of course, Mammy and Eithne had gone to visit Auntie Aoife. She went into the kitchen and immediately lit the fire. It was nice to have some space.

EITHNE

Granny died when I was four. I only have one clear memory of my grandmother. She is sick, as usual, and seated by the range in the kitchen. She has a rug over her knees, and I am sitting on her lap. I remember the tug of her fingers on my waist. For someone so ill, she still possessed a strong grip. Every so often she coughs, then shakes and I wobble, but I do not want to get off. As I suck my thumb, she starts to play with my hair. It is something I have always loved, having my hair brushed, plaited and twisted around someone's fingers. I find it the most comforting thing in the world. Granny and I are both looking across the kitchen table at Beatrice. She is nine years old. She is wearing her school uniform, and her hair is in pigtails. She stands to attention, her hands behind her back. She is reciting a poem. What is it now? Let me think . . .

> *Oh to have a little house!*
> *To own the hearth and stool and all!*
> *The heaped-up sods upon the fire,*
> *The pile of turf against the wall!*
>
> *To have a clock with weights and chains*
> *And pendulum swinging up and down!*
> *A dresser filled with shining delph,*
> *Speckled and white and blue and brown!*

I could be busy all the day
Clearing and sweeping hearth and floor,
And fixing on their shelf again
My white and blue and speckled store!

I could be quiet there at night
Beside the fire and by myself,
Sure of a bed and loth to leave
The ticking clock and the shining delph!

Och! but I'm weary of mist and dark,
And roads where there's never a house nor bush,
And tired I am of bog and road,
And the crying wind and the lonesome hush!

And I am praying to God on high,
And I am praying Him night and day,
For a little house — a house of my own —
Out of the wind's and rain's way.

The room is full of women. Mammy and my aunts Bríd, Aoife and Mary sit at the table sharing a pot of tea. Mammy's eyes sparkle with pride. Aoife's two little girls are under the table, tugging each other's skirts and whispering; her boys are running around, wild and noisy. Someone kicks them outside to play, and then the room is peaceful again. We are all spellbound.

The poem is sad and Beatrice delivers it beautifully. Of course, I didn't understand the poem, just words here and there. I was only four. But I understood about Beatrice, that she was special. We all knew it.

Granny died just a few weeks later. Daddy and Uncle Jack came back from England for the funeral. I hardly knew my father and I had never met my uncle. When Daddy arrived home, he got out of the car and came straight over to me, not to Mammy, not to Beatrice, but to me first. He smoothed my hair, bent down and looked me straight in the eyes. There was recognition, immediately, like two animals from the same species.

As we walked behind the coffin, Daddy held my hand. He was shaking but he did not cry. In the church, Beatrice recited the poem again. But the words rang hollow. Without Granny they fell flat, the poem seemed slight and empty among the shuffling and inattentive crowd.

All those things were Granny — the hearth, the stool, the heaped-up sods on the fire, the big clock on the wall, and the dresser stacked with shining delph. That's what she means to me now — a bunch of quaint old things. Will it ever be that way with Beatrice? Will she ever be the trail she left behind? Pearls, scarf, beret, sketchbook. All bound together in Mammy's kitchen drawer.

I wake up and look out of the window. All I can see is the blank white of a thick fog. There is not a breath of wind, and a heavy mist has descended upon the landscape. I open the window. The air is moist yet freezing, a cloying cold. I shut it quickly.

The house is completely quiet. Mammy must still be asleep. Lisa is snoring softly, in the bed next to mine, Beatrice's bed. I hope Daddy got home all right.

I try to go back to sleep but it's no good, I need to clear my head. I fling on a few clothes, and pick up the car keys.

The roads are treacherous, people are crawling to work and I wish I had not gone out now. I slide down the hill, past Jakob Rudin's house. A For Sale sign is up. Driving conditions are terrible. The fog is so dense I can barely see in front of me. I put on my lights. Suddenly I see movement in the fog.

Something is coming towards me. I do exactly the wrong thing and brake. The car starts to skid, quickly I go down a gear and try to steer. The car slides across the road in a graceful semi-circle and cuts out. I take three deep breaths and start her up again. I turn the car, and start driving back towards the village. In my rear-view mirror I can see a stray sheep emerging out of the fog. It peers at me.

As I go back up the hill, light begins to break through the fog. A rosy cascade floods the road, yet I cannot see the sun. It is almost a divine sign – so utterly singular and incomparable is the light. To my left, very slowly, the fog begins to lift. The tip of Witch's Hill appears, wreathed in mist. It looks preternatural. I have lived here all my life, and yet this landscape has an aspect to it I have never seen before. Even though the heating in the car is on full, I shiver. Something terrible has happened.

Both Jack and Joseph came home for good when their mother died. She died in May, her favourite season, Our Lady's month.

The two men were shocked to find that the May Bush was still as it always had been, every year since they were children. They remembered, vividly, being sent out to collect bluebells, cowslips and buttercups. Running barefoot across the thistly heath to reach a copse of trees, which would yield up their flowery treasure. Then they would decorate the same old bush every year. It wasn't a special bush, just an evergreen. They tied the flowers into bunches using coloured wool, and attached them to the bush.

This tradition had never died. For years Granny had made the May Bush herself and, since she could walk, Beatrice had helped her. That year Beatrice and I had made the May Bush. Really she had done it on her own as I was only able to pick the flowers (and then I picked far too many dandelions). I could not reach most of the bush, and I couldn't tie the wool.

Jack had not been home for a few years, having devoted all his energy towards his failing marriage. Besides, his wife hated Ireland. But now that she had finally left, Jack had decided he might as well throw in the towel and come home. He always regretted not seeing the light sooner, and missing out on his mother's last years. But he had had to make a choice – his little boy, Philip, or his ailing mother.

Now he had effectively lost them both.

At the funeral Jack cried. He was a smaller man than Joseph, but more expressive. I liked my Uncle Jack from the day I met him. Apart from Daddy, he was the only other person who believed in me, and told me I was special. Joe and Jack were close. When I was smaller they were very alike, you would have thought they were twins from their gestures and animated story-telling. But as Daddy's heart slowly turned to lead he spoke less and almost shunned his brother's company. Jack's determination to be positive in the face of losing his wife and child was almost too much to bear. Daddy had everything – a family, a house, land – yet he felt he could not look forward to one single thing in his life. Each time he looked to the future, he drew a blank. His wife hated him. Where could it end?

Jack was one of nature's philosophers. He had an encyclopedic knowledge of natural history, but his approach was not purely scientific. He treated nature with a reverence that was quite unusual in a farmer's son.

He said to me once, 'There is enough beauty, truth and nourishment in one small flower to last a lifetime.'

He always put things into perspective. When Uncle Jack lived in England he worked in a bank, even attaining as high a position as assistant manager. Back home he seemed to have no interest in finance. He got a job as a barman in a pub in town and seemed quite content with that. He said he preferred to work in the evening because it left the daylight hours free for him to wander about. He loved walking.

Like me.

Uncle Jack moved in with us when he first came home. We all lived in Granny's house, Mammy, Daddy, Beatrice, Bríd, Jack and me. It was a squeeze, but I loved the gatherings we would have in the evenings, before I was put to bed. Jack and Beatrice would sing, Bríd would play the fiddle. I had a little tin whistle which I could barely play (to be honest I ruined the ensemble). Daddy would tap his feet and Mammy would watch. Now I look back, I remember how strange they both were. Rigid and miserable amid such joy and love. It never once occurred to either of them that they should separate.

When Daddy finally built our house and we moved in, Jack stayed on in Granny's house. It was just himself and Bríd. Bríd would be out all day with Daddy, working the land and looking after the stock. Jack would clean and cook and walk. When Bríd came home, they would eat dinner and then Jack would head off into town on a battered old bike. They were an odd couple. Sometimes Bríd would follow him into town a few hours later. She'd pull up outside the pub on her tractor. She always sat at the bar with the men and drank pints. At the time, you could be sure Daddy would be there as well. His brother and sister let him drink. It was the only time they ever saw him smile.

SARAH

The summer of her second pregnancy, Sarah slept with Noel Chaney every day for two weeks. The dust gathered, the house remained unswept, the sheets unlaundered. Upon her return the housekeeper could never quite work out what on earth Sarah Kelly had been doing every morning in Mr Chaney's dirty Georgian house.

Sarah was living out her dreamworld. When she lay in Noel Chaney's bed, and let him caress her, she closed her eyes and imagined her fantasy life. Noel Chaney was Anthony, the baby was theirs. They were living in a country manor, somewhere in England. She didn't have a dull mundane life and a loveless marriage. Instead, she had shiny hair, a beautiful wardrobe and a man who admired her. Beatrice was their lovely daughter. She had a pony, and played the piano. Every day that Sarah visited Noel Chaney her fantasy gathered momentum. She was in ecstasy, and approached their love-making with a devout enthusiasm.

Noel Chaney was bowled over. He had never thought a local girl would be so willing; then again, she *was* English.

He had been bored all summer and now this was a delicious diversion. He was engaged to his childhood sweetheart, Lizzie, and they were to be married in September. This was the perfect opportunity to have a little fun before he had to settle down. Besides, there were things Sarah would do which he could never imagine Lizzie agreeing to. The fact that she was married and pregnant was even better — no complications or possible accidents. The husband was conveniently away in England. It was the perfect set-up.

Each day started the same way. Noel Chaney would be downstairs in the library when Sarah arrived. She would go upstairs to his bedroom to make the bed. He followed her a few minutes later. They would spend an hour or two in bed and then Sarah would get up and go downstairs to get his lunch.

On Sarah's last day, Noel opened a bottle of wine. They drank it in bed, in between their love-making.

'Will I come again after today?' Sarah asked.

'I think not,' said Noel

'Right,' she said. Her voice was suddenly cold.

'Sarah,' he said, 'you know that to think we might have a future together would be ridiculous?'

'I know.'

'I'm getting married in September, remember, and you, of course, are married yourself.'

'I would hardly call it a marriage.'

'But you're having his baby . . . you must be intimate.'

'I hate him,' she spat. 'He is thick and ignorant. I didn't choose to get pregnant. He forced himself on me.'

'Oh, Sarah,' he said. 'I am so sorry.' He paused, embarrassed. 'We will always be friends. I am very fond of you.'

His last words hit her. It was like a flashback. Noel was not Anthony, but Jonathan. All of a sudden, Sarah was seventeen again, broken-hearted and destitute in a cafe in Oxford.

'No, you're not,' she said sourly.

He put his arm on hers.

'Sarah!'

She pushed him off, got out of the bed and dressed quickly.

'Don't be like that,' said Noel. 'Don't ruin our last hour together.'

'You've spoilt everything!' she said, her eyes blazing, and strode out of the room, leaving his lunch to burn to a cinder in the oven.

For two weeks, Sarah's anger kept her going. She shoved Noel Chaney to the back of her mind and tried to focus on her family. She took Beatrice for walks in the woods, where they would collect wildflowers and press them when they got home. She tried to get as excited as her daughter about the new baby.

'I hope it's a girl,' Beatrice would say. 'I want a little sister to play with. But then,' she'd add, 'I don't mind if it's a boy either . . . if it's a boy, Mammy, can we call him Peter like Peter Pan?'

Sarah winced. She put her hand on her belly. She had been trying her best to feel ambivalent about the new life inside her, but she could feel already the seeds of resentment in her heart. She didn't want this baby.

The third week, there was a full moon. Sarah hadn't been able to sleep for three days. She was being driven crazy by moon-fever. Her dream-world was over, and she felt suffocated by the mundane world she inhabited. Here she was, her life ticking away, sitting in the small front room – Margaret coughing in the corner, Aoife talking about babies, Mary about the hospital, Bríd about the farm. She had to get out.

She waited until the others went to bed, then crept out of the house. She cycled the four miles to Noel Chaney's house in her nightdress; a ghost in the moonlight. When she got there she crept round the back, and threw pebbles at his window. After a few minutes it opened. Noel stuck his head out. When he saw her he closed the window. She waited. A few seconds later the back door opened.

'Sarah, what's wrong?'

'Noel . . . please can I come in?'

'Have you taken leave of your senses? Of course you can't come in. You're in your nightdress, for Heaven's sake.'

'I can't bear it,' she whined.

'Go home, Sarah.'

She turned and walked back down the drive. She was sobbing. At the gate Noel caught up with her. He took her by the hand, and led her behind a thick stand of rhododendrons.

'All right, all right. Just once more,' he said. They fell down onto the soft, mossy ground. Sarah sat on top of him, guided him inside her and rode Noel Chaney as though she was going to the ends of the earth. She closed her eyes and saw everything crashing around her: Anthony – the manor house – being a lady. It was all demolished. Now all she could see was the moon-shadowed night, and all she could hear were Noel Chaney's gasps. He came inside her. She sat for a minute, then got up, wiping herself with the hem of her nightdress.

'I'm fine now,' she said calmly and walked through the rhododendron wall. She got her bicycle and mounted it. Noel came out of the bushes. He was bemused. His head on one side.

'Good luck, Sarah,' he said.

Sarah smiled. A car passed them, a dirty old Ford Escort. Then everything was quiet again.

'Goodbye,' said Sarah and pushed off down the lane on her bicycle.

EITHNE

Lisa leaves the day before the funeral, wanting to forget all about us. When she had recovered from the shock of Lisa's identity, Mammy had gone into overdrive, saying that she was going to get the Gardaí to open the case again. After wanting to find out the truth for so long, I had suddenly felt fearful . . . something about Daddy's behaviour had worried me terribly. Now all Lisa wanted to do was get away from us. I could hardly blame her.

My father has died, and they cannot tell me whether it was an accident or suicide. They say he would have known it was madness to go wandering on the bog on a night as cold as that. Either that or he was so drunk he did not know where he was going. They found him lying rigid in the reeds. He was cradling the whiskey bottle.

Maybe we killed him: Mammy, Beatrice and I.

I had seen him angry before, but never like that. I daren't think what it could mean. Has Daddy been hiding something all these years?

Uncle Jack was the first to find out about what had happened to Daddy. He came with the Gardaí to tell us. I was just back from my drive. Only Lisa was shocked, and then she was embarrassed. I had been expecting this all my life. My mother was very matter of fact. After about five minutes she asked what we had to do next – the post-mortem, the inquest, the funeral.

Had she ever loved him?

Leo grew up within the shelter of a loving family. Sometimes he finds my fear of attachment and of having children hard to understand. I try to explain. But he asks, 'Did your father hit your mother?'

'No.'

'Did he beat you or your sister?'

'Well, he slapped us a couple of times and shouted at us, and he and Mammy argued all the time.'

'All couples have rows. You should know that.'

'There was no love.'

'Did your parents love you?'

'Yes, but . . .'

'That's what's important. Myself and Clara don't love each other any more, but we love Shauna. She knows that and she's happy. That's what counts.'

'But you and Clara don't live together. Our family home was like living in a cold war. It was awful to watch.'

Leo would shake his head. You could tell he thought I was being melodramatic. He wanted another child and found it hard to understand my reluctance.

I have to ring him now. I haven't spoken to him since our row on the phone the other night. He has hurt me. I don't understand why he can't accept Lisa. Maybe he is sick of it all . . . I know he has a point. But at the moment he has made me feel deserted, more alone than I have ever felt in my life.

*

This morning Daddy died. We sit at the kitchen table, brandy in our tea, Uncle Jack, Mammy, Lisa, the poor Garda and me. Even Uncle Jack cannot cry. The fog still hangs heavy around the house. I am cold in my bones and shivering. Daddy has betrayed me. He walked his own lonely path into the bog without telling me where or why he was going. Has he forgotten the stories he told me when I was little? Has he completely forgotten my reverence? Suddenly I feel I will choke. I walk out of the back door, and stumble across our dirty patch of lawn. In the field next door, cattle loom out of the fog. They eyeball me. Leaning against the fence is Daddy's spade. It is old, the handle splintered and worn. It is a fitting symbol and focus for my grief. I pick it up and hurl it towards the startled cattle.

BEATRICE

He had been drinking for hours and could hardly hold himself straight. He crashed through the front door. The house was dark and quiet. There was a fire glowing in the range. He thought he was alone until he saw her sitting on a stool next to it. She watched him. He could see disgust in her eyes.

'Little whore!' he spat.

'Excuse me,' she said. 'What did you just call me?'

'I called you a fucking whore,' he shouted.

'Oh really, and where did you pick that up from? From the throngs of people in this shit-hole who have nothing better to do than make up lies about me? You're my bloody father, you should defend me.'

'You're no daughter of mine!'

'Yes, I am. You chose me! You took Mammy and me from that hospital, almost by force, I would say. So you made me your daughter. Like it or lump it.'

'I saw you tonight,' he said.

'What are you talking about?'

'I saw you with my nephew, Philip. I saw you corrupting him.'

'God, now he's rambling. We were sitting in a field . . . we had a sleep. Okay, so we took our clothes off. Big deal.'

'You're bad through and through. You turned your mother against me.'

'Don't talk rubbish. Go to bed, Joseph. You're making a scene. Just get out of my sight.'

She turned her back to him and huddled in front of the fire. He went towards her, and kicked the stool from under her. She fell, cried out, and hit her head on the hearth. She lay on her side unconscious. Joe pushed her onto her back. He continued to shout at her, 'Don't think you can do this to me. You bitch! I'm in charge, not you.'

He lifted Beatrice's skirt, and pulled down her pants. He began to undo his trousers. Then he stopped. He rose, as quickly as he could, and stumbled across the kitchen to the sink, vomiting into it. What was he thinking of? He must be demented. He lunged across to the other side of the room, and went into the sitting room. He had to get away from her. Joe fell onto the sofa and passed out. His last thought was, 'Thank God.'

When Beatrice opened her eyes it was completely dark. The fire had gone out. Her head hurt. There was blood on her lips. She shivered; the stone floor was freezing. She shifted her body. Why was the hem of her skirt brushing her lips? Why were her pants around her ankles? Beatrice started to whimper. She stood up, and put her clothes straight. Her hands were shaking. There was a terrible smell in the room. Banging into the table, into the chairs, she managed to get out of the house. It was brighter outside, her head still hurt, and her teeth were chattering. She began to cry. What had happened? What had he done to her? Beatrice picked up her bicycle, and fled. She was never coming back.

FIVE: THE COMPACT

EITHNE

Mammy possessed one family heirloom. It was a small brass compact, inlaid with mother-of-pearl, which had belonged to her grandmother. Nothing precious, but then the Quigleys had never been wealthy.

Its cheap metal is tarnished now, the clasp is broken, the mirror is cracked and the mother-of-pearl butterfly on its lid is incomplete. The thin puff is long gone, but there are traces of face powder still in the bottom. Forensics had a field day with that.

Sarah's father had given it to his daughter when she was a little girl. He thought she could play with it. Sarah always carried her compact with her, from childhood to adulthood. She did not wear much make-up but she always dusted her face with powder before she went out. Just to take the shine off it.

When Beatrice went off to college Mammy gave her the compact. It was a grand gesture and Beatrice knew this. She gave it to Beatrice as she was getting on the bus for Dublin, weighed down with bags. Nothing was ever said. The elder woman just handed it over. Beatrice began to cry. She seemed so pale. Ever since she'd decided to stay with the Artist – in preparation for art college, so she said – she had not seemed herself. Mammy had not wanted her to stay there, but Beatrice had insisted. Mammy had grudgingly agreed, but said that Daddy would never comply. Surprisingly he did.

The compact was found open, sitting on a stone by the spring in Baile Fobhair. You might think it had been left there as a charm. The cracked mirror gleamed in the fairy-tale light, and reflected back the dingy spring full of coppers. But whoever found it thought it might mean something to someone. They handed it in at the local pub. It was the pub where Mammy worked.

We went to see the Seven Wonders of Fore or Baile Fobhair, the day before Beatrice left for art college. It was just Beatrice and I. Phil had gone back to England a couple of weeks earlier. Since Beatrice had been staying with the Artist she had not seen Phil, and he never called at the house any more.

I missed Phil. Although I had moaned on our walks, he had paid me some attention. He was *so* charming. And the two of them made me feel as though I was part of something special. But since he had gone, things were dull. I was back at school, and dreading Beatrice's departure.

Beatrice did not go to Mass any more. Mammy had given up trying to make her go, and surprisingly Daddy had said nothing. It was like he had given up on her completely. The Sunday before Beatrice left, Mammy and Daddy stopped off at Glenamona on the way home from Mass. I went on ahead. Beatrice was waiting for me.

'Get your bike,' she said. 'We're going to St Feichin's place.'

St Feichin had founded Baile Fobhair, town of the spring. This very special valley was home to seven mysterious 'wonders': the monastery in a bog, the mill without a race, the water that flows uphill, the tree that won't burn, the water that won't boil, the anchorite in the stone, and the stone raised by St Feichin's prayers.

Uncle Jack had brought us here first, and it was one of our favourite places. Although the wonders can be described as folklore at best, hogwash at worst, there is no doubt that Fore has a unique energy.

We cycled down the hill, into the valley of Fore. The ruined abbey lay nestled below the hills, its stone was a soft-focus grey, and it seemed to me like a gentle mist drifted out from the ruins. It looked like something from a mystical world; a place that could just disappear during the blink of an eye.

We got off our bicycles.

'I felt it was important we spend my last day here. I thought we should each make a wish,' Beatrice said.

She walked up to a wizened old tree, known as the tree that won't burn. I followed her. Beatrice thrust a copper into the gnarled trunk, and closed her eyes. I watched her lips moving. She opened one eye.

'Come on, make a wish.'

I found a tuppence in my pocket, leant forward and pushed it into the spongy bark. We were not the only ones. The tree was riddled with coins. There were all sorts of things attached to its branches – hair scrunchies, plastic bags, scraps of material, even crisp packets tied and twisted. It looked like a head of hair in rags. I closed my eyes and hunted for a wish. It took a while.

'Finished?' She nudged me.

'Why do they do that?' I said, pointing to the decorations on the tree.

'I'm not sure. I think they're charms. The travellers tie them to the tree so their prayers or wishes will come true.'

'I'd like to be a traveller,' I said.

'You'd never survive,' Beatrice said, authoritively. She started to walk towards the abbey. I caught up with her.

'Beatrice?'

'Yes.'

'Now that you're going away to college, you won't forget about me, will you?'

She turned suddenly, and hugged me fiercely. 'Don't be daft.' She cradled my face in her hands. 'Eithne, sweet, you're my sister.' Her eyes were dark limitless pools. 'You're the most important person in my life, apart from Mammy.'

'You won't go away and never come back?'

'I'm only going to be in Dublin. I'll be down all the time. You're being silly.'

'But, well, what about Daddy?'

'What do you mean?'

'Do you have to hate him so much?'

'I don't hate him. It's just . . . Eithne, I really can't talk about this.'

'It's not his fault that he isn't your real Daddy, but he loves you, I know he does.'

'I don't think so.'

Her mood changed, and she looked away from me, at the abbey, the hills, the clouds, who knows?

'Be careful, Eithne,' she said. 'Daddy has lots of problems.'

'I know,' I said. 'About the drink.'

'Just be careful,' she replied.

'Is that why you won't stay at home any more? Is it because of Daddy? Has something happened?'

'Nothing happened, Eithne. I have just . . . grown up, and seen our father for what he is, a pathetic drunk. If you can't see that, you're a fool. Why should I have to spend time in the company of that man?'

She charged ahead, and began to climb the hill opposite the abbey, going faster and faster. Eventually I gave up trying to catch her, and sat on a stone by the mausoleum.

This was where the anchorite's cell had been. He never left his stone, and survived on food left out for him by the locals.

That would be the thing. Hide in a stone. I looked at Beatrice. She was a speck now, climbing higher and higher, bearing her stony heart with her. I could hardly carry my conflicting feelings for a father and a sister. They weighed me down so that all I managed was one heavy sob.

BEATRICE

The dark village. As they drive past she closes her eyes. It is night, a dark one, but she does not want to see even the house lights from the road. They would remind her of what home once was. They would remind her of Eithne, and of how she wishes to tell her. How did her life all of sudden get to be so serious?

She thinks of the summer she has just spent and how she felt so free and full of excitement at her approaching independence. Now that's all spoilt. Her college days have hardly begun and they are ruined. She shrinks back in her seat, and clutches herself. The tears roll down her cheeks but she says nothing. Her heart is depleted while something else grows inside her. It horrifies her to think of it.

She knows well the laws of nature; her granny had taught her much about folklore, and the good and the evil that lurks in the land about. Her granny had seen a banshee once, the night old Mrs O'Reilly, her neighbour, had died. It made Beatrice's blood curdle to remember Granny's description, 'I heard the banshee's cry. I was in bed and I got up. I wanted to see her for once. I was curious.'

'What did it sound like, Granny?'

'It's hard to describe, a scream, not unlike a vixen's howl, but on the same note, holding it, and going on and on, until it finally faded away.'

'And did you see her, Granny?'

'Oh yes, I did, to be sure. The banshee was outside the back door of the house. Child, she was a fright to see. Oh my Lord, I crossed myself I did, and she leered at me, her face pulled into the most horrific scream, her eyes red as a wild wolf, and her hair, white and lank. But worst of all, she had no body at all. Oh sweet Jesus, I believed then, so I did. I believed in it all after that.'

'But Mammy said that the banshee's not bad. She said she's a little old woman who just combs her hair. She says she only comes when someone good is dying.'

'Well, there's some that see her like that, and then there's others who see her like I did.'

Beatrice knows well how something bad can get inside you. She is sure that is what she is carrying – pure evil. She shivers, pulls down the sun-visor, and peers into its little mirror. She does look different.

Out of the corner of her eye she can see the village disappearing behind them as they drive down the hill. She can see the pub on the corner; an old lad goes in. That'll be him, she thought, in a couple of years, that's what he'll be, an old piss-head. Well, I shan't let him get away with it.

The handball alley is on the other side of the road, for once there are no teenagers hanging about outside. They drive past the small council estate. Everything is quiet in there, two lorries and a tractor sit parked and silent. But there are hardly any lights on in the houses. She can see them all in the field behind the estate, standing around their Hallowe'en bonfire. It was a good one this year, the kids had been collecting stuff for weeks, and now it was piled high and fiercely blazing. Sparks shot up into the dark night, and Beatrice imagined all those people she had grown up with standing around the fire. She was not close to anyone; they were all so different from her. The girls didn't want to travel, and the boys just wanted to marry you. And, anyway, because the Kellys did not actually live on the estate they were treated a bit differently, which was ridiculous because they were probably worse off than any of them. But that was how it was. They owned their own house and that meant a lot.

Now the car turns a corner, and everything is gone, all of a sudden. Now there is just black behind them, a slate wiped clean.

EITHNE

I drive Lisa into town to catch the bus to Dublin. Daddy is going to be buried tomorrow. Leo is on his way down. Even Phil is coming from England. I haven't seen him since the summer before Beatrice disappeared.

It is snowing, a white blizzard envelops the car.

'Are you sure you're okay taking the bus back?' I ask.

'It's no problem,' says Lisa. 'I don't want to be in the way.'

'You wouldn't be,' I say, and I mean it, although I can imagine what some of the relatives would say if they knew who she was.

'I have to get back,' she says. 'You see, Steve's expecting me.'

'Right,' I say.

'We're getting married in a few months.'

'So soon!' I say, thinking she's too young.

'That's why I wanted to find my real mum,' she says. 'I had a dream that she'd be at my wedding – instead of Lorraine and Paul.'

'But they're your parents as well.'

'Only on paper.' She gets out her cigarettes, and lights one up. 'They wouldn't bloody come anyway,' she says, puffing out the window. 'They wanted me to go to college, not get married.'

'What do you want to do?' I ask her.

'I don't want to go to college. I've had enough of school. I want to get out into the real world.'

Freezing air streams into the car. I shiver.

'All I want is to have my own kids,' she adds.

'It's hard work.'

'I know . . . that's what Lorraine keeps saying. But I can't wait to have my own little baby.'

'Babies scare me,' I say. 'They're such a huge responsibility.'

'Ah, they're easy. All they need is to be loved.'

'But they can't talk to you, that's what frightens me. How do you know if they're okay?'

'You know, cos you're their mum. It's all instinct!'

'Maybe you're right.'

'Course I'm right. You're practically a mum anyway, don't you have that little girl all the time, your husband's daughter?'

'That's different . . . she's not a baby.'

'You'd be a great mum, Eithne, I know it,' she says definitively. 'I wish that it was you I had been looking for – I wish you were Beatrice.'

I blush, and accept her praise.

'I just don't understand,' she continues, throwing her butt out the window, and winding it up.

'What?'

'How she could give me up?'

'I don't know, Lisa. I don't understand anything any more. I thought Beatrice was dead.'

'There must have been someone or something that made her do it.'

We drive in silence. I know we are both thinking the same thing. Neither of us has forgotten Daddy's scene the night he died. It is almost too much to bear. Daddy would never have done *that*.

242

We arrive in town as the bus pulls up. We get out of the car, and Lisa takes her bag out of the boot.

'Thanks, Eithne,' she says.

'I didn't do anything,' I say.

'You believed me.' She crosses the road, and then turns and runs back.

'Sorry about your dad,' she blurts out. 'Sorry if it was me . . . being there . . . that made him—' She stops.

'No, Lisa, don't think that. It had nothing to do with you.' She looks doubtful.

'Come back, Lisa,' I say. 'Come back sometime when things are better here. You've my number.'

'Yeah, thanks.'

She hesitates, and then, nearly knocking me over, she wraps her arms around my chest and squeezes me tightly. A Beatrice hug. She smells of cigarettes and soap. Then she lets go, turns and runs across the road.

'We will find her one day. I promise,' I call after her.

She doesn't hear me. I am shaking, trying to push the tears back. I rub my elbows through my jumper and coat. She has already boarded the bus without a backward glance.

I head into the hotel for a cup of coffee. Leo is arriving in an hour and I may as well wait. People look at me as I sit down. A couple of them come over and offer their condolences. I feel very removed.

I had no business making Lisa that promise. It was one I could not keep.

SARAH

Sarah was scared again. The day after she gave birth to the new baby, Joe came to visit her in the hospital. He brought her a big show of flowers, but no smile on his face.

Sarah held the baby in her arms while she fed. Joe sat in the chair next to the bed. He said nothing, just glowered at his wife.

'Let's hope this one's mine,' he growled under his breath.

Sarah started, and the child unlatched.

'You know exactly *when* this child was conceived.'

'Maybe, maybe not.'

His breath stank of whiskey fumes.

'Will Noel Chaney be visiting you?' he suddenly demanded. Sarah immediately coloured, he had caught her off guard.

'Tommy told me,' he whispered. 'He saw you, Sarah, last summer. Tell me – wife – what were you doing visiting Noel Chaney in the middle of the night, in your underwear? Cleaning his house at midnight? Or were you getting a few perks with the job?'

'He's lying, Tommy is lying,' Sarah countered quickly.

'Now why would he do that? He's my friend.'

'Because he hates me.'

'He only hates you because he knows you're a tart, and he thinks I deserve better than that.'

'He tried to kiss me once but I pushed him away. He's resented me ever since.'

'Stop lying, bitch,' he hissed.

'Can you not see she's yours?' Sarah sobbed. She offered the squirming bundle up to him.

Joe looked down at the tiny baby. His anger dissipated. Something in the little girl's shiny dark eyes reached through all the pain to his heart. He took the child into his arms.

'You're right,' he said, 'she is mine.' He held her for a minute, and stroked her downy cheeks. 'She's to be called Eithne, after my granny.' Then he handed the baby back to Sarah. 'But, Sarah,' he whispered, 'you know what they say: there's no smoke without a fire.'

EITHNE

I glance at myself in the mirror in the hotel toilets. I look dreadful: my skin is almost jaundiced; my eyes are smudged by dark shadows; I have an unsightly cold sore on my upper lip. As for the rash it is out of control, even though I have lathered my arms in special creams. I hunt around in my bag for a bit of make-up. My hand knocks against the compact. I had forgotten it was in there. Mammy had given it to me after Beatrice went. She could not bear to keep it herself.

I hardly ever use it. I never wear foundation or face powder. But I keep it in my bag, always, like a talisman.

I take the compact out now, and click it open. I peer inside at the tarnished and cracked mirror. It gives a kinder reflection, and I do not look so battered, just sad. I finger the rim of the compact, its sharp 'O'. What could this tiny treasure tell me? If only its mirror could rewind reflections. What might it show us? It was the last thing found, open and perfectly balanced on a tiny stone by the brook in Fore. All her things . . . in so many different places, miles from each other. She must have put them there herself – or someone who knew her very well.

Lisa's appearance has turned my world upside down. I like life tidy: home, college, print-making, marriage, exhibitions. Lisa does not fit into any of my boxes. The neatest thing would have been if Beatrice had died. Awful . . . but at least there would have been an end to it. What drives me mad are all the loose ends. They bind me like ropes, and throw the rest of my life into complete disarray. I feel different about everyone – Daddy, Mammy, Beatrice, even Leo.

I don't want to see him.

I rang him before I left for the bus with Lisa. He didn't even mention our row. He told me he was sorry, he told me he loved me, and that he would come right there and then. That very minute.

My good husband, who has done so much for me, who is dropping everything to be by my side, yet his impending arrival troubles me. It stresses me. Leo always knows best, but this time I do not want his advice. I should be needing him – my father has died for God's sake. Yet I just want to be alone. Once I speak to Leo he'll start to analyse everything. I'm not ready . . . I don't want him to put two and two together, as he inevitably will. I don't want his 'help'.

I click the compact shut and finger the iridescent pearl on the lid. Why did she not take this and all the other things with her? I put it away, and dig out a lipstick and mascara.

As I come out of the toilet there is a text message for me. It is from Mammy. Leo has phoned to say he'll be down early tomorrow morning. He tried my phone, but I must have been out of coverage. Shauna is unwell, and he has to take her to the doctor. His friend Mick is driving him down tomorrow, and his mother will mind Shauna. He is sorry, so sorry, but his daughter needs him.

I am relieved. Then guilty, that I feel so. And then I am cross.

Why do I always come second?

There is more to Mammy's message. Phil is arriving on the next bus. Can I stay in town and meet him? I go back into the hotel bar and order a whiskey. Now I need a drink.

LISA'S LOOKING GLASS

For a moment she is still.

Her presence has the same quality as a gazelle about to take flight. Her muscles are tensed; she balances on her toes. Lisa gazes at the rippling water. She likes to see herself like this, disguised with cap and goggles. Poised in her sports swimwear. She waits until the pool is virtually still, and then she gazes into her perfect looking glass.

I want to break through the blue.

Lisa can see the tiles on the bottom of the pool. She sees a lost wedding ring, a sharp bright light amid the floating reflections.

She has seen that film, *The Big Blue*, where the two friends compete against each other, diving deeper and deeper, pushing themselves way past the limit. The hero was like a sea creature, she had thought at the time. Awkward on land, among people. Lisa knew how he felt.

If only she could see me now, as I shoot forward and slice the water. My arms cut a white path, and I know where I am going.

Lisa did not like her life to hold too much time for reflection. It was only here, when she stood on the edge of the pool, toes squeezed tight, that she dared to look in at herself.

She narrowed her vision until it contained nothing but blue. She closed her ears to the splashing of others swimming and she shut out the smell of chlorine. She was on a white cliff, a sparkling contrast to the Mediterranean blue sea. She was high up, the sun on her head, and dreams in her heart. Yes, she loved that film.

She had seen it only once, and Steve had said it was boring but she thought it was great. There *were* those who weren't earthbound.

She found people hard work. It had been difficult in Ireland, meeting that family, trying to be tough. She had built her hopes so high. Now she had had enough.

I want to be like everyone else.

Lisa raised her arms, pressing her hands together, pointing her fingers like an arrowhead, and bent her knees. She sprang into a graceful arch, and entered her haven. Folded in blue. The water carried and soothed her.

Lisa's limbs began to work; she glided swiftly, effortlessly forwards.

If she could have dived for her mother, she would have swum ten thousand fathoms.

SARAH

After Eithne was born Sarah changed.

A tiny spark inside her, which she had let Noel Chaney ignite, finally went out. She cut her hair and dedicated herself to her children, in particular to Beatrice. It was her little girl who kept her alive, who gave her the love she needed to keep going on. Now that she was five, each little advance Beatrice made excited Sarah. Her first day at school, the first book she was able to read, and all the funny, witty things she said – they were the reasons she was able to get up every morning and face each day. Joe went back to England, but his threats had frightened her. She knew what he was capable of when he was angry. She had seen him watching her with Beatrice, and she knew their intimacy taunted him. A couple of times she was certain he was jealous of the child. So maybe the baby's arrival wasn't such a bad thing . . . at least he had a little girl too now.

Sarah felt so different about this baby. She had bonded with Beatrice as soon as she laid eyes on her. But she found it hard to accept Eithne into her heart. Even at three months the baby still felt like a stranger. She had long given up on breastfeeding, and much to Margaret's approval the baby was now being bottle fed. When Sarah felt guilty about her lack of feeling for her new-born she consoled herself with the fact that Beatrice adored her little sister, and spent as much time as she could lavishing affection on her. Sarah prayed that one day her love for Eithne would expand.

As money was still tight, she got a part-time job in the pub in Fore, as well as keeping on some cleaning jobs. It was great to get out in the evening, and Margaret and Bríd were happy to mind the two girls. Sarah made friends in the pub. For once she was part of a small but lively scene. The landlady was a cheerful and robust little woman, Katie Sykes, and she liked the young Englishwoman. Each evening she left out old magazines for Sarah to take home with her to read and study what was happening in the outside world, even if it was only fashion.

When Sarah locked up the pub, she would circle the village of Fore, just so she could pass the abbey. It was a place of such rare beauty, and completely unappreciated by her neighbours. Sarah imagined the monks, and the harshness of their lives. It must have been so cold inside that old stone in the winter.

By the side of the abbey was a pigeon house. It was similar to a miniature round tower, with openings all the way around it for the pigeons. Sarah imagined the panicked flapping of the doomed birds. They were the monks' only form of sustenance in the long, winter months. Now the birdhouse stood empty and calm.

At that time you could still go into the mausoleum and Sarah would often sit on a tomb, kneading her fingers, shaking her head. At times she felt so low that if it had not been for her two little girls, she would happily have climbed inside the tomb and settled herself among the dusty old bones.

One night, when Eithne was only about four months old, Tommy O'Reilly came into the pub. Tommy had been in England and Sarah had not seen him since long before the baby was born. At first he acted as if nothing was the matter.

'How ye doing, Sarah!' he said cheerily. 'Fix us up a pint there, will ya?'

Sarah started pulling the pint; she said nothing.

'I believe congrats are in order,' he continued. 'Will you have a drink, on me, to wet the baby's head?'

'No, thank you,' she said stiffly.

'Ah, come on. I haven't seen ye in ages. Have a drink, why not? For old friends' sake.'

'I have nothing to celebrate with you, Tommy O'Reilly.'

'Jaysus, what's up with you?'

He scratched his head. Sarah finished pulling his pint, and almost slammed it in front of him.

'Steady on,' he said. 'You'll ruin me pint.'

She started to walk to the other side of the bar.

'Oh, I get it,' he shouted after her. 'You're sore cos of what I told Joey.'

The bar was fairly empty. Everyone looked up. Sarah turned and walked quickly back to Tommy.

'For God's sake, haven't you done enough damage?'

'Sure, I was only having a laugh with Joey. I only said what I saw. Where's the harm?'

'Don't pretend you're a fool,' she hissed.

Tommy's red face deepened. She glared at him.

'You know what he can be capable of.'

He shook his head, picked up his pint and joined his buddies. All night long he kept looking over at her.

When Sarah had finished work it was about one in the morning. She took her usual stroll around Fore. She crossed the brook and walked towards the abbey. She was stepping over a low wall, when she heard someone behind her. 'Who's there?' she called out, turning.

'It's only me.' Tommy O'Reilly stood behind her, a cigarette glowed between his fingers.

'What are you doing here?'

'You shouldn't have done that,' said Tommy. 'I don't like to be humiliated in front of me pals. You should have taken the drink and shut up.'

'You had no right to tell Joseph you saw me with Noel Chaney—' she began.

'But it's true, isn't it?' he sneered. 'I did see ye – in yer nightie.' He started to laugh. 'Joey's right, he's married a right tart who chucks it around to anyone who'll ask.'

Sarah froze.

'So I'm asking yer.' He took a last drag, and then threw his cigarette away. He stepped towards her.

'Are you mad?' she spluttered. 'I'm married to your best friend.'

'I won't tell, will you?'

Her lie to Joe had come true. Tommy grabbed her arm and tried to kiss her.

'Get off me.'

'What's wrong? Am I not good enough for you? Will you only go with the likes of Noel Chaney?'

Sarah felt sick. She pulled away from him.

'Please, Tommy – this is stupid. I'll tell Joe and he'll kill you.'

Tommy let go suddenly. He spat.

'Guess you're right,' he said. 'He is me friend and all. Anyway, I don't go with whores.'

He turned and strolled away, as cool as they come. Sarah's legs gave way. She crumbled among the ruins of the abbey. Somewhere else had been taken away.

EITHNE

I met Phil first. Beatrice was still on holiday in Majorca when he arrived. He was every country girl's fantasy, so suave. Uncle Jack brought him down to the house to meet us the day he arrived. I have never seen Jack so pleased, he was positively beaming. We sat in the front room and Mammy made a special tea, scones, barm brack and, as always, ham sandwiches.

Phil lived in London with his mother and step-father. We had heard that they were rich. They had a house in a place called Chelsea, which impressed Mammy a lot. She said that they must move in 'high circles'. Phil, though, regarded himself a radical. He was almost immediately at loggerheads with Daddy over Margaret Thatcher. Phil said she was a fascist, whereas Daddy admired her hard-line politics. Uncle Jack speedily changed the subject.

'Eithne, why don't you give your cousin a tour of the village?'

'Okay.'

Phil didn't look too keen, but he got up and followed me. He was eighteen and absolutely gorgeous to my thirteen-year-old eyes. I was incredibly conscious of a spot on my nose. We walked out of the door, and Phil put these mad, mirror sunglasses on. He still managed to look cool.

'How old are you?' he said, taking out a packet of cigarettes and lighting up.

'Thirteen.'

'And your sister, Beatrice?' He offered me a cigarette.

Flattered, I shook my head. 'She's seventeen, nearly eighteen.'

'When'll she be back?'

'Saturday. She's in Majorca.'

'The poet Robert Graves lived there.'

I nodded my head, knowledgeably. I had never heard of Robert Graves.

'I could have gone to Italy this summer,' he continued, 'with my mother and step-father, they've a villa near Rome. But I decided to come here instead.'

I looked at him. His hair was blond and devilishly tousled. I felt weak.

'Why?' I could not possibly imagine giving up a free trip to the sun.

'Because I wanted to get to know Jack. Anyway, my step-father bribed me. He's as sick of me as I am of him. He's going to buy me a car when I get back. I can't wait to have wheels.'

We had circled the village.

'Is this it?' he asked.

'I'm afraid so.'

'Any pubs?'

'Two.' I pointed them out.

'Let's go for a drink.'

I hesitated.

'Sorry, I forgot you were only thirteen. You look older.'

I blushed with pleasure.

'We can still go in. I'll have a lemonade,' I said.

'Deal,' he replied. 'I hope my other cousin is as pretty as you.'

I glowed, colouring from head to toe.

*

Nearly twenty years later and Joni Mitchell sings across the airwaves as the radio blasts from behind the bar.

I have been waiting in the hotel, with my single whiskey, for well over an hour. I have butterflies. It is still snowing — maybe the bus was cancelled.

A flurry of people arrive . . . here he comes now. Philip. I would recognize him anywhere. A more rugged, filled-out version of the eighteen-year-old boy strolls into the hotel. The same blue eyes. There is something instantly familiar about them. Of course he does not recognize me. I have changed, I am glad to say, since I was thirteen.

'Phil!' I wave. He sees me and comes over.

'Eithne?' he says, questioningly.

'It's me,' I say.

We embrace.

'My God!' he says. 'You look so different. It's been a long time.'

He carries a camera bag on his shoulder.

'Are you planning to make a film of the funeral?' I ask.

'No, no. I bring it with me everywhere. Just habit; you know, being a journalist dash film-maker.'

'Poser . . .' I tease him.

'Let's have a drink,' he says.

'I'd better not. I'm driving.'

'Please . . . go on — I can't face Jack just yet. I haven't seen him in so long.'

'Too long,' I say.

'I know . . . I just couldn't bear to come back, after Beatrice went. We've spoken on the phone often, and he's come over to see me — I've been away a lot — but I just couldn't handle this place after what happened to Beatrice.'

I look away. It always comes back to that.

'I see her everywhere,' he whispers.

'So do I.' My eyes glisten. 'I have something to tell you about Beatrice.'

He looks up. 'What?'

'Get the drinks first. I'll have a Coke.'

He goes to the bar. I fiddle with my hands; I look at the clock, and then at Phil's back. It is so strange seeing him again after all this time. I still think he is gorgeous; my thirteen-year-old taste can't have been too bad. We have spoken on the phone a couple of times, and emailed now and again, but he was always too busy, Phil said, to come back. He even missed my wedding because he was filming in the Ukraine. In all our correspondence we carefully skirt round the Beatrice issue. It is too much pain for us both.

Phil comes back with the drinks, and we sit in silence for a few minutes.

'I'm sorry about your father, Eithne,' he says, eventually.

'Me too.'

'What happened?'

'Well, he died of the cold, so to speak. He collapsed on the bog, the night before last. He was full of the drink as usual. He got hypothermia and his heart stopped.'

'The demon drink.'

'It killed his dreams.'

'Is he at home?'

'No, he's in the church. I'll be glad when this is all over,' I say shakily.

He puts his hand over mine, and then he asks softly, 'What were you going to tell me about Beatrice?'

'I wanted to ask you something.' I pause. 'It's a bit personal . . .'

'You know you can ask me anything. Go on spit it out.' He smiles.

'Did you and Beatrice . . . well . . . were you an "item"?'

'An "item"? Do you mean were we sleeping together?'

'Yes . . . so?'

'You might remember that Beatrice lived in your house, and I lived with Jack and Bríd.'

'You know what I mean, there were plenty of opportunities.'

'This all seems a bit irrelevant now.'

'Did you?' I press.

'No . . . well, at least, I don't think so. We were so high on magic mushrooms that summer I can't remember much, to be honest.'

He pauses, taking a sip from his drink.

'We did take our clothes off once, but that wasn't really sexual, it was more like getting down to nature. Anyway, then we both conked out on the grass. Nothing happened . . . no, nothing at all,' he adds more firmly.

'Well, you two did spend ninety per cent of the time stoned,' I say. 'It's possible . . .'

'No, I really don't think so. I remember that was the day we fell out over that artist chappy. If she was sleeping with anyone, it was probably him.'

'You think so?'

'Well, we rowed over him.'

Jakob Rudin, the father of my sister's child? But why had Jakob stayed and she had gone? It made no sense.

'Are you going to tell me what this is all about?' Phil asks.

I take a deep breath.

'Four days ago a girl turned up on my doorstep, called Lisa. She claims she is Beatrice's daughter.'

'What!' He nearly knocks over his drink.

'She says she was adopted just after she was born.'

258

'But I thought Beatrice was dead,' he says. 'I mean she has to be dead . . .' He trails off.

'She had her birth certificate with Beatrice's name, and copies of the adoption papers. Phil, she *is* Beatrice's daughter.'

'Beatrice is alive?' he speaks slowly, in shock.

'It seems so,' I say.

'Oh my God!' He gulps. 'So you thought I might be the father of this girl?'

'I was hoping . . .'

'She must be Jakob Rudin's child. He might know where Beatrice is. Did you ask him?'

'He's dead . . . and I don't think he is. I think Beatrice would have told him she was pregnant, and I don't think he would have rejected her . . . Anyway, if Beatrice was having Jakob Rudin's child, why did she run away? There was no need to go. He would have looked after her and we would never have shunned her.'

'It does seem strange. Beatrice was never one to mind what other people thought. But how will we ever know now that Jakob is dead? Was there anything about the father on this girl's birth certificate?'

'No . . . there was nothing under the father's name or address.'

'I can't believe that Beatrice could be alive.' Phil grips my hand. 'Eithne, we have to find her.'

'Did Beatrice ever tell you that Daddy wasn't her real father?'

'Yes, I always knew.'

'I thought she might have gone there – to her real father's house in London – so I rang yesterday morning but there was no one in. And now . . . I don't know what to do – I don't know whether we should just leave it all.'

'What do you mean? Eithne, your sister could be alive, why on earth do you want to leave it now?'

'There's something else,' I say. 'All this has something to do with Daddy. I think he knew something, which he has been keeping from us all these years.'

I tell Phil about Daddy attacking Lisa the night he died.

'I know I never saw eye to eye with your father, but he had his principles. I don't think he would have done what you think he might,' Phil says carefully.

'I don't know what to think any more.' I begin shaking, and take a slug of his whiskey. 'I'm scared, Phil,' I whisper. 'All I know is that sometimes the drink made Daddy lose sight of himself. It took him over, and he became someone dark, not nice.'

'No, Eithne,' says Phil. 'You mustn't believe that.'

I tremble, smearing tears with the back of my hand. We sit quietly. Phil hands me a tissue. I try to claw back from the edge.

'Eithne,' he whispers. 'If Beatrice is alive then maybe she will turn up tomorrow morning.'

I gasp. 'Oh, Phil. I hadn't even thought of that.'

BEATRICE

Dear Jakob

I did it. I'm here in London. Thanks for helping me. You're the only person I can trust, Jakob.

I wish you were here. I know you said you didn't want to come, and you're scared. But so am I. Couldn't we go somewhere together, until this whole thing is over? We could be like Frida Kahlo and Diego Rivera. We could go and live in Mexico, and you could be the famous artist, and I could paint as well. And we would have lots of Bohemian artist friends, and just be free. Please come, Jakob, please . . . please . . .

Every night I have really weird dreams. They're not nightmares. Just strange dreams about funny-looking birds — and creatures that look as though they've come straight out of a Bosch painting. I suppose it makes sense — doesn't it? I mean there's someone else inside me — so there's two brains ticking away. It's bound to make my head go funny.

I want him to think I'm dead. I want him to think he made me die. He deserves to think it's all his fault. I will tell Mammy and Eithne soon. But not yet . . . You see he has to tell them why first. I want him to have to confess.

God, Jakob. Have you ever hated someone this much? When I think about him and what he did to me, I just feel sick. I mean I feel sick all the time anyway — but when I realized I was pregnant . . . You see, up till then I had tried to forget all about

*it; pretend it didn't really happen — I mean, I don't remember it
happening so it was easy to forget. But then — when I didn't get
my period, and I was in college, in the loos, throwing up . . .
Oh, Jesus, Jakob, it all came back — and I knew — and I kept
thinking, he's put some kind of monster inside me. And it's
making me go mad.*

*I'll never forget the day I found out — I got one of those kits
and did it in the bathroom in my digs. Jesus, when it went blue,
do you know what I did? I just charged out of the flat, and went
straight into a shop, and bought a huge bottle of gin. Then I
went home, and ran a boiling-hot bath — I scalded myself getting
in — and I drank that whole bottle of gin. And I waited, and
nothing happened — I just threw up again. Whatever he's put
inside me has stuck fast.*

*That's why I'm here. I'm going to do it, Jakob. I'm going to
get rid of this thing in me. It has to be bad.*

*This is my address for now. I'm in a hostel just round the
corner from where my real father lives. I'm going to go and see
him tomorrow. He won't turn his back on me, not his own flesh
and blood.*

*Take care, Jakob, and write to me soon or come. Please come.
Let me know what's happening at home, and when he tells them
why I've gone.*

Love B

EITHNE

We walk the fields, which are laced with ice, in total silence. I look at Phil and he seems so out of context. This man I remember as a boy reaching adulthood, like a son of the summer sun, shining, golden and warm, appears now as ethereal as a ghost. The night chill casts a blue shadow across him. His hair is white in the moonlight, and he moves with precision like an Arabian stallion. Phil takes my hand. There is warmth still in his fingertips.

It has been a long evening. Mass first in the church, followed by refreshments at our house, with the family commemorating my father through alcohol. Strangely fitting. I am as drunk as the rest of them. Tommy O'Reilly is singing, Mammy retreats to bed, while Jack cries at last.

Phil and I escape. We run out of the house like two wild children – whooping and shrieking. Then we take each field at a time, sprinting like nocturnal animals, stiff blades of grass crunching beneath our feet. We stop. Without a word, Phil turns to face me. The moon slips behind a cloud, and then slowly emerges again. The landscape is thrown into high relief. Our cheeks glow silver. He strokes my face, and his eyes entreat me.

Where is Leo? He should be here now, comforting me. He is my husband.

There is an empty cottage on the ridge of the field. Phil leads me towards it. He kicks open the door. The grate is filled with an ancient bird's nest and twigs and leaves. Phil lights the humble kindling. We squat side by side. Smoke starts to billow out into the room.

'The chimney must be blocked,' he says.

I start to cry, hot rushed tears. It is all too much for me.

'Eithne . . . Eithne . . .' he whispers.

Phil begins to kiss me. It is like drinking a case of wine.

'No,' I say, pulling back. 'No, Phil, we mustn't.'

Phil takes my hand, and holds it against his heart.

'You're right, Eithne,' he says. 'I'm sorry . . .'

'It's okay.' I gulp back my tears.

'I really loved her,' Phil says, beginning to shake. 'Oh God! Why did I have to be so proud?'

He cries, and I hold him, crying too. We cling to each other, and wallow in our grief, new and old. Our sorrow soars high above us, like a shooting star. It burns a hole in the seamless frozen night. Snow begins to fall through the ragged cottage roof. It pads around us, keeps safe our secret wake.

BEATRICE

Dear Jakob

Did you get my letter? I know I only sent it yesterday, but if you get this one and have not replied yet, please write to me. Has Daddy told them what happened yet? I suppose there's no way you'll know that. They'll probably call off the search. I wonder if he'll get sent to prison. Eithne will hate me.

You told me to tell the Gardaí when I found out. But, Jakob, you should know by now that no one would believe me. They'd have sent down the priest and he would have given me a big talk. Then they wouldn't have let me out of their sight so I wouldn't have been able to come here and get an abortion. No, Daddy has to tell them. He'll have to.

The woman who runs this hostel is Greek. She's pregnant as well. Jakob, she looks so huge. Her name's Alexa. She gave me dinner last night and didn't ask me to pay for it. It was delicious. I hadn't eaten all day and I was starving.

Today I wandered around London. It's so big. I went to the National Gallery like you told me. It was brilliant — I had no idea Van Eyck's Arnolfini Marriage *was so small. I saw so many paintings, it was exhausting but I was inspired as well. I can't wait to get back to painting again, after all this.*

I was thinking of going to Cambridge to see Phil. But I'm still cross with him, and then how could I explain this? He might tell Uncle Jack where I am. I can't face anyone, not just yet.

I know what you're thinking. No, I haven't been to see my father yet.

I can't decide what to wear. I don't want to look shabby. I walked past the house in Hampstead yesterday. It's so posh around there. I have to look good, Jakob. I want him to like me. I don't want it to be just about money, I want him to want to know me.

Please write soon, Jakob. I feel so alone. I wish I was sitting in your garden, drawing, and drinking your special lapsang souchong tea.

Love B

EITHNE

Leo and Mick arrive an hour before the funeral.

The weather has turned mild, and the landscape is sluiced with moisture. They are sitting drinking tea with my mother in the kitchen as I come in through the back door, my face speckled with rain.

'Eithne.' Leo rises, comes over and embraces me.

'I'm all wet,' I say.

'I'm so sorry, love,' he says. I move away from him. I feel strange.

'I'm sorry about your father,' says Mick. 'How are you doing?'

'I'm okay.'

'Do you want some tea?' Mammy asks me.

'Yes, please, Mam.'

She gets a mug and pours another cup.

'How's Shauna?' I ask Leo.

'She's fine now. It was just a twenty-four-hour bug. She sends her love; so does my mother.'

'Shauna'll be making her communion this year?' asked Mammy.

'In May.'

'That's something to look forward to,' Mammy says. She appears incredibly calm and distant. I look at the kitchen clock.

'We'd better get ready,' I say to her.

'Yes, we'd best,' she says. 'Help yourselves, lads.' She indicates a bottle of Hennessey on the countertop.

I know that both Leo and Mick feel uneasy at our apparent normality, our lack of histrionics. They exchange glances. Myself and Mammy glide up the stairs. We are so far removed that we could be phantoms. We dress in silence. When I am ready I go into Mammy's room. She is putting on her lipstick. She looks really well. She is wearing a soft, slate-grey dress in wool. I had never seen it before.

'That's nice,' I say.

'Thank you,' she says. 'I got it in Carrolls in the sale.'

I walk over to the wardrobe. Daddy's things are still hanging up inside. I touch the sleeve of his best jacket and smell it. It smells of mothballs. He hadn't worn it in so long. I put my hand in the pocket – there's an old lotto slip, over a year old. In the corner of the pocket there is a small witch's stone. It is shiny and rubbed smooth, with a tiny hole in the centre. He must have picked it up on one of his rambles. It is so perfect that it could have been man-made; its surface is so highly polished by his heavy fingering that it could be pure ebony. I take the stone and hold it in the palm of my hand. I hold it there all day.

An hour later we stand rigid in the church. Tension sears through my body.

Will she come?

I stand next to Leo. He holds my hand. Phil is behind me. I sense his breath on the back of my neck. It comforts me.

Few cry. Surprisingly Aunt Bríd is in floods. The priest is talking about Daddy. The whole thing is totally surreal. I look at the coffin. He is in there.

I squeeze my eyes tight and let my memory return me to a

different time. I am a little girl walking hand in hand with my daddy. I am a daddy's girl like Shauna, confident of his protection and love. We are walking in high boggy grass and tall-stemmed bog cotton. We are searching for frogs.

Daddy has promised to build a pond in our back garden. We are going to have waterlilies, and fish *and* frogs. Maybe we'll get an ornament, or a little fountain, and some fairy lights to hang in the tree. I carry a large Tupperware box. I am hoping our hunt will be successful.

Daddy and I sing as we wade through the reeds.

> *When I was but a little boy*
> *And washed my mammy's dishes*
> *I put my finger in my eye*
> *And pulled out golden fishes.*

He doesn't care if I get wet and muddy. Things like that are not important, because we are busy hunting frogs.

Daddy finds one. It is tiny. In my nature books they looked so big. This wee frog is shining and green. He picks it up, and slips it into my box, which I have lined with grass and leaves for my frogs' comfort.

I put the lid on – we have made holes in it so that the frogs can breathe. Mammy won't be pleased we've ruined her best Tupperware, but that doesn't matter now. We are explorers, battling against the elements, an adventurer and his adventuress daughter.

> *Hey, diddle, diddle*
> *The cat and the fiddle,*
> *The cow jumped over the moon,*
> *The little dog laughed*

> *To see such sport,*
> *And the dish ran away with the spoon!*

Daddy lifts me up on the last beat of the rhyme and swings me through the air. Sky and land collide in my vision. I laugh, he laughs.

We find three more frogs. Daddy says that is enough for now. I am tired. He crouches on the ground, and I climb onto his back. We canter home.

> *When I was but a little boy*
> *And washed my mammy's dishes*
> *I put my finger in my eye*
> *And pulled out golden fishes.*

This is our song.

BEATRICE

Dear Jakob

Thanks for your letter. I can't believe he hasn't told anyone yet. God he's a pig — what a mess. Mammy must be going mad. But I can't ring her, Jakob, not yet.

Everything's going to be okay — I'm meeting my real father tomorrow.

I spoke to him! And yes, Jakob, he's going to meet me. Tomorrow afternoon at 3 o'clock in the Waldorf Hotel for tea. There now, I will be taking tea with my father this time tomorrow.

Once I tell my father everything he'll help me. Then I can ring Mammy.

I know what you're thinking. Why didn't he turn up to our meeting in Majorca? Well, he explained that. He just got the hotels mixed up. He thought he'd said the Continental, but in fact he had said the Europa. A simple mistake.

It's night-time, but the streets of London are still alive with people. My room's on the top floor, it's an attic room. I've a tiny balcony, well it's more like a gangway slotted between two roofs. I'm sitting here now, on a chair I've brought out from the room. It's fab sitting here, among the rooftops of London. The street lights sparkle below me, it's as though there's an orange haze hanging above the city. It never really gets dark here, not like at home.

I can still smell autumn. It's different from home. There's no bog here, no decay. Instead, the leaves fly about me, they're light and golden, cast off the trees by a gentle breeze. They spin like dancers in the air, one last flurry before they land, and are swept away by the street cleaners. The odd leaf remains. It withers to become a fragile skeleton. I've been picking up these delicate things and drawing them.

I'm also sketching people. Alexa lets me draw her. She says I'm very good, and I should set myself up in Piccadilly Circus, drawing portraits for money. Well, if things get desperate . . .

It's starting to rain. I'm going in to bed. Think of me tomorrow and my big day. I'm not nervous. I feel so weird at the moment. Really out of it as though I'm on something. I really want to be myself again.

Write soon,

Love B

EITHNE

The wind picks up as soon as Daddy is buried. It pushes us out of the graveyard, hurling hats, flapping coats, obscuring faces with flyaway hair. I remember Granny used to say that a strong wind was a portent of bad news. I believe I have already heard the worst.

Darkness falls early as the family make their way to Daddy's favourite hostelry. Safe inside, away from the hostile wind, we group around long tables, and sip at steaming bowls of soup. I sit in between Leo and Mammy. Phil is opposite me. Uncle Jack is talking about when he and Daddy were boys, and the pranks they got up to. It is hard to imagine Daddy as a child, carefree and mischievous. Since Beatrice disappeared, even before that, he had become so apathetic. I begin to eat my soup; it scalds my throat and brings tears to my eyes.

'I have to talk to you,' Leo whispers.

'Now?' I ask.

'Can we go somewhere to talk in private?' he says.

'Okay . . . I'll meet you outside the back door.'

He gets up and makes his way towards the Gents. Phil glances over at me, and his eyes hold no apology. His look is warm and direct. I smile at him, and he smiles back.

I get up from the table, and excuse myself. I walk through the pub, and out of the back door. The wind has grown even more ferocious. Leo stands under the back-door light; his face wears a worried expression.

'What's up?' I ask. 'It's freezing out here.'

'I have to tell you something,' he says.

'I can't hear you.'

The wind howls. Leo raises his voice.

'I have to tell you something,' he repeats. 'But before I do, you have to remember I was thinking of you, that's why I couldn't tell you.'

'What are you on about?'

'You worshipped your father, and he was good to you. I didn't want to be responsible for damaging your relationship.'

I am completely in the dark. My husband makes no sense to me.

'Leo, what is this all about?'

'These.' He takes a sheaf of paper out of his coat pocket. He grips them tightly, as their edges flap in the wind, then he hands them to me.

I look at the first page. It is regular copybook paper, torn down one side and slightly discoloured from age.

I immediately recognize the handwriting. It belongs to Beatrice. I read, 'Dear Jakob . . .' I look up at Leo. I am completely stunned.

'I found them in Jackob Rudin's attic when I was down that time with Mick,' he says. 'I couldn't give them to you, Eithne. Not after I read them. It would have destroyed you. I didn't think it would do anyone any good if you saw them. But now your father is dead you should read them, I think.'

He steps back. Has he any idea what he has done?

'Are these letters from my sister?' I say very slowly.

'Yes.'

'You had these letters all this time and you didn't tell me?'

'I couldn't, Eithne – what she says in them, I couldn't let you find out—'

'But you had these letters, you knew she was alive all along. Why did you say Lisa was a fake?'

'Because the truth is too ugly. I didn't want you to get hurt.'

'*Hurt!*' I scream in unison with the wind. 'The one person in my life I thought I could trust has been lying to me and hiding things from me. I thought we had no secrets. How could you?'

'I haven't lied to you. I just didn't tell you. Calm down, Eithne, please. You'll understand why when you have read the letters.'

'I don't need to read them to know that you have betrayed me.'

'Don't be so melodramatic.' He holds my shoulders. 'I was trying to protect you.'

I push him away.

'From the truth. Aren't you always telling me that you must be honest; that it is the most important thing.'

'But this is different.' Leo is exasperated. 'What Beatrice writes in the letters – it's so dreadful, Eithne, I couldn't let you know while your father was still alive. It was just too terrible—'

'*No!*' I interrupt him. What is he saying? What does he mean? Something snaps and I slap him with all the strength of my free hand. He steps back, shocked. I run into the wind, driving myself against it, the horror of my husband's words propelling me. I run through the town, up the hill, and fold up beneath the round tower. Trees lash at each other, as my heart rips apart.

BEATRICE

Dear Jakob
  He never came.
  *I am too upset to write about what happened. I am coming
home, and then I will tell you everything.*
  Love B

When she got back to the hostel, Beatrice phoned Jonathan.

'Where were you?'

'I thought it best if I didn't come. I'm sorry I couldn't contact
you.'

'But, why don't you want to meet me? I'm your daughter.'

There was a pause, then he said slowly, 'I think it's best not
to get emotionally involved at this stage.'

What did that mean? Didn't he become emotionally involved
the day she was conceived?

'You have to meet me,' she said. She was getting desperate
now. 'I won't go away until you meet me, at least once.'

'I'm afraid that's out of the question,' he said, and hung up.

So she went to the house, the next morning.

He came to the front door. When he saw her, he looked
appalled. He glanced behind him and opened the porch door.

'What the hell are you doing here?'

He knew who she was immediately. He must have been
expecting her.

'I have to talk to you,' Beatrice whispered, shaking.

He made her stand in the porch, with her coat still on.

'So?' he stood questioningly. 'What is it you want?'

'I'm your daughter,' she said, quietly.

'Maybe by blood. But the man who married your mother and brought you up is your real father.'

'Never,' she hissed.

He was taken aback. They stood in silence. Beatrice composed herself.

'I need your help,' she said.

'What is it?'

'I've nowhere to go,' she said.

'Why don't you go home, back to Ireland?'

'I can't go back. I can't . . .'

To her shame, she began to cry.

He shook his head; he was getting agitated. This was not what Beatrice had dreamt about, this was a nightmare. She could hear voices in the hall.

'For goodness' sake, what's wrong?' he said, impatiently.

'I'm pregnant.'

The words fell out of her mouth. Heavy . . . clumsy . . . awful.

'Oh,' he said, embarrassed.

'I can't go home because Joseph – my step-father – he's a drunk, and he hits me, and . . . well . . . and it was him, you see, who made me pregnant.'

'Good Lord!' he exclaimed. 'That's appalling, of course, but I'm sorry, I can't do anything about it. No, no, it's much better if I was not involved. You should report it to the police and leave it up to the authorities.'

She started to laugh, manically.

'Shush . . .' he said, glancing over his shoulder nervously. 'Will you please be quiet.'

'No one would believe me.'

'I really don't think that I can help you at all—'

He was interrupted by a clear voice singing out from the hall.

'Daddy, who's at the door?'

He turned to close the front door, but before he did so, it swung open. A girl about three years younger than Beatrice faced her. She was blonde and blue-eyed.

'Hello,' she said, smiling.

Beatrice stared back at her, and said nothing.

Jonathan Voyle took out his wallet. He thrust some notes into Beatrice's hand.

'There you go now,' he said. 'Get yourself sorted out with that.'

Humiliated, Beatrice turned and left, still clutching the notes. She could hear the sing-song voice of her sister say, 'Who was that girl?'

'Just a gipsy, begging at the door,' replied her father.

'She looked so sad.'

'Well, she's in trouble, so to speak.'

Beatrice turned her head and saw the girl embrace her father.

'Oh, Daddy, you're so good to help her out,' she said. 'I do love you.'

SIX: THE PURSE

EITHNE

I sit on a gravestone and listen to the birds sing. This is not where Daddy is buried. He is behind the large Catholic church in town. This little Protestant graveyard is in the middle of nowhere, tucked behind a small ruined church. It is a place where you can step back in time. People are still buried here, but it is the very old graves I like to sit by.

I am in the far corner, surrounded by creaking yew trees.

If I walk to the other side of the plot, the trees clear and I have a timeless view of the hills, a few cottages and the ruined church. In the winter light, the mountains are deep blue, the ground is intense green and the trees are brown-feathered skeletons.

A tractor passes. Nobody else is around for miles. I hear its engine trail into the distance.

I have been sitting here all morning, reading. I am still clutching the bundle of letters, staring off into the middle distance. I am scared. I don't know what to do.

I see my mother walking towards me, crossing the road, her jacket is loose and flaps about her. Instinctively I take out a cigarette lighter and, sheltering behind a gravestone, I light one corner of one of the letters. I make a little fire then with a few sticks and twigs, and by the time Mammy reaches me, the letters have all gone up in flames.

'What are you doing, Eithne?' she asks. 'What is it you're burning?'

'Nothing.'

She stands above me, head on one side, staring down at me.

'What's going on? Why has Leo left without you, Eithne? You never even said goodbye to him.'

'He's gone, then.'

'Yes, he's gone. He waited and waited for you, but you never came back, and your phone was switched off . . . so he went. He looked quite upset, Eithne. What's happened?'

'It's too complicated to go into.'

She sits down next to me on the gravestone, and sighs.

'He lied to me,' I say. 'He kept things from me and didn't tell me.'

'Was he unfaithful?' she asks.

'No, it's nothing like that.'

'Why did he lie?'

'I don't know . . . he said he was trying to protect me.'

A bunch of rooks take off suddenly, cawing wildly.

'Maybe he was,' Mammy says. 'Is that such a bad thing?'

'It feels like it is.'

'What's important, Eithne, is, do you love Leo? Because, if you do, any deceit is worth overcoming . . . if there is love. So many of us lose that chance to really love someone. Once it's gone, it's very hard to get it back again. You might never get it back ever.'

She speaks very quietly, so softly I can hardly hear her. I put my arms about her.

'Mammy,' I ask her. 'Did you love Daddy?'

'No, darling,' she says sadly. 'I never did, though he loved me. I have that on my conscience.'

'Do you think Daddy was a good man?'

'Yes, he was, though he would have been a better man if he hadn't chosen me. I brought out the worst in him, and you brought out the best.' She smiles wistfully. 'He adored you, Eithne, don't forget that.'

'I know,' I say.

'And he loved Beatrice too,' she adds. 'It was very hard for him when she disappeared.'

I say nothing. There seems absolutely no point in shattering her illusions.

She gets up.

'Come on back to the house,' she says. 'I'm making tea.'

'In a minute.'

I watch her as she heads back up the lane, and then I am on my own again. I get up, and circle the graveyard. Although it is still daylight, there is frost on the tips of the blades of grass. I smell woodsmoke, and another night approaching.

I go over to the darkest corner of the graveyard, as a vague memory stirs. Pulling aside some creepers, I see an oval marble slab, slanting out of the ground. I move towards it. The grave belongs to a young woman who died when she was only twenty-seven. Beatrice and I used to spend time at this grave, thinking how awful that was, to die so young. As I bend down to read the inscription again, I notice something buried under a pile of moss, a tiny corner of red velvet.

My heart beats faster. I recognize the fabric. Surely not?

I pull away the moss and then a heavy stone, underneath is a cellophane bag, inside is a small, embroidered purse. Air has got into the bag so that most of the purse is rotten, but a corner of red velvet remains intact.

There is no doubt – it is a purse I gave to Beatrice. I made it out of a piece of velvet Mammy cut up from an old dress. I had just learnt how to cross-stitch and I had enthusiastically decorated the tiny thing. It had been my going-away present to my sister.

It hurt me to think that she had expelled this too – like all the other things. Did she leave them as a code for me to decipher, or was it just a process of forgetting all about us?

I think back to the last letter I read. She had said she was coming home, but she never did. The only two people who could help me solve the mystery were dead now: my father and the Artist.

I look at the rotten purse, and then, surprising myself, I don't pick it up. I leave it there. Let the birds pick at it, the slugs rot it, what can it do for me now? My survival instinct is strong. I know that if I want my life back, I will have to relinquish the past.

As I pass the fire of letters, it is all ashes now. Soon the wind will blow them away. I wish it could do the same to what I now know.

SARAH

Five days after her husband died, Sarah changed the sheets.

She missed him.

Although she had never loved Joseph, now he was gone she felt even more lonely than before. More than anything else, she felt an overwhelming sense of guilt. Maybe she had pushed him towards his death? When she could think about Joseph, just as a man, not as her husband, she felt incredibly sad and even sorry for him, despite what he had done to her in the past.

All these years, since the day Eithne was conceived, she had never let him touch her, and he had respected that, although they had always shared a bed. Sarah missed his presence next to her; his child-like slumber, when she could watch his oblivion and regret the day they had ever met. When he was drinking he would sleep downstairs on the sofa, but if it was a good week, if he managed to stay away from the pub, he would sleep upstairs. He liked to prop himself up with two pillows, and read the daily paper. As his black curls greyed, he began to wear reading glasses. He would scan the arts pages, looking for a mention of Eithne in some exhibition or other. Although he could not really understand her work, he was incredibly proud of her. And he had taught Sarah something, to look at her second daughter in a different light, to appreciate her talent.

For four nights after Joe died, Sarah slept on his side of the bed. She could smell him in the bed still. She hoped that by lying there, maybe some answers would come to her. What was it Joseph had not told her about Beatrice?

On the fifth day she rose, and stripped the bed. She washed the sheets, by hand, in the bath. She wrung them out until her knuckles were red and her nose ran. Then she went outside to hang them. It was windy still. She pegged the sheets up, and they fluttered like a row of angels. It was crazy really, they would never dry out here. It had already begun to rain. But she needed them aired so that when she ironed them their scent would be crisp and new.

Sarah stood by the back door, holding her empty laundry basket, and staring into space. The sheets flapped loudly in front of her, they obscured her view of the garden, and the road beyond. But she sensed someone.

As the sheets lifted with the rhythm of the wind, she saw a figure walking up the road towards the house that was all hers now. She could not make out who it was but she felt an air of expectancy encompass her. A particularly strong gust of wind lifted the corner of one sheet, and twisted it around the line. Now she had a perfect view.

The figure had reached her garden gate. It was a man, not much older than herself. He was dark. He looked at her. Sarah dropped her basket and her mouth fell open. She had longed for this moment for over thirty years.

There he stood on her front lawn, the line of laundry between them. The sheets slapped and clapped in the wind as Anthony Voyle walked towards her. She raised her hands to her mouth. Speechless.

BEATRICE

In Eithne's wood she walks like a queen. Her feet bounce up and down, cushioned by a carpet of old moss and discoloured needles. She begins to run again, weaving in and out of the trees. She hears the birds, but there is silence behind the sound, like a veil ready to lift on the day. Cobwebs catch on her cheeks, and stray pine needles spin on single threads around her. The trees are tight, already bare and spiky, ready to tear her skin. In this part of the wood they are so close together. She can see shadows. She senses that she is not alone.

The land lifts, and she climbs over a rabbit warren, careful not to lose her footing. Pushing her way through the tangled undergrowth and vines, which hang like wispy grey hair, she comes out at a clearing. She stands at the foot of the big lime tree, surveying its majesty. Eithne always called it the Grandpa Tree, Beatrice called it the Ancient Tree. They always made wishes here. Sometimes they came true.

She goes up to it now and touches it. There is barbed wire behind it and a fairy-tale view of rolling green hills, with the cairns perched on the top and evergreen woods at their base. She doesn't know what to ask for, she just wants some peace. She wants a rest from all the shadows following her, night and day, when she is awake and asleep.

BEATRICE

In the clearing the wind picks up and leaves start to whirl around her. It sounds like it's raining, a big downpour, but it is just the lime tree, creaking, swaying and dropping his leaves. It is just the sound of release.

PHIL

Phil left the day after the funeral. He still found it hard to be in that place. When he looked at the landscape of Ireland, he was immediately locked into his eighteen-year-old heart. Beatrice was the first girl he had ever loved, and he had found it impossible to forget her, even maybe to forgive her.

When he first heard she was missing he had been angry with her. It was just typical of Beatrice, and he had expected her to turn up on his doorstep at his digs in Cambridge any day. But she never came. And then he began to believe what everyone else was saying – that she had been murdered.

But they had had a pact that if either of them were on the other side, they would contact the other – show them somehow that they were dead. He had never seen a sign, and so Beatrice's disappearance confirmed his atheism: from now on he would only believe in what he saw right before him.

Phil was dedicated to his career. He approached his work as a documentary film-maker with the same commitment as a military man. He wasn't afraid . . . because someone had to go out there and show the world what was going on. What frightened him was not what he saw in the war zones, not the devastation or the human suffering, what frightened him was being back at home, and every man's indifference.

He had hoped that Beatrice would show up at his uncle's funeral – but even as he had said those words to Eithne he had doubted them. She had been absent for too long. Wherever she was she was never going back to Ireland.

However, his documentary mind told him there was a chink of hope, a possible breakthrough – the Voyles. For Eithne's sake, Phil decided to pay them a visit. If he found nothing out, then he would never have to tell Eithne. He knew she was too afraid now to take it any further. She had loved her father. So he would do it for her, because he had loved her sister.

Phil lived in Kilburn. It only took him ten minutes to drive up the Finchley Road and head into Hampstead. The address had been easy to find – they were in the phone book. All along, right under his nose.

There was the house. A huge mansion: two marble columns gleamed in the winter sunlight, and the garden was exquisitely manicured. These people had money. Phil parked his old Volvo estate, which looked even shabbier here. He took a deep breath, walked up to the door, and knocked. It opened almost immediately, as if someone had been waiting for him.

'Jonathan Voyle?' he asked.

He was looking at a dark grey-haired man who must have been in his late fifties, yet he had the physique of a younger man; tall and erect. He reminded Phil of some of the older army men he had come across. It was his face and hair which gave his age away. He was completely grey, and his skin was etched with deep worry lines.

'No,' said the man. 'Who are you?'

'Pardon me, my name is Philip Kelly.' His voice wavered, he was nervous.

'Well, what do you want?' the man asked abruptly.

'I'm looking for Jonathan Voyle,' Phil repeated.

'I'm afraid he died five years ago,' he said. 'I'm his brother.'

Phil could have walked away, but instinct stopped him. He came straight to the point.

'Can you tell me . . . do you know where Beatrice Kelly lives?' he asked. 'I'm her cousin.'

Anthony Voyle stared at the younger man.

'Beatrice Kelly?' he said. 'Sarah Kelly's daughter? Do you know Sarah?'

'Of course, I'm her nephew,' he said.

The older man seemed lost for words. What colour was in his cheeks quickly faded.

'Come in, then,' he said finally, each word followed by a choked rasp. Phil followed him into a huge sitting room, with a big fire.

'Sit down, please.'

Phil sat on one of the sofas.

Anthony remained standing. He said nothing for a couple of minutes, then went over to one of the bay windows, leant against the shutters and looked at the bare trees. The clock ticked. Phil coughed.

'How is Sarah?' Anthony asked, his voice barely rising above a whisper.

'Not great,' Phil replied. 'Her husband just died.'

'Oh.' Anthony turned; he looked shocked.

Phil began to wonder whether this had been such a good idea. He had been expecting Jonathan, and now he wasn't sure how much his brother knew. Anthony stood staring at him. Phil began to shift his feet. Maybe he should go? Then as if reading his thoughts, Anthony came out of his trance.

'So how can I help you?' he asked stiffly, pulling himself up to his full height.

'We lost Beatrice, Sarah's daughter,' Phil blurted out, 'years ago now – eighteen years ago to be precise. I discovered that your brother was her real father. I thought maybe she might have come here, that maybe your family might know where she went . . .'

'I see,' Anthony said nodding. He was very odd. He didn't seem surprised at all, and was less shocked than when Phil had mentioned Sarah. He didn't deny the fact that Jonathan was Beatrice's father either.

'But I'm sorry,' he said. 'I've already told you my brother died – of cancer – a few years ago.'

He began walking around the room. Round and round. Phil got up.

'I'm sorry to have disturbed you,' he said. 'It was just a long shot.'

Anthony didn't reply, instead he kept circling the room. Phil stood hesitant, unsure what to do.

'She did come here once,' he said eventually. 'But Jonathan just gave her money and sent her away.'

'Why didn't you contact her parents? Surely you must have realized something was wrong?' Phil said accusingly.

'He didn't tell me about Beatrice's visit until he was on his deathbed. If I had known at the time I would, of course, have found her and helped her. I would have brought her home . . . to Sarah. But by then it was too late.'

'Didn't you ever see her again?'

'No, not once. I think Jonathan did come to regret his actions, especially after Vicky died.'

He stopped walking and stared out of the window again.

'Who was Vicky?' Phil asked.

'His daughter . . . my niece. She was killed in a car crash when she was only nineteen.'

'I'm sorry . . .' Phil plunged on, 'but, please Mr Voyle, think again – did your brother ever mention Beatrice again?'

He said nothing for a while. Then he said, sadly, 'No, I'm sorry.' He sighed. 'There's been a lot of tragedy in this house. The last day I saw Sarah was the day before my mother died. She fell down the stairs in the middle of the night. She was going to get a glass of water. What a stupid way to go.'

Again silence. Finally, he walked over to a table, and opened a drawer.

'I suppose you should have this,' he said, taking out a small brown purse. He handed it to Phil.

The purse was very ugly. It was made of brown plastic, and, although it was old-fashioned, it looked as though it had hardly been used.

'It belonged to Beatrice,' said Anthony.

Phil opened it. Inside there was money. They were old notes – some green one-pound notes, and a few of the large five-pound and ten-pound notes . . . there was about sixty pounds in the purse in all.

'Jonathan gave this to me on the day he died. He told me to mind it until, one day, Beatrice might return,' he explained. 'I don't think she ever will.'

'But the money?'

'My brother had given her money,' he said. 'To have an abortion.'

'I still don't understand.'

'The day after he gave it to her, he found this pushed through the door. There was a note with it. It's inside.'

There was a small piece of paper twisted inside the notes. Phil pulled it out.

I don't want your money, or your love.

He looked at Anthony. The older man shook his head.

'I'd better go,' Phil said, a lump inside his throat.

'You must give me your aunt's address in Ireland.'

'Sure.'

Anthony coughed and shuffled his feet.

'Maybe I should wait until she gets over her husband's death, before getting in touch with her.'

'It wasn't a match made in heaven,' Phil told him. 'She could do with a friend.'

'Really?' Anthony replied, his expression lifting.

Phil could see that Anthony had something in his pocket. He kept touching it. He took it out, and twisted it round his fingers. It was a gold chain, with a locket.

'What's that?' Phil asked.

But the older man said nothing. Looking embarrassed, he thrust the locket back in his pocket and showed Phil the way out.

Phil walked back to his car, gripping the brown plastic purse. There was no point telling Eithne about it, there was no point telling anyone.

'Where are you, Beatrice?' he whispered, and looked up at the sky. It had gone completely white. All of sudden his face was struck by small sharp stones of ice and the heavens opened. He ran to the car and sat inside while giant hail slammed on his roof. He sat in his car, angry. *Why didn't you come to me? Why didn't you come to Cambridge?*

When the storm stopped everything melted, except for one large hailstone lodged in his wipers. It was there all the way home. He took it as a sign.

EITHNE

All Souls' Week, 1981. We went to the graveyard every day and prayed for the dead people; all those held hostage in purgatory. We were doing our duty, Mammy, Daddy and I, sending out our plenary indulgences, messages to the unknowable. It was the only time Mammy would leave the house. She clung on to her shaky faith, because that's all she had.

'If she is dead, please save her soul, help her to heaven, let her be free.'

Years later I made an etching called 'All Souls' Day'. It is the only picture I've made with the three of us in it. I used the small Protestant graveyard as the setting for the composition. The dense green yew trees create a striking contrast with the cool grey hues of the gravestones. We are heavily etched, outlined in black, and bowed down with sorrow. What is nice about the picture is that Mammy and Daddy stand either side of me. At least we are united.

It takes me a long time to forgive Leo, but I do.

We head west for a while after the funeral. Leo's sister Marta has a house in Connemara, which she lets to us for a month. He takes leave from college, and tells Clara he can't take Shauna for a while. He is going to incredible lengths though, at first, I just don't see it. My pain makes him a shadow, and I feed off the landscape for solace. Now I know why Mammy sat at the back door for so many years.

The wet moorlands of Connemara suit my mood with their grey skies and soft relentless rain; the rich and staggeringly brilliant browns of the bogs are a comfort to me. The space is wide and I need this.

I let Leo walk with me. Every day we go down to the sea's edge. At first we say little to each other. Our relationship is struggling on shifting sands, one wrong word could sink it.

Then, hesitantly, Leo begins to talk. About little things at first – a shell, the waves, a seagull singing above, a stray wild-flower in the sand. We pay attention to the small things. We use them to nourish our relationship.

One day Leo takes my hand and I don't pull away. Then I begin to draw. I take photographs of the sea, film after film. And then I cannot stop painting. I try to use other colours but in the end all I see is blue, blue, blue. I end up with an eternal blue abyss. There is no structure to the work, just vigorous brush strokes, and what Leo calls 'an abandoned energy'. It is different from anything I have ever made.

I let go.

And then, one day, all of a sudden, it is spring. We shed our heavy coats and go for a hike by the sea. The sun is strong and golden, and everything around us is budding. This day is fresh and new.

We have brought food and it is warm enough to sit on the sand and picnic. Leo has even brought a bottle of wine. He pops it open and fills two beakers.

'Eithne,' he says after a while, 'I have to go back.'

He is missing Shauna.

He looks at me, with his Slavic eyes, and his clear, pearly skin.

'Will you come with me?' he asks.

I look out at the Atlantic. What he has done has not been wrong, but can I ever trust him again?

'Do you understand why I did it?' he asks.

'Yes.' I chew my salty lips. 'Yes, I know you thought it was the right thing to do. It's okay,' I say. 'It's all over now. We can go on.'

We huddle together on the dunes. Then he turns and kisses me. I half close my eyes, his yellow hair is streaked against the blue sky. I kiss him back for the first time in months.

Relief, emotion, love floods us. We lie back on the sand, and let it sink around us. It is sticky and damp. We cling to each other like two lost children.

It is different from before. Maybe then I made love blind. Now my eyes are open and I look at the face of the man who decided to become involved in my suffering. It no longer matters whether he was right or wrong. Wordless, we look at each other as our bodies fuse and we conceive our first child.

JOSEPH

No one had thought to look in what Beatrice and Eithne had called the secret garden. Of course Joe knew about it. He had heard them at night in their bedroom, whispering about the hidden door at the back of the shed, and their wild sanctuary behind. He had smiled to himself at the time, pleased that the children had found somewhere of their own. He had never violated their privacy. Not until today.

Beatrice had been missing for two weeks. By now all her things had been found, and the Gardaí were on an extensive hunt for any further clues. Sarah was beside herself. Eithne was pale and quiet. Everyone assumed Beatrice had been killed.

But, guiltily, he thought there might be other reasons why she was gone. She had always overreacted. What had happened had been an accident, but she seemed to have totally gone off the deep end: moving into that foreign artist's house – if anyone knew where she was Jakob did – and refusing to speak to him. Joe had not told anyone about that night, and he wasn't going to now. She'd come back.

He had to force the door open because he couldn't find where the girls had put the key. Joe was shocked at how overgrown the little garden was: you couldn't see daylight. He went back into the shed and got a torch, then he returned to the garden and began to look.

It didn't take long to find the box. Beatrice had left it in an

obvious spot so that Eithne would see it. He prised it open.
There was a letter inside.

Dear Eithne

*I've wanted to tell you so much but I just couldn't say it to
your face. I have to warn you, though, and I know you'll come
here and find this — don't trust Daddy. I know you love him but
he did a terrible thing to me, Eithne, and I'm worried for you.*

*Do you remember the night that you and Mammy went to see
Aunty Aoife last summer, some time after that rock concert? Well,
that night Daddy came home very drunk, we argued and he
knocked me out. Eithne, he did an awful thing. I can't even say
it. But now I'm pregnant. I can't tell anyone because I'm going
to England to have an abortion.*

Then I'll come back.

*Please don't show anyone this letter. Tell Mammy that you
know I'll be back soon. Hopefully, Daddy will tell you why I
had to go, because I suppose the Gardaí will be looking for me,
and everything.*

I love you loads and loads, and I'll see you soon.

Love Beatrice

Joe began to shake. What was she saying? He didn't do it. He
hadn't touched her in that way. How could she accuse him of
such a thing? The little witch was trying to turn Eithne against
him. He wanted to rip the letter into shreds, but for some
reason he didn't. Instead he took out a pencil end from his
trouser pocket, and scrawled at the bottom of the letter.

*I, Joseph Padraig Kelly, swear that I never harmed one hair
on the head of my daughter, Beatrice Kelly. She is a liar, no true
Kelly.*

I know who the father is. I saw with my own eyes that sinner

*of a daughter, God forgive her, corrupting my brother's son. I've
not said one word out of respect for my brother, and for the
shame I feel on behalf of my daughter.*

*No doubt she'll come back soon enough, tail between her legs.
But we'd all be better off without her.*

14 November 1981

Then he put the letter back in the box, and dug a deep hole
underneath a bed of ivy. He buried the box there. He was sure
it would never be found.

EITHNE

Thirty pieces hang against the stark white walls of the Wright Gallery. The press release describes the divergence in style of the work and their range in colour and tone. It proclaims the exhibition as an ambitious first solo show, and the artist as an emerging new talent.

I don't want success, that's not what I'm after. I just want to be able to practise my craft and improve. I just want my pictures to mean something to someone.

The exhibition is split into two halves – my etchings comprise the first half called 'Underearth' and are explorations of the land around home, some with reference to Beatrice's missing objects. The second half of the show, 'Underwater', are the paintings I made when I was in Connemara. It is this part of the show which particularly pleases Eliza Wright.

'I wasn't expecting any paintings, Eithne,' she says. 'I love them. They're super. They remind me of some of Camille Souter's work. Excellent. And good sales, I see.'

The show has nearly sold out and it is still only opening night. Shauna is flying around the place, overexcited and thrilled by all the attention from her parents' friends. Clara comes over to me.

'Well done,' she says. 'I love your new work, Eithne.'

'Thanks,' I reply.

'I'm so glad you guys worked things out.' She squeezes my

hand and moves away. I could be offended or annoyed that Leo confided in her, but none of that stuff matters any more.

'I'm so proud of you,' Mammy says, coming up from behind. She looks wonderful, literally ten years younger; an exquisite duck-egg-blue shawl is around her shoulders. 'We bought number seventeen and number twenty-two.'

'Mammy, I would have given them to you,' I say.

'Oh, let him.' She giggles. 'He can afford it. Especially now I've sold the house. You will go down and sort everything out, won't you?'

'Yeah, Mammy, I'll even gut the secret garden.'

'The what?'

'It's a place myself and Beatrice used to hang out.'

'God knows what you'll find in there, but you keep it all, Eithne; I don't want to go back, ever.'

I look over at Anthony Voyle, who is talking to Sasha, who looks cool in a knitted pink outfit full of holes. Anthony is taller than Daddy, but I am struck by how similar they look – dark grey hair, striking eyes, what I would call beautiful.

'Where's Jack?' Mammy asks. 'I'll get him to buy one as well.'

'He's over with Phil. But, Mammy, please don't bully him. I don't want anyone to buy anything unless they actually like it.'

'Of course he likes them, it's just a matter of deciding which one he likes best.'

She goes over to Jack and Phil, while Leo comes towards me.

'You look gorgeous,' he says, putting his arm around my thickening waist.

'I feel like a dumpling,' I say.

'Rubbish, you're blooming,' he says, pleased as punch. It has been a good week for us. His public art commission is well under way, the latest scan at the hospital went well, and now my opening is packed and selling out.

'Nearly time for speeches,' he says.

'Get me another Ballygowan, will you? My throat has all dried up.'

But before he has a chance, Eliza Wright takes the floor.

'Good evening, ladies and gentlemen. I would like to welcome you to "Underearth: Underwater", a breathtaking exhibition of work by an emerging artist, Eithne Kelly, who it seems is equally talented as a print-maker and a painter.'

She speaks for a few minutes, and as she is talking the door of the gallery opens and I see Lisa come in with a tall, good-looking guy who must be Steve.

I am really surprised to see them. Lisa and I have been emailing each other regularly, and I had told her about the opening, but I had never expected her to come all this way. I am pleased. Particularly as she is pregnant as well and, although she is two months behind me, she is already bigger than I am. I can see a big flashy engagement ring on her finger, and I smile to myself. It seems that some of her dreams are coming true. She is very pretty in her own way, but I still can't get over how different she looks from Beatrice. And when I think about it, she doesn't look a bit like Daddy either.

A big gang of relatives has congregated in one corner of the gallery, and as Eliza introduces me and I go forward to make a speech I notice Phil out of the corner of my eye. He is standing right next to Lisa.

All of a sudden I see it. It is as plain as day. They have exactly the same keen blue eyes, the same shape of the brow, and the same rounded chin, the full lips and the turned-up nose. It is unmistakable. I am looking at a father and his child.

A wave of relief almost knocks me over. 'Thank you, Daddy,' I whisper as I take the podium.

BEATRICE

Being in water always made her feel better. She remembered when she was a little girl, playing with Eithne and her cousins in the stream at Granny's house. It was a beautiful clear brook. Beside it was a well of sweet spring water, which the family used. There was no comparison to the metallic-tasting water which came out of a tap.

A tiny stone bridge crossed the stream and this led the way to the house. Beatrice liked to think that the stream was their moat, and if needs be, they could pull the bridge up, and keep everyone outside the family away.

The children played on the far side of the bridge. They'd scramble down the brambly bank and start gathering stones. Beatrice was always the fastest, even though she had to help Eithne, who was still in nappies. Her baby sister didn't like the water much, she was happy to sit on the bank and play with the reeds. Beatrice and her younger cousins ran like mad things, collecting stones, as large as they could find, and building a dam as far from the bridge as they could manage. Then they'd sit back and watch the water rise. Eventually they could wait no longer and, flinging off their clothes, they'd jump into the soft bog water, splashing and screaming with sheer delight.

Beatrice had never forgotten how this thrilled her.

She loved to submerge herself completely. And with her eyes open she would let herself sink to the bottom. Slowly, slowly, blue sky became brown water. All you could see were muddy clouds kicked up by the children. She longed to go to the sea, where she knew she'd be able actually to see what was there — sea horses and starfish and such like.

Sometimes when she did this — sinking to the bottom like a dead thing — she frightened her cousins. They'd plead with her to stop, and Eithne would start to cry. Beatrice loved to tease them. They were such babies.

But the stream was a dangerous place. If one of the children couldn't be found it was always the first place the women looked. And they were constantly warned never to go on their own, never to go too far down where the stream-bed turned to thick, boggy quicksand, and you could get stuck and pulled down.

Nevertheless, it was impossible to keep the children away from the water. In the summer, they lived in the stream and built whole cities on its surface. Piling stone upon stone they created a fantasy world of citadels, and castles decorated with wild flowers. They populated the city with reed folk, who travelled in reed boats. They even filled the boats with tiny wild strawberries, which they imagined their people eating. They built them twig houses, in their water-city, and pathways of stone across the stream, with tiny little bridges made of shiny, bright pebbles.

Each day, if the weather stayed fine, the children worked away extending their fairy city into a magic land. If it was a rare week of hot sunshine, then Aunt Aoife would let her brood stay in Glenamona. The children were so dedicated to their mission that they went to bed when they were told and rose early, racing down to the stream as soon as they had finished their breakfasts. At night, they chatted and wriggled in their beds, and on mattresses on the floor, telling stories about their fairyland. After the others had fallen asleep, Beatrice would listen hard, sitting up by the window, and staring out into the completely black night. She could hear tiny voices, tinkling in the distance, she was sure she could see miniature lights bobbing above the stream. She longed to be tiny as well, then she could sail down the stream in one of the reed boats.

But such a good thing could never last for ever, and when the weather broke there would be tears. Just one strong gust of wind could wipe out their world. It was a miracle it had survived for seven whole days. It was so fragile.

Epilogue

Midsummer's day. Dawn. She woke to the angry lap of water, and the motion of a rough sea which had dominated her sleep. She felt dizzy and sick. She stumbled out of the hold and onto the deck. She hung over the side and vomited.

It hadn't all been like this. There had been beautiful days, when she had lain in the sun, on the roof of the boat, and soaked up its rays. On those days, she had felt as though she was healing from all the hurt and sadness she had endured over the past year. She had felt positive, and was glad she had followed Alexa's advice and taken this crewing job. It was a good way to get over things.

Here, in the middle of the deep blue sea there was nothing to focus on, just the vast expanse of water and the vast expanse of sky. It helped to get things into perspective.

But now they were near land. In fact, they had been able to see land for several days but the sea had been so agitated it had been unsafe to go any closer to the shore. They had to wait until it settled.

She felt as though she was going crazy. She wanted so badly to feel terra firma under her feet. Every day she felt more and more nauseous. They said this always happened, that everyone got seasick, no matter how good a sailor they were. But she just wanted to get off the boat.

She had come to her senses. She wanted her baby back. And

she wanted to go home. She closed her eyes and saw her mammy in the kitchen. She could almost smell her — sweet pink roses — that's what she smelt like. She wanted her mammy to hold her so badly it made her gasp.

Beatrice stared down at the water. There was nothing left in her stomach to throw up. She looked at the shadows beneath the sea's surface. There was no reason to be afraid. She got up quickly and fetched a plastic bag. She collected together her few possessions and put them in it. Then she tied it to her waist. She was going to go home. She was a good swimmer, and she was sure she could make it to land. She did not fear the water.

She climbed onto the edge of the boat. She could hear the crew calling her, but she did not pause to listen. She sprang into the air and dived into the sea.

The water was waiting for her. She had not expected it to challenge her so. She floundered as the current pulled and twisted her limbs. The ocean filled her mouth, her lungs. A wave lifted her up, a last flash of day. It rolled her up in a tomb of foam.

Then she went down.

All the way.